KEATS

John Keats was born in October 1795, son of the manager of a livery stable in Finsbury. His father died in 1804 and his mother of tuberculosis in 1810. By then he had received a good education at John Clarke's Enfield private school. In 1811 he was apprenticed to a surgeon, completing his professional training at Guy's Hospital in 1816. His decision to commit himself to poetry rather than a medical career was a courageous one, based more on a challenge to himself than any actual achievement.

His genius was recognized and encouraged by early friends like Charles Cowden Clarke and J. H. Reynolds, and in October 1816 he met Leigh Hunt, whose *Examiner* had already published Keats's first poem. Only seven months later *Poems* (1817) appeared. Despite the high hopes of the Hunt circle, it was a failure. By the time *Endymion* was published in 1818 Keats's name had been identified with Hunt's 'Cockney School', and the Tory *Blackwood's Magazine* delivered a violent attack on Keats as a lower-class vulgarian, with no right to aspire to 'poetry'.

But for Keats fame lay not in contemporary literary politics but with posterity. Spenser, Shakespeare, Milton and Wordsworth were his inspiration and challenge. The extraordinary speed with which Keats matured is evident from his letters. In 1818 he had worked on the powerful epic fragment *Hyperion*, and in 1819 he wrote 'The Eve of St Agnes', 'La Belle Dame sans Merci', the major odes, *Lamia*, and the deeply exploratory *Fall of Hyperion*. Keats was already unwell when preparing the 1820 volume for the press; by the time it appeared in July he was desperately ill. He died in Rome in 1821.

Keats's final volume did receive some contemporary critical recognition, but it was not until the latter part of the nineteenth century that his place in English Romanticism began to be recognized, and not until this century that it became fully recognized.

JOHN KEATS

SELECTED POEMS

———

EDITED WITH AN INTRODUCTION
AND NOTES BY
JOHN BARNARD

PENGUIN BOOKS

PENGUIN BOOKS

Published by the Penguin Group
27 Wrights Lane, London W8 5TZ, England
Viking Penguin Inc., 40 West 23rd Street, New York, New York 10010, USA
Penguin Books Australia Ltd, Ringwood, Victoria, Australia
Penguin Books Canada Ltd, 2801 John Street, Markham, Ontario, Canada L3R 1B4
Penguin Books (NZ) Ltd, 182–190 Wairau Road, Auckland 10, New Zealand

Penguin Books Ltd, Registered Offices: Harmondsworth, Middlesex, England

Published in Penguin Books 1988
3 5 7 9 10 8 6 4 2

Filmset in Ehrhardt (Linotron 202) by
Rowland Phototypesetting Ltd, Bury St Edmunds, Suffolk
Printed and bound in Great Britain by
Cox & Wyman Ltd, Reading, Berks

Contents

CONTENTS

Introduction

On 29 May 1815 church bells all over England rang out in celebration of the Restoration of Charles II. In the same year Napoleon had escaped from Elba, forcing Louis XVIII to flee France for asylum in London. There he was welcomed by huge crowds. Keats, then nineteen, denounced the nation-wide celebrations of the re-establishment of 'legitimate' kingship in a savage extempore. For him, Charles's Restoration, which led to the execution for treason of the 'republican' heroes Sir Henry Vane, Algernon Sidney and Lord William Russell, was Britain's 'direst, foulest shame', an infatuated rejection of the true patriotism betrayed by the Restoration. In what is now believed to be his last poem, 'In after-time, a sage of mickle lore', Keats prophesied the eventual defeat of tyranny and injustice by the combined forces of democracy and a free press in a mock Spenserian allegory. These pieces open and close this selection. Neither were meant for publication. They both reject the repressive rule of a Tory ministry which, threatened by social unrest, employed spies and the law in an attempt to prevent legitimate protest in print or at public meetings.

Keats, who was born in 1795 and died prematurely, of tuberculosis, in 1821, lived the whole of his life under the shadow of the Napoleonic wars and their immediate aftermath. Like Shelley, Leigh Hunt and Hazlitt he was a liberal in his political views, and, while not an atheist, had little time for Christianity. His poetry is frequently an indirect commentary on the conventional political and religious beliefs which governed his society. It also reacts against the growing forces of prudery in the Regency period. While Regency high society was notable for sexual excess and licence, the middle and lower-middle classes had a strongly demarcated view of male and female roles and a sexual double standard, clearly foreshadowing 'Victorian' attitudes. The virulent review in *Blackwood's* in August 1818 was, from a Tory and culturally conservative viewpoint, right to see Keats as a lower-class 'Cockney', an 'ignorant and unsettled pretender' to culture, a writer of 'prurient and vulgar lines' unfit for the ladies, a 'bantling' who has 'already learned to lisp sedition', a poet who vulgarized classical poetry and mythology.

This is not to say that Keats was, like Shelley, a political poet. Throughout his life Keats always believed that true poetry was written for posterity, and that its 'realms of gold', whether created by Homer, Dante, Spenser or Shakespeare, existed in a sphere independent of the accidents of history. Keats is the one great English Romantic poet whose prime belief was in Art and Beauty. 'A thing of beauty is a joy for ever', the opening line of *Endymion: A Poetic Romance*, published in April 1818, is probably Keats's best known line. It suggests that his poetry inhabits a timeless world of Art, one endorsed by the Grecian Urn's conviction that 'Beauty is Truth, Truth Beauty'. This was certainly the case for Keats's nineteenth-century critics, and an emphasis upon Keats as a poet preoccupied by the nature of the imagination and poetry continues to the present.

Yet *Endymion*, which Keats dismissed as immature even as he published it, is more than that. It *is* loosely structured, and its self-excited dreams of poetry, love and sexual satisfaction can easily be read as adolescent fantasizing, an escape from early-nineteenth-century realities to the supposed natural freedom of ancient Greece. But it is also the most ambitious long poem Keats completed. Its reanimation of Greek mythology is a serious effort to imagine a non-Christian religion based on animism and celebrating love. At the same time, it is an implicit criticism of conventional political, religious and sexual beliefs in the contemporary world. Keats himself thought that the opening of Book III was a clear expression of his attitude to the 'present ministry', and it was precisely this passage which led the *Blackwood's* reviewer to accuse him of sedition.

Keats's later re-telling of the classical myth of Hyperion leads first to an epic fragment based on an optimistically evolutionary view of history, and then to the intensely subjective self-examination of *The Fall of Hyperion*, which is at the same time a debate about the role of contemporary poetry, and about the nature of religion and myth.

Keats's poetry does seek to believe in and embody the 'dreams of art', but it also provides a critique of the claims of poetry and the imagination, and remains aware of human suffering.

One aim of this anthology, then, is to emphasize Keats's place as a second-generation Romantic. This has meant annotating *Endymion* and the two 'Hyperion' fragments more heavily than Keats's best known works, partly to explain the allusions to contemporary events and obscure allegorical passages, partly to explain what Keats was attempting to make of his material. In differing ways, Keats's neo-Hellenism is shared by Byron, Leigh Hunt and Shelley, as is his political stance. He also resembles them in his mixed reaction to Wordsworth. Wordsworth's achievement was undeniable but his active support of the Tory government was seen as a betrayal of his earlier radicalism, and his later poetry seemed to have retreated into gloomy subjectivity. It is significant that the older poet rejected Keats's 'Hymn to Pan' in Book I of *Endymion* as a 'Very pretty piece of Paganism'.

This focus has necessitated a highly selective approach to Keats's earliest poetry, and has also meant giving rather less space to his later unpublished verse than I would have liked. The problem is caused by the length of *Endymion*. Even when represented, as here, by Book I, followed by excerpts from the other three books, there are still two thousand lines of poetry. This abbreviated version, coupled with the commentary, attempts to give a sense of the poem's overall shape and meaning. *Endymion* calls for a sympathetic and generous reading (the main point made by Keats's published and unpublished Prefaces is right). Its diction can be uncertain, arch or coy. Its basic theme, a kind of sensual Platonism in which human love and poetry are manifestations of the same power, giving access to immortal truth, makes the allegorical level liable to slip over into fantasizing. Yet it is a remarkable achievement, more serious than it first appears, and essential to Keats's development as a mythological poet.

Of Keats's earliest unpublished verse, only the attack on the celebration of Charles II's Restoration and the sonnet 'Written in Disgust of Vulgar Superstition', which attacks conventional Christianity, are included. The remaining early poems are all taken from those published in Keats's first volume. *Poems* (1817) is something of a rag-bag. Album verse, verse epistles to Keats's family and friends, Spenserian narrative fragments and a group of sonnets are all sandwiched between 'I stood tip-toe' and 'Sleep and Poetry'. The latter two, the most ambitious poems in the volume, have been given in their entirety. 'I stood tip-toe' is a catalogue of characteristic early Keatsian 'luxuries'. 'Sleep and Poetry' announces Keats's self-dedication to poetry, and includes his assessment of the achievements and shortcomings of contemporary poetry. Both works are indebted to Leigh Hunt, a sonnet to whom ('Glory and loveliness have passed away') Keats placed as the dedication to *Poems* (1817). Otherwise, the early poetry is represented by a selection from the sonnets, notably by the rapt astonishment of 'On First Looking into Chapman's Homer'.

Poems (1817) outlines Keats's ambitions and hopes, but goes little way towards fulfilling them. The extraordinary courage with which Keats committed himself to writing a full-scale allegorical work of four thousand lines was, on the evidence of his earlier work, remarkable to the point of foolhardiness. Yet Keats did succeed in drafting *Endymion* between April and November 1817 and found himself as a poet in the course of doing so. Without that experience he could not have attempted the epic scale of *Hyperion* the following autumn, nor would he have written the important speculative letters in 1817 and early 1818.

Keats's final volume, *Lamia, Isabella, The Eve of St Agnes, and Other Poems*, published in July 1820, contained most of Keats's mature poems with the exception of *The Fall of Hyperion*. It also printed some weaker pieces. The major odes and narrative poems were accompanied by the vapid medievalizing of 'Robin Hood' and the celebratory 'Lines on the Mermaid Tavern', both written in February 1818 when Keats was revising *Endymion*, and the two 'rondeaus', 'Fancy' and 'Bards of Passion and of Mirth', written late in 1818. Surprisingly, it did not contain 'La Belle Dame sans Merci' published a few months earlier in Leigh Hunt's *Indicator*, or the strange and powerful 'A Dream, after reading Dante's Episode of Paolo and Francesca', also published by Hunt.

It is not known whether Keats or his publishers were responsible for the selection and ordering of the poems (a note by the publishers told the public that *Hyperion* was included against the poet's wishes, and Taylor and Hessey refused to print Keats's alterations to *The Eve of St Agnes* making it more sexually explicit. The selection probably represents a compromise between Keats's own uncertain critical taste and that of his publishers.

Keats's undependable sense of his own poetry reflected and was caused by the instability of literary standards evident in a new and growing reading public, of which he was himself a representative. The young Keats had shared the 'ladies'' taste for 'romance' as his youth fantasies in 'Calidore', of Spenserian knights saving and serving 'lovely woman' show. But the Keats who wrote *Lamia* in 1819 no longer wished to appeal to the readers of that kind of poem. He told Richard Woodhouse that the changes to *The Eve of St Agnes* were made because 'he does not want ladies to read his poetry: that he writes for men . . .' The violence of Keats's reaction is precisely because one side of his poetic imagination shared the 'ladies'' liking for romance. The medieval stories, *Isabella*, *The Eve of St Agnes* and 'La Belle Dame sans Merci', all deal with closely related plots – young lovers whose love is opposed by the real or everyday world. *Isabella* ends in madness and death but asks for the reader's pity. In *The Eve of St Agnes* the lovers escape but into a storm, and La Belle Dame is an ominous, possibly demonic, lover. All are about people possessed by love. Keats's final 'romance' poem, *Lamia*, has a classical setting, and is more self-knowing, ironic and objective. The result is unsettling and unsettled. *Lamia* seems to reject the possibility of romantic lover or the imagination functioning in the actual world. These poems can be read very differently, and some recent readers have seen in *The Eve of St Agnes* an ironic account of Madeline as foolish virgin, self-deceived by superstition. This seems to me wrong (the point of Keats's alterations was to introduce a mocking note): *The Eve of St Agnes* celebrates youthful love while perceiving its vulnerability.

Disagreements over the meaning of Keats's romantic narratives reflect his own ambivalences. *Lamia*, a critique of romantic love and the fancy, stands at the beginning of the 1820 collection: *Hyperion*, with its faith in progress and beauty, is placed at the end, an affirmation of what the opening poem attacks. Keats's longing to believe in the consolation offered by poetry and the imagination is set against a suspicion of their insufficiency as an answer to human suffering. The major odes are invocations of, and powerful meditations upon, the subjects which preoccupy Keats's poetry – love, art, song, sorrow and the natural world. Each poses questions, but only 'To Autumn' seems to imply a resting point.

The poetry which Keats published during his lifetime is various, but is united by two features: it is uniformly 'poetic' and serious. His high conception of 'Poesy' and of 'Fame' has its constrictions. The sense of humour and the responsiveness to everyday language and life so evident in the letters are absent from the published poems. When Keats could forget the demands of high art, he was capable of a wider range of effects, from the light-hearted to the satirical. 'The Gothic looks solemn', written while he was working on *Endymion* in Benjamin Bailey's rooms at Oxford, is a quizzical look at the comforts of college life. The slight but charming 'To Mrs Reynolds's Cat' shows a talent for light verse. Keats also wrote sprightly nonsense verses in his letters to Fanny, his fifteen-year-old sister ('A Song about Myself', 'Two or three posies'). The 'Character of Charles Brown', written extemporaneously, is a good-natured private joke among friends, while a passage in the satirical 'Fragment of the "Castle Builder"' gives a vivid comic portrait of Covent Garden. Two other satirical pieces, 'And what is love? It is a doll dressed up' and 'Pensive they sit, and roll their languid eyes', mock the affectation of fashionable lovers. 'Nebuchadnezzar's Dream' is a strongly felt, if oblique, attack on George IV and his ministry.

This area of Keats's verse is most interesting when he is writing for himself or for friends. The long unfinished fantasy, 'The Cap and Bells', though written for amusement, seems to have been written in hope of eventual pseudonymous publication. The result is obscure and prolix. However, the disjointed and disturbed verse letter which Keats wrote to J. H. Reynolds on 24 March 1818, between finishing *Endymion* and starting *Isabella*, vividly describes a nightmare in which Keats saw 'too distinct' into nature's 'eternal fierce destruction'.

There is a final group of four poems. They are 'The day is gone, and all its sweets are gone', 'I cry your mercy, pity, love – ay love', 'What can I do to drive away', and 'To Fanny'. All of these were written in late 1819 or early 1820, and reflect Keats's distraught and confused feelings towards Fanny Brawne. Keats was engaged but had no secure financial future, and 'To Fanny' was probably written when seriously ill and confined to bed, while living next door to her in Hampstead. None of these poems can be understood without reference to Keats's life, and all four belong to Keats's biography rather than his poetry. He was suffering not only from jealousy, but from an obsessional fear that love was incompatible with a career in poetry. Only one of these poems is given, 'What can I do to drive away', partly as an example, partly for the remarkable passage it contains on the New World, which Keats believed to be a waste region, empty of tutelary gods.

The penultimate piece, 'This living hand, now warm and capable', probably a dramatic fragment, seeks to reach out from the past. Its poignancy is matched by Keats's final unawareness of what he had achieved. The line which he dictated to Joseph Severn on his death-bed, and which he wished to have inscribed on his tombstone, reads –

'Here lies one whose name was writ on water.'

Note on the Text

Text and chronological ordering based on my edition of *John Keats: The Complete Poems* (1973: 3rd edition, 1988). Since first editing Keats in 1973 I was able to correct my edition against Jack Stillinger's *The Texts of John Keats* (1974) in 1977, and subsequently to make further minor corrections from his edition of the poems in 1987. I now believe that the 'Bright Star' sonnet was written earlier rather than later, and date it July 1819.

Chronology

1792   Shelley born.

1794   Blake, *Songs of Experience*. Fall of Robespierre.

1795   Keats born 31 October.
         Speenhamland system of poor relief introduced.

1796   Death of Burns.

1798   Wordsworth and Coleridge, *Lyrical Ballads*. Battle of the Nile.

1799   Napoleon becomes First Consul.

1802   Scott, *Minstrelsy of the Scottish Border*, I and II.

1804   Death of Keats's father, 16 April. Mother remarries, 27 June, and her four children are sent to live with their grandparents. Napoleon proclaimed Emperor.

1805   Scott, *Lay of the Last Minstrel*. Battle of Trafalgar, 21 October.

1807   Wordsworth, *Poems in Two Volumes*; Crabbe, *The Parish Register*.

1809   Byron, *English Bards and Scotch Reviewers*; Coleridge, *The Friend*.

1810   Keats's mother dies mid-March, buried 20 March; Richard Abbey appointed guardian in July.
         Crabbe, *The Borough*; Scott, *The Lady of the Lake*.

1811   Keats leaves Enfield School and is apprenticed to Thomas Hammond, a surgeon in Edmonton.
         Jane Austen, *Sense and Sensibility*. Shelley sent down from Oxford.
         Luddite riots.

1812   Byron, *Childe Harold*, I and II. Napoleon invades Russia.

1813   Byron, *The Giaour*; Shelley, *Queen Mab*. Southey made Poet Laureate.

1814   Wordsworth, *The Excursion*; Scott, *Waverley*. Napoleon abdicates.

1815   Keats writes sonnet on Leigh Hunt's release from prison,

2 February; enters Guy's Hospital as a student, 1 October.
Byron, *Hebrew Melodies*. Battle of Waterloo; Napoleon exiled to St Helena.

1816   Keats's first poem published in the *Examiner*, 5 May. Completes medical education, 25 July. Completes 'Sleep and Poetry', December.
Coleridge, *Christabel*, *Kubla Khan*; Shelley, *Alastor*.

1817   Keats's first volume, *Poems*, published by C. and J. Ollier, 3 March. Taylor and Hessey become his future publishers, *c.* 13 April.
Plans to begin *Endymion*, 18 April.
Shelley, *Laon and Cyntha*; Coleridge, *Biographia Literaria*; Jane Austen dies.

1818   Keats attends Hazlitt's *Lectures on the English Poets*, January–February. Writes *Isabella* March–April. *Endymion* published *c.* 27 April. Walking tour, with Charles Brown, of Scotland, 24 June–18 August. Virulent review by 'Z.' in *Blackwood's Edinburgh Magazine*, August 1818. Working on *Hyperion*.
Death of Tom Keats from tuberculosis, 1 December.
Byron, *Beppo*; Mary Shelley, *Frankenstein*; Jane Austen, *Northanger Abbey*, *Persuasion*.

1819   Keats writes *The Eve of St Agnes*, January; and the great spring odes. Summer spent working on *Lamia*, *Otho the Great* (a play jointly written with Charles Brown) and *The Fall of Hyperion*. Writes 'To Autumn', 19 September, and on 21 September gives up *The Fall of Hyperion*. By the end of December engaged to Fanny Brawne. 'Rather unwell' on 22 December.
Byron, *Don Juan*, I and II; Wordsworth, *Peter Bell*; Crabbe, *Tales of the Hall*. Peterloo Massacre, 16 August.

1820   *Otho the Great* rejected by Drury Lane, January. Haemorrhage, 3 February. Offers to break off engagement, *c.* 13 February. *La Belle Dame sans Merci* published in Hunt's *Indicator*, 10 May. Corrects proofs of *Lamia* volume, *c.* 11 June. Attack of blood-spitting, 22 June. *Lamia, Isabella, The Eve of St Agnes, and Other Poems* published by Taylor and Hessey, July. Ordered to leave for Italy for his health, 5 July. Sails for Italy,

13 September. Eventually reaches Rome, 15 November. Relapse, 10 December.

Clare, *Poems Descriptive of Rural Life*; Shelley, *Prometheus Unbound*; Blake, *Jerusalem*. Accession of George IV.

1821   Dies, 23 February. Buried in Rome's Protestant Cemetery, 26 February.

Lines Written on 29 May
The Anniversary of the Restoration
of Charles II

Infatuate Britons, will you still proclaim
His memory, your direst, foulest shame?
    Nor patriots revere?

Ah! when I hear each traitorous lying bell,
'Tis gallant Sidney's, Russell's, Vane's sad knell,
    That pains my wounded ear.
                (Not published by Keats)

On First Looking into
Chapman's Homer

Much have I travelled in the realms of gold,
   And many goodly states and kingdoms seen;
   Round many western islands have I been
Which bards in fealty to Apollo hold.
Oft of one wide expanse had I been told
   That deep-browed Homer ruled as his demesne;
   Yet did I never breathe its pure serene
Till I heard Chapman speak out loud and bold:
Then felt I like some watcher of the skies
   When a new planet swims into his ken;
Or like stout Cortez when with eagle eyes
   He stared at the Pacific – and all his men
Looked at each other with a wild surmise –
   Silent, upon a peak in Darien.

To my Brothers

Small, busy flames play through the fresh-laid coals,
    And their faint cracklings o'er our silence creep
    Like whispers of the household gods that keep
A gentle empire o'er fraternal souls.
And while, for rhymes, I search around the poles,
    Your eyes are fixed, as in poetic sleep,
    Upon the lore so voluble and deep,
That aye at fall of night our care condoles.
This is your birth-day Tom, and I rejoice
    That thus it passes smoothly, quietly.
Many such eves of gently whispering noise
    May we together pass, and calmly try
What are this world's true joys – ere the great voice,
    From its fair face, shall bid our spirits fly.

Addressed to [Haydon]

Great spirits now on earth are sojourning;
    He of the cloud, the cataract, the lake,
    Who on Helvellyn's summit, wide awake,
Catches his freshness from Archangel's wing:
He of the rose, the violet, the spring,
    The social smile, the chain for Freedom's sake:
    And lo! – whose steadfastness would never take
A meaner sound than Raphael's whispering.
And other spirits there are standing apart
    Upon the forehead of the age to come;
These, these will give the world another heart,
    And other pulses. Hear ye not the hum
Of mighty workings? –
    Listen awhile ye nations, and be dumb.

'I stood tip-toe upon a little hill'

Places of nestling green for Poets made
          'The Story of Rimini'

I stood tip-toe upon a little hill,
The air was cooling, and so very still,
That the sweet buds which with a modest pride
Pull droopingly, in slanting curve aside,
Their scantly leaved, and finely tapering stems,
Had not yet lost those starry diadems
Caught from the early sobbing of the morn.
The clouds were pure and white as flocks new shorn,
And fresh from the clear brook; sweetly they slept
On the blue fields of heaven, and then there crept   10
A little noiseless noise among the leaves,
Born of the very sigh that silence heaves:
For not the faintest motion could be seen
Of all the shades that slanted o'er the green.
There was wide wandering for the greediest eye,
To peer about upon variety;
Far round the horizon's crystal air to skim,
And trace the dwindled edgings of its brim;
To picture out the quaint, and curious bending
Of a fresh woodland alley, never ending;   20
Or by the bowery clefts, and leafy shelves,
Guess where the jaunty streams refresh themselves.
I gazed awhile, and felt as light, and free
As though the fanning wings of Mercury
Had played upon my heels: I was light-hearted,
And many pleasures to my vision started;
So I straightway began to pluck a posy
Of luxuries bright, milky, soft and rosy.

A bush of May flowers with the bees about them;
Ah, sure no tasteful nook would be without them;
And let a lush laburnum oversweep them,
And let long grass grow round the roots to keep them
Moist, cool and green; and shade the violets,
That they may bind the moss in leafy nets.

A filbert hedge with wild briar overtwined,
And clumps of woodbine taking the soft wind
Upon their summer thrones; there too should be
The frequent chequer of a youngling tree,
That with a score of light green brethren shoots
From the quaint mossiness of agèd roots:
Round which is heard a spring-head of clear waters
Babbling so wildly of its lovely daughters
The spreading blue-bells – it may haply mourn
That such fair clusters should be rudely torn
From their fresh beds, and scattered thoughtlessly
By infant hands, left on the path to die.
Open afresh your round of starry folds,
Ye ardent marigolds!
Dry up the moisture from your golden lids,
For great Apollo bids
That in these days your praises should be sung
On many harps, which he has lately strung;
And when again your dewiness he kisses,
Tell him, I have you in my world of blisses:
So haply when I rove in some far vale,
His mighty voice may come upon the gale.

Here are sweet peas, on tip-toe for a flight:
With wings of gentle flush o'er delicate white,
And taper fingers catching at all things,
To bind them all about with tiny rings.

Linger awhile upon some bending planks
That lean against a streamlet's rushy banks,
And watch intently Nature's gentle doings:
They will be found softer than ring-dove's cooings.
How silent comes the water round that bend;
Not the minutest whisper does it send
To the o'erhanging sallows: blades of grass
Slowly across the chequered shadows pass –
Why, you might read two sonnets, ere they reach
To where the hurrying freshnesses aye preach   70
A natural sermon o'er their pebbly beds;
Where swarms of minnows show their little heads,
Staying their wavy bodies 'gainst the streams,
To taste the luxury of sunny beams
Tempered with coolness. How they ever wrestle
With their own sweet delight, and ever nestle
Their silver bellies on the pebbly sand.
If you but scantily hold out the hand,
That very instant not one will remain;
But turn your eye, and they are there again.   80
The ripples seem right glad to reach those cresses,
And cool themselves among the emerald tresses;
The while they cool themselves, they freshness give,
And moisture, that the bowery green may live:
So keeping up an interchange of favours,
Like good men in the truth of their behaviours.
Sometimes goldfinches one by one will drop
From low-hung branches; little space they stop;
But sip, and twitter, and their feathers sleek –
Then off at once, as in a wanton freak: 90
Or perhaps, to show their black, and golden wings,
Pausing upon their yellow flutterings.
Were I in such a place, I sure should pray
That naught less sweet, might call my thoughts away,
Than the soft rustle of a maiden's gown
Fanning away the dandelion's down;

Than the light music of her nimble toes
Patting against the sorrel as she goes.
How she would start, and blush, thus to be caught
Playing in all her innocence of thought.
O let me lead her gently o'er the brook,
Watch her half-smiling lips, and downward look;
O let me for one moment touch her wrist;
Let me one moment to her breathing list;
And as she leaves me may she often turn
Her fair eyes looking through her locks aubùrn.

What next? A tuft of evening primroses,
O'er which the mind may hover till it dozes;
O'er which it well might take a pleasant sleep,
But that 'tis ever startled by the leap
Of buds into ripe flowers; or by the flitting
Of diverse moths, that aye their rest are quitting;
Or by the moon lifting her silver rim
Above a cloud, and with a gradual swim
Coming into the blue with all her light.
O Maker of sweet poets, dear delight
Of this fair world, and all its gentle livers;
Spangler of clouds, halo of crystal rivers,
Mingler with leaves, and dew and tumbling streams,
Closer of lovely eyes to lovely dreams,
Lover of loneliness, and wandering,
Of upcast eye, and tender pondering!
Thee must I praise above all other glories
That smile us on to tell delightful stories.
For what has made the sage or poet write
But the fair paradise of Nature's light?
In the calm grandeur of a sober line,
We see the waving of the mountain pine;
And when a tale is beautifully staid,
We feel the safety of a hawthorn glade:
When it is moving on luxurious wings,

The soul is lost in pleasant smotherings:
Fair dewy roses brush against our faces,
And flowering laurels spring from diamond vases;
O'er head we see the jasmine and sweet briar,
And bloomy grapes laughing from green attire;
While at our feet, the voice of crystal bubbles
Charms us at once away from all our troubles:
So that we feel uplifted from the world,
Walking upon the white clouds wreathed and curled.   140
So felt he, who first told, how Psyche went
On the smooth wind to realms of wonderment;
What Psyche felt, and Love, when their full lips
First touched; what amorous, and fondling nips
They gave each other's cheeks; with all their sighs,
And how they kissed each other's tremulous eyes;
The silver lamp – the ravishment – the wonder –
The darkness – loneliness – the fearful thunder;
Their woes gone by, and both to heaven upflown,
To bow for gratitude before Jove's throne.   150
So did he feel, who pulled the boughs aside,
That we might look into a forest wide,
To catch a glimpse of Fauns and Dryadès
Coming with softest rustle through the trees,
And garlands woven of flowers wild, and sweet,
Upheld on ivory wrists, or sporting feet:
Telling us how fair, trembling Syrinx fled
Arcadian Pan, with such a fearful dread.
Poor nymph – poor Pan – how he did weep to find,
Naught but a lovely sighing of the wind   160
Along the reedy stream; a half-heard strain,
Full of sweet desolation – balmy pain.

What first inspired a bard of old to sing
Narcissus pining o'er the untainted spring?
In some delicious ramble, he had found
A little space, with boughs all woven round;

And in the midst of all, a clearer pool
Than e'er reflected in its pleasant cool
The blue sky here and there serenely peeping
170   Through tendril wreaths fantastically creeping.
And on the bank a lonely flower he spied,
A meek and forlorn flower, with naught of pride,
Drooping its beauty o'er the watery clearness,
To woo its own sad image into nearness:
Deaf to light Zephyrus it would not move:
But still would seem to droop, to pine, to love.
So while the Poet stood in this sweet spot,
Some fainter gleamings o'er his fancy shot;
Nor was it long ere he had told the tale
180   Of young Narcissus, and sad Echo's bale.

    Where had he been, from whose warm head out-flew
That sweetest of all songs, that ever new,
That aye refreshing, pure deliciousness,
Coming ever to bless
The wanderer by moonlight? to him bringing
Shapes from the invisible world, unearthly singing
From out the middle air, from flowery nests,
And from the pillowy silkiness that rests
Full in the speculation of the stars.
190   Ah! surely he had burst our mortal bars;
Into some wondrous region he had gone,
To search for thee, divine Endymion!

    He was a Poet, sure a lover too,
Who stood on Latmos' top, what time there blew
Soft breezes from the myrtle vale below;
And brought in faintness solemn, sweet, and slow
A hymn from Dian's temple; while upswelling,
The incense went to her own starry dwelling.
But though her face was clear as infant's eyes,
200   Though she stood smiling o'er the sacrifice,
The Poet wept at her so piteous fate,

Wept that such beauty should be desolate:
So in fine wrath some golden sounds he won,
And gave meek Cynthia her Endymion.

   Queen of the wide air! thou most lovely queen
Of all the brightness that mine eyes have seen!
As though exceedest all things in thy shine,
So every tale, does this sweet tale of thine.
O for three words of honey, that I might
Tell but one wonder of thy bridal night!   210

   Where distant ships do seem to show their keels,
Phoebus awhile delayed his mighty wheels,
And turned to smile upon thy bashful eyes,
Ere he his unseen pomp would solemnize.
The evening weather was so bright and clear,
That men of health were of unusual cheer;
Stepping like Homer at the trumpet's call,
Or young Apollo on the pedestal:
And lovely women were as fair and warm,
As Venus looking sideways in alarm.   220
The breezes were ethereal, and pure,
And crept through half-closed lattices to cure
The languid sick; it cooled their fevered sleep,
And soothed them into slumbers full and deep.
Soon they awoke clear-eyed: nor burnt with thirsting,
Nor with hot fingers, nor with temples bursting:
And springing up, they met the wondering sight
Of their dear friends, nigh foolish with delight;
Who feel their arms, and breasts, and kiss and stare,
And on their placid foreheads part the hair.   230
Young men, and maidens at each other gazed
With hands held back, and motionless, amazed
To see the brightness in each other's eyes;
And so they stood, filled with a sweet surprise,
Until their tongues were loosed in Poesy.
Therefore no lover did of anguish die:

But the soft numbers, in that moment spoken,
Made silken ties, that never may be broken.
Cynthia! I cannot tell the greater blisses,
That followed thine, and thy dear shepherd's kisses:
Was there a Poet born? – but now no more,
My wandering spirit must no further soar. –

240

Sleep and Poetry

As I lay in my bed slepe full unmete
Was unto me, but why that I ne might
Rest I ne wist, for there n'as earthly wight
[As I suppose] had more of hertis ese
Than I, for I n'ad sicknesse nor disese.
                                        Chaucer

What is more gentle than a wind in summer?
What is more soothing than the pretty hummer
That stays one moment in an open flower,
And buzzes cheerily from bower to bower?
What is more tranquil than a musk-rose blowing
In a green island, far from all men's knowing?
More healthful than the leafiness of dales?
More secret than a nest of nightingales?
More serene than Cordelia's countenance?
More full of visions than a high romance?
What, but thee Sleep? Soft closer of our eyes!
Low murmurer of tender lullabies!
Light hoverer around our happy pillows!
Wreather of poppy buds, and weeping willows!
Silent entangler of a beauty's tresses!
Most happy listener! when the morning blesses
Thee for enlivening all the cheerful eyes
That glance so brightly at the new sun-rise.

10

   But what is higher beyond thought than thee?
Fresher than berries of a mountain tree?   20
More strange, more beautiful, more smooth, more regal,
Than wings of swans, than doves, than dim-seen eagle?
What is it? And to what shall I compare it?
It has a glory, and naught else can share it:
The thought thereof is awful, sweet, and holy,
Chasing away all worldliness and folly;
Coming sometimes like fearful claps of thunder,
Or the low rumblings earth's regions under;
And sometimes like a gentle whispering
Of all the secrets of some wondrous thing   30
That breathes about us in the vacant air;
So that we look around with prying stare,
Perhaps to see shapes of light, aërial limning,
And catch soft floatings from a faint-heard hymning,
To see the laurel wreath, on high suspended,
That is to crown our name when life is ended.
Sometimes it gives a glory to the voice,
And from the heart up-springs, 'Rejoice! Rejoice!' –
Sounds which will reach the Framer of all things,
And die away in ardent mutterings.   40

   No one who once the glorious sun has seen,
And all the clouds, and felt his bosom clean
For his great Maker's presence, but must know
What 'tis I mean, and feel his being glow:
Therefore no insult will I give his spirit,
By telling what he sees from native merit.

   O Poesy! for thee I hold my pen
That am not yet a glorious denizen
Of thy wide heaven – Should I rather kneel
Upon some mountain-top until I feel   50
A glowing splendour round about me hung,
And echo back the voice of thine own tongue?
O Poesy! for thee I grasp my pen

That am not yet a glorious denizen
Of thy wide heaven; yet, to my ardent prayer,
Yield from thy sanctuary some clear air,
Smoothed for intoxication by the breath
Of flowering bays, that I may die a death
Of luxury, and my young spirit follow
60   The morning sunbeams to the great Apollo
Like a fresh sacrifice; or, if I can bear
The o'erwhelming sweets, 'twill bring to me the fair
Visions of all places: a bowery nook
Will be elysium – an eternal book
Whence I may copy many a lovely saying
About the leaves, and flowers – about the playing
Of nymphs in woods, and fountains; and the shade
Keeping a silence round a sleeping maid;
And many a verse from so strange influence
70   That we must ever wonder how, and whence
It came. Also imaginings will hover
Round my fire-side, and haply there discover
Vistas of solemn beauty, where I'd wander
In happy silence, like the clear Meander
Through its lone vales; and where I found a spot
Of awfuller shade, or an enchanted grot,
Or a green hill o'erspread with chequered dress
Of flowers, and fearful from its loveliness,
Write on my tablets all that was permitted,
80   All that was for our human senses fitted.
Then the events of this wide world I'd seize
Like a strong giant, and my spirit tease
Till at its shoulders it should proudly see
Wings to find out an immortality.

     Stop and consider! life is but a day;
A fragile dew-drop on its perilous way
From a tree's summit; a poor Indian's sleep
While his boat hastens to the monstrous steep

Of Montmorenci. Why so sad a moan?
Life is the rose's hope while yet unblown; 90
The reading of an ever-changing tale;
The light uplifting of a maiden's veil;
A pigeon tumbling in clear summer air;
A laughing school-boy, without grief or care,
Riding the springy branches of an elm.

    O for ten years, that I may overwhelm
Myself in poesy; so I may do the deed
That my own soul has to itself decreed.
Then will I pass the countries that I see
In long perspective, and continually 100
Taste their pure fountains. First the realm I'll pass
Of Flora, and old Pan: sleep in the grass,
Feed upon apples red, and strawberries,
And choose each pleasure that my fancy sees;
Catch the white-handed nymphs in shady places,
To woo sweet kisses from averted faces –
Play with their fingers, touch their shoulders white
Into a pretty shrinking with a bite
As hard as lips can make it, till, agreed,
A lovely tale of human life we'll read. 110
And one will teach a tame dove how it best
May fan the cool air gently o'er my rest;
Another, bending o'er her nimble tread,
Will set a green robe floating round her head,
And still will dance with ever varied ease,
Smiling upon the flowers and the trees:
Another will entice me on, and on
Through almond blossoms and rich cinnamon;
Till in the bosom of a leafy world
We rest in silence, like two gems upcurled 120
In the recesses of a pearly shell.

    And can I ever bid these joys farewell?
Yes, I must pass them for a nobler life,

Where I may find the agonies, the strife
Of human hearts – for lo! I see afar,
O'er-sailing the blue cragginess, a car
And steeds with streamy manes – the charioteer
Looks out upon the winds with glorious fear:
And now the numerous tramplings quiver lightly
130   Along a huge cloud's ridge; and now with sprightly
Wheel downward come they into fresher skies,
Tipped round with silver from the sun's bright eyes.
Still downward with capacious whirl they glide;
And now I see them on a green-hill's side
In breezy rest among the nodding stalks.
The charioteer with wondrous gesture talks
To the trees and mountains; and there soon appear
Shapes of delight, of mystery, and fear,
Passing along before a dusky space
140   Made by some mighty oaks: as they would chase
Some ever-fleeting music on they sweep.
Lo! how they murmur, laugh, and smile, and weep –
Some with upholden hand and mouth severe;
Some with their faces muffled to the ear
Between their arms; some, clear in youthful bloom,
Go glad and smilingly athwart the gloom;
Some looking back, and some with upward gaze;
Yes, thousands in a thousand different ways
Flit onward – now a lovely wreath of girls
150   Dancing their sleek hair into tangled curls;
And now broad wings. Most awfully intent
The driver of those steeds is forward bent,
And seems to listen: O that I might know
All that he writes with such a hurrying glow.

     The visions all are fled – the car is fled
Into the light of heaven, and in their stead
A sense of real things comes doubly strong,
And, like a muddy stream, would bear along

My soul to nothingness: but I will strive
Against all doubtings, and will keep alive   160
The thought of that same chariot, and the strange
Journey it went.

          Is there so small a range
In the present strength of manhood, that the high
Imagination cannot freely fly
As she was wont of old? Prepare her steeds,
Paw up against the light, and do strange deeds
Upon the clouds? Has she not shown us all?
From the clear space of ether, to the small
Breath of new buds unfolding? From the meaning
Of Jove's large eye-brow, to the tender greening   170
Of April meadows? Here her altar shone,
E'en in this isle; and who could paragon
The fervid choir that lifted up a noise
Of harmony, to where it aye will poise
Its mighty self of convoluting sound,
Huge as a planet, and like that roll round,
Eternally around a dizzy void?
Ay, in those days the Muses were nigh cloyed
With honours; nor had any other care
Than to sing out and soothe their wavy hair.   180

   Could all this be forgotten? Yes, a schism
Nurtured by foppery and barbarism,
Made great Apollo blush for this his land.
Men were thought wise who could not understand
His glories: with a puling infant's force
They swayed about upon a rocking horse,
And thought it Pegasus. Ah, dismal souled!
The winds of heaven blew, the ocean rolled
Its gathering waves – ye felt it not. The blue
Bared its eternal bosom, and the dew   190
Of summer nights collected still to make

The morning precious: beauty was awake!
Why were ye not awake? But ye were dead
To things ye knew not of – were closely wed
To musty laws lined out with wretched rule
And compass vile: so that ye taught a school
Of dolts to smooth, inlay, and clip, and fit,
Till, like the certain wands of Jacob's wit,
Their verses tallied. Easy was the task:
A thousand handicraftsmen wore the mask
Of Poesy. Ill-fated, impious race!
That blasphemed the bright Lyrist to his face,
And did not know it! No, they went about,
Holding a poor, decrepit standard out
Marked with most flimsy mottoes, and in large
The name of one Boileau!

                O ye whose charge
It is to hover round our pleasant hills!
Whose congregated majesty so fills
My boundly reverence, that I cannot trace
Your hallowed names, in this unholy place,
So near those common folk – did not their shames
Affright you? Did our old lamenting Thames
Delight you? Did ye never cluster round
Delicious Avon, with a mournful sound,
And weep? Or did ye wholly bid adieu
To regions where no more the laurel grew?
Or did ye stay to give a welcoming
To some lone spirits who could proudly sing
Their youth away, and die? 'Twas even so.
But let me think away those times of woe:
Now 'tis a fairer season; ye have breathed
Rich benedictions o'er us; ye have wreathed
Fresh garlands: for sweet music has been heard
In many places – some has been upstirred
From out its crystal dwelling in a lake,

By a swan's ebon bill; from a thick brake,
Nested and quiet in a valley mild,
Bubbles a pipe – fine sounds are floating wild
About the earth: happy are ye and glad.

    These things are doubtless: yet in truth we've had   230
Strange thunders from the potency of song;
Mingled indeed with what is sweet and strong,
From majesty: but in clear truth the themes
Are ugly clubs, the poets Polyphemes
Disturbing the grand sea. A drainless shower
Of light is Poesy; 'tis the supreme of power;
'Tis might half-slumbering on its own right arm.
The very archings of her eye-lids charm
A thousand willing agents to obey,
And still she governs with the mildest sway: 240
But strength alone, though of the Muses born,
Is like a fallen angel: trees uptorn,
Darkness, and worms, and shrouds, and sepulchres
Delight it; for it feeds upon the burrs,
And thorns of life; forgetting the great end
Of Poesy, that it should be a friend
To soothe the cares, and lift the thoughts of man.

    Yet I rejoice: a myrtle fairer than
E'er grew in Paphos, from the bitter weeds
Lifts its sweet head into the air, and feeds   250
A silent space with ever sprouting green.
All tenderest birds there find a pleasant screen,
Creep through the shade with jaunty fluttering,
Nibble the little cuppèd flowers and sing.
Then let us clear away the choking thorns
From round its gentle stem; let the young fawns,
Yeaned in after times, when we are flown,
Find a fresh sward beneath it, overgrown
With simple flowers: let there nothing be
More boisterous than a lover's bended knee;   260

Naught more ungentle than the placid look
Of one who leans upon a closèd book;
Naught more untranquil than the grassy slopes
Between two hills. All hail delightful hopes!
As she was wont, th' imagination
Into most lovely labyrinths will be gone,
And they shall be accounted poet-kings
Who simply tell the most heart-easing things.
O may these joys be ripe before I die.

270   Will not some say that I presumptuously
Have spoken? that from hastening disgrace
'Twere better far to hide my foolish face?
That whining boyhood should with reverence bow
Ere the dread thunderbolt could reach? How!
If I do hide myself, it sure shall be
In the very fane, the light of Poesy:
If I do fall, at least I will be laid
Beneath the silence of a poplar shade;
And over me the grass shall be smooth-shaven;
280   And there shall be a kind memorial graven.
But off, Despondence! miserable bane!
They should not know thee, who, athirst to gain
A noble end, are thirsty every hour.
What though I am not wealthy in the dower
Of spanning wisdom; though I do not know
The shiftings of the mighty winds that blow
Hither and thither all the changing thoughts
Of man: though no great minist'ring reason sorts
Out the dark mysteries of human souls
290   To clear conceiving – yet there ever rolls
A vast idea before me, and I glean
Therefrom my liberty; thence too I've seen
The end and aim of Poesy. 'Tis clear
As anything most true; as that the year
Is made of the four seasons – manifest

As a large cross, some old cathedral's crest,
Lifted to the white clouds. Therefore should I
Be but the essence of deformity,
A coward, did my very eye-lids wink
At speaking out what I have dared to think.   300
Ah! rather let me like a madman run
Over some precipice! let the hot sun
Melt my Dedalian wings, and drive me down
Convulsed and headlong! Say! an inward frown
Of conscience bids me be more calm awhile.
An ocean dim, sprinkled with many an isle,
Spreads awfully before me. How much toil!
How many days! what desperate turmoil!
Ere I can have explored its widenesses.
Ah, what a task! upon my bended knees,   310
I could unsay those – no, impossible!
Impossible!

       For sweet relief I'll dwell
On humbler thoughts, and let this strange assay
Begun in gentleness die so away.
E'en now all tumult from my bosom fades:
I turn full-hearted to the friendly aids
That smooth the path of honour; brotherhood,
And friendliness the nurse of mutual good.
The hearty grasp that sends a pleasant sonnet
Into the brain ere one can think upon it;   320
The silence when some rhymes are coming out;
And when they're come, the very pleasant rout:
The message certain to be done to-morrow –
'Tis perhaps as well that it should be to borrow
Some precious book from out its snug retreat,
To cluster round it when we next shall meet.
Scarce can I scribble on; for lovely airs
Are fluttering round the room like doves in pairs;
Many delights of that glad day recalling,

330 When first my senses caught their tender falling.
And with these airs come forms of elegance
Stooping their shoulders o'er a horse's prance,
Careless, and grand – fingers soft and round
Parting luxuriant curls – and the swift bound
Of Bacchus from his chariot, when his eye
Made Ariadne's cheek look blushingly.
Thus I remember all the pleasant flow
Of words at opening a portfolio.

        Things such as these are ever harbingers
340 To trains of peaceful images: the stirs
Of a swan's neck unseen among the rushes;
A linnet starting all about the bushes;
A butterfly, with golden wings broad parted,
Nestling a rose, convulsed as though it smarted
With over-pleasure – many, many more,
Might I indulge at large in all my store
Of luxuries: yet I must not forget
Sleep, quiet with his poppy coronet,
For what there may be worthy in these rhymes
350 I partly owe to him: and thus, the chimes
Of friendly voices had just given place
To as sweet a silence, when I 'gan retrace
The pleasant day, upon a couch at ease.
It was a poet's house who keeps the keys
Of Pleasure's temple. Round about were hung
The glorious features of the bards who sung
In other ages – cold and sacred busts
Smiled at each other. Happy he who trusts
To clear Futurity his darling fame!
360 Then there were fauns and satyrs taking aim
At swelling apples with a frisky leap
And reaching fingers, 'mid a luscious heap
Of vine leaves. Then there rose to view a fane
Of liny marble, and thereto a train

Of nymphs approaching fairly o'er the sward:
One, loveliest, holding her white hand toward
The dazzling sun-rise: two sisters sweet
Bending their graceful figures till they meet
Over the trippings of a little child:
And some are hearing, eagerly, the wild   370
Thrilling liquidity of dewy piping.
See, in another picture, nymphs are wiping
Cherishingly Diana's timorous limbs –
A fold of lawny mantle dabbling swims
At the bath's edge, and keeps a gentle motion
With the subsiding crystal, as when ocean
Heaves calmly its broad swelling smoothness o'er
Its rocky marge, and balances once more
The patient weeds, that now unshent by foam
Feel all about their undulating home.   380

    Sappho's meek head was there half smiling down
At nothing; just as though the earnest frown
Of over-thinking had that moment gone
From off her brow, and left her all alone.

    Great Alfred's too, with anxious, pitying eyes,
As if he always listened to the sighs
Of the goaded world; and Kosciusko's worn
By horrid sufferance – mightily forlorn.

    Petrarch, outstepping from the shady green,
Starts at the sight of Laura; nor can wean   390
His eyes from her sweet face. Most happy they!
For over them was seen a free display
Of out-spread wings, and from between them shone
The face of Poesy: from off her throne
She overlooked things that I scarce could tell.
The very sense of where I was might well
Keep Sleep aloof: but more than that there came
Thought after thought to nourish up the flame

400

Within my breast; so that the morning light
Surprised me even from a sleepless night;
And up I rose refreshed, and glad, and gay,
Resolving to begin that very day
These lines; and howsoever they be done,
I leave them as a father does his son.

_____

Written in Disgust of Vulgar Superstition

The church bells toll a melancholy round,
 Calling the people to some other prayers,
 Some other gloominess, more dreadful cares,
More hearkening to the sermon's horrid sound.
Surely the mind of man is closely bound
 In some black spell; seeing that each one tears
 Himself from fireside joys, and Lydian airs,
And converse high of those with glory crowned.
Still, still they toll, and I should feel a damp –
10 A chill as from a tomb – did I not know
That they are dying like an outburnt lamp;
 That 'tis their sighing, wailing ere they go
 Into oblivion – that fresh flowers will grow,
And many glories of immortal stamp.

     (Not published by Keats)

_____

To Kosciusko

Good Kosciusko, thy great name alone
 Is a full harvest whence to reap high feeling;
 It comes upon us like the glorious pealing
Of the wide spheres – an everlasting tone.
And now it tells me, that in worlds unknown,
 The names of heroes burst from clouds concealing,

And change to harmonies, for ever stealing
Through cloudless blue, and round each silver throne.
It tells me too, that on a happy day,
   When some good spirit walks upon the earth,   10
     Thy name with Alfred's and the great of yore
   Gently commingling, gives tremendous birth
To a loud hymn, that sounds far, far away
     To where the great God lives for evermore.

===

'After dark vapours have oppressed our plains'

After dark vapours have oppressed our plains
   For a long dreary season, comes a day
   Born of the gentle South, and clears away
From the sick heavens all unseemly stains.
The anxious month, relieving from its pains,
   Takes as a long-lost right the feel of May,
   The eyelids with the passing coolness play,
Like rose leaves with the drip of summer rains.
And calmest thoughts come round us – as of leaves
   Budding – fruit ripening in stillness – autumn suns   10
Smiling at eve upon the quiet sheaves –
Sweet Sappho's cheek – a sleeping infant's breath –
   The gradual sand that through an hour-glass runs –
A woodland rivulet – a Poet's death.

===

To Leigh Hunt, Esq.

Glory and loveliness have passed away;
   For if we wander out in early morn,
   No wreathèd incense do we see upborne
Into the east, to meet the smiling day:
No crowd of nymphs soft voiced and young, and gay,

In woven baskets bringing ears of corn,
   Roses, and pinks, and violets, to adorn
The shrine of Flora in her early May.
But there are left delights as high as these,
   And I shall ever bless my destiny,
That in a time, when under pleasant trees
   Pan is no longer sought, I feel a free,
A leafy luxury, seeing I could please
   With these poor offerings, a man like thee.

On the Sea

It keeps eternal whisperings around
   Desolate shores, and with its mighty swell
   Gluts twice ten thousand caverns, till the spell
Of Hecate leaves them their old shadowy sound.
Often 'tis in such gentle temper found,
   That scarcely will the very smallest shell
   Be moved for days from where it sometime fell,
When last the winds of Heaven were unbound.
Oh ye! who have your eye-balls vexed and tired,
   Feast them upon the wideness of the Sea –
     Oh ye! whose ears are dinned with uproar rude,
   Or fed too much with cloying melody –
     Sit ye near some old cavern's mouth and brood,
Until ye start, as if the sea-nymphs quired!

═══════

'The Gothic looks solemn'

The Gothic looks solemn –
The plain Doric column
Supports an old Bishop and crosier;
The mouldering arch,
Shaded o'er by a larch
Stands next door to Wilson the Hosier.

Vicè – that is, by turns –
O'er pale faces mourns
The black-tassled trencher and common hat;
The chantry boy sings,   10
The steeple bell rings,
And as for the Chancellor – *dominat.*

There are plenty of trees,
And plenty of ease,
And plenty of fat deer for parsons;
And when it is venison,
Short is the benison –
Then each on a leg or thigh fastens.

(Not published by Keats)

Endymion:
A Poetic Romance

'The stretched metre of an antique song'
INSCRIBED TO THE MEMORY OF THOMAS
CHATTERTON

PREFACE

Knowing within myself the manner in which this Poem has been produced, it is not without a feeling of regret that I make it public.

What manner I mean, will be quite clear to the reader, who must soon perceive great inexperience, immaturity, and every error denoting a feverish attempt, rather than a deed accomplished. The two first books, and indeed the two last, I feel sensible are not of such completion as to warrant their passing the press; nor should they if I thought a year's castigation would do them any good; – it will not: the foundations are too sandy. It is just that this youngster should die away: a sad thought for me, if I had not some hope that while it is dwindling I may be plotting, and fitting myself for verses fit to live.

This may be speaking too presumptuously, and may deserve a punishment: but no feeling man will be forward to inflict it: he will leave me alone, with the conviction that there is not a fiercer hell than the failure in a great object. This is not written with the least atom of purpose to forestall criticisms of course, but from the desire I have to conciliate men who are competent to look, and who do look with a zealous eye, to the honour of English literature.

The imagination of a boy is healthy, and mature imagination of a man is healthy; but there is a space of life between, in which the soul is in a ferment, the character undecided, the way of life uncertain, the ambition thick-sighted: thence proceeds mawkishness, and all the thousand bitters which those men I speak of must necessarily taste in going over the following pages.

I hope I have not in too late a day touched the beautiful mythology of Greece, and dulled its brightness: for I wish to try once more, before I bid it farewell.

Teignmouth, 10 April 1818

BOOK I

A thing of beauty is a joy for ever:
Its loveliness increases; it will never
Pass into nothingness; but still will keep
A bower quiet for us, and a sleep
Full of sweet dreams, and health, and quiet breathing.
Therefore, on every morrow, are we wreathing
A flowery band to bind us to the earth,
Spite of despondence, of the inhuman dearth
Of noble natures, of the gloomy days,
Of all the unhealthy and o'er-darkened ways   10
Made for our searching: yes, in spite of all,
Some shape of beauty moves away the pall
From our dark spirits. Such the sun, the moon,
Trees old, and young, sprouting a shady boon
For simple sheep; and such are daffodils
With the green world they live in; and clear rills
That for themselves a cooling covert make
'Gainst the hot season; the mid forest brake,
Rich with a sprinkling of fair musk-rose blooms:
And such too is the grandeur of the dooms   20
We have imagined for the mighty dead;
All lovely tales that we have heard or read –
An endless fountain of immortal drink,
Pouring unto us from the heaven's brink.

   Nor do we merely feel these essences
For one short hour; no, even as the trees
That whisper round a temple become soon
Dear as the temple's self, so does the moon,
The passion poesy, glories infinite,

30 Haunt us till they become a cheering light
Unto our souls, and bound to us so fast,
That, whether there be shine, or gloom o'ercast,
They alway must be with us, or we die.

      Therefore, 'tis with full happiness that I
Will trace the story of Endymion.
The very music of the name has gone
Into my being, and each pleasant scene
Is growing fresh before me as the green
Of our own valleys: so I will begin
40 Now while I cannot hear the city's din;
Now while the early budders are just new,
And run in mazes of the youngest hue
About old forests; while the willow trails
Its delicate amber; and the dairy pails
Bring home increase of milk. And, as the year
Grows lush in juicy stalks, I'll smoothly steer
My little boat, for many quiet hours,
With streams that deepen freshly into bowers.
Many and many a verse I hope to write,
50 Before the daisies, vermeil-rimmed and white,
Hide in deep herbage; and ere yet the bees
Hum about globes of clover and sweet peas,
I must be near the middle of my story.
O may no wintry season, bare and hoary,
See it half finished; but let Autumn bold,
With universal tinge of sober gold,
Be all about me when I make an end.
And now at once, adventuresome, I send
My herald thought into a wilderness –
60 There let its trumpet blow, and quickly dress
My uncertain path with green, that I may speed
Easily onward, thorough flowers and weed.

Upon the sides of Latmos was outspread
A mighty forest; for the moist earth fed
So plenteously all weed-hidden roots
Into o'er-hanging boughs, and precious fruits.
And it had gloomy shades, sequestered deep,
Where no man went; and if from shepherd's keep
A lamb strayed far a-down those inmost glens,
Never again saw he the happy pens   70
Whither his brethren, bleating with content,
Over the hills at every nightfall went.
Among the shepherds, 'twas believèd ever,
That not one fleecy lamb which thus did sever
From the white flock, but passed unworrièd
By angry wolf, or pard with prying head,
Until it came to some unfooted plains
Where fed the herds of Pan – aye great his gains
Who thus one lamb did lose. Paths there were many,
Winding through palmy fern, and rushes fenny,   80
And ivy banks; all leading pleasantly
To a wide lawn, whence one could only see
Stems thronging all around between the swell
Of turf and slanting branches: who could tell
The freshness of the space of heaven above,
Edged round with dark tree tops? through which a dove
Would often beat its wings, and often too
A little cloud would move across the blue.

Full in the middle of this pleasantness
There stood a marble altar, with a tress   90
Of flowers budded newly; and the dew
Had taken fairy fantasies to strew
Daisies upon the sacred sward last eve,
And so the dawnèd light in pomp receive.
For 'twas the morn: Apollo's upward fire
Made every eastern cloud a silvery pyre
Of brightness so unsullied, that therein

A melancholy spirit well might win
Oblivion, and melt out his essence fine
100   Into the winds: rain-scented eglantine
Gave temperate sweets to that well-wooing sun,
The lark was lost in him; cold springs had run
To warm their chilliest bubbles in the grass;
Man's voice was on the mountains; and the mass
Of nature's lives and wonders pulsed tenfold,
To feel this sun-rise and its glories old.

    Now while the silent workings of the dawn
Were busiest, into that self-same lawn
All suddenly, with joyful cries, there sped
110   A troop of little children garlanded;
Who gathering round the altar, seemed to pry
Earnestly round, as wishing to espy
Some folk of holiday: nor had they waited
For many moments, ere their ears were sated
With a faint breath of music, which even then
Filled out its voice, and died away again.
Within a little space again it gave
Its airy swellings, with a gentle wave,
To light-hung leaves, in smoothest echoes breaking
120   Through copse-clad valleys – ere their death, o'ertaking
The surgy murmurs of the lonely sea.

    And now, as deep into the wood as we
Might mark a lynx's eye, there glimmered light
Fair faces and a rush of garments white,
Plainer and plainer showing, till at last
Into the widest alley they all passed,
Making directly for the woodland altar.
O kindly muse! let not my weak tongue falter
In telling of this goodly company,
130   Of their old piety, and of their glee:
But let a portion of ethereal dew
Fall on my head, and presently unmew

My soul – that I may dare, in wayfaring,
To stammer where old Chaucer used to sing.

   Leading the way, young damsels danced along,
Bearing the burden of a shepherd song;
Each having a white wicker over-brimmed
With April's tender younglings; next, well trimmed,
A crowd of shepherds with as sunburnt looks
As may be read of in Arcadian books,   140
Such as sat listening round Apollo's pipe,
When the great deity, for earth too ripe,
Let his divinity o'erflowing die
In music, through the vales of Thessaly;
Some idly trailed their sheep-hooks on the ground,
And some kept up a shrilly mellow sound
With ebon-tippèd flutes; close after these,
Now coming from beneath the forest trees,
A venerable priest full soberly,
Begirt with ministering looks: alway his eye   150
Steadfast upon the matted turf he kept,
And after him his sacred vestments swept.
From his right hand there swung a vase, milk-white,
Of mingled wine, out-sparkling generous light;
And in his left he held a basket full
Of all sweet herbs that searching eye could cull:
Wild thyme, and valley-lilies whiter still
Than Leda's love, and cresses from the rill.
His agèd head, crownèd with beechen wreath,
Seemed like a poll of ivy in the teeth   160
Of winter hoar. Then came another crowd
Of shepherds, lifting in due time aloud
Their share of the ditty. After them appeared,
Up-followed by a multitude that reared
Their voices to the clouds, a fair-wrought car,
Easily rolling so as scarce to mar
The freedom of three steeds of dapple brown.

Who stood therein did seem of great renown
Among the throng. His youth was fully blown,
170   Showing like Ganymede to manhood grown;
And, for those simple times, his garments were
A chieftain king's: beneath his breast, half bare,
Was hung a silver bugle, and between
His nervy knees there lay a boar-spear keen.
A smile was on his countenance; he seemed,
To common lookers-on, like one who dreamed
Of idleness in groves Elysian:
But there were some who feelingly could scan
A lurking trouble in his nether lip,
180   And see that oftentimes the reins would slip
Through his forgotten hands: then would they sigh,
And think of yellow leaves, of owlets' cry,
Of logs piled solemnly. Ah, well-a-day.
Why should our young Endymion pine away?

Soon the assembly, in a circle ranged,
Stood silent round the shrine: each look was changed
To sudden veneration: women meek
Beckoned their sons to silence; while each cheek
Of virgin bloom paled gently for slight fear.
190   Endymion too, without a forest peer,
Stood, wan, and pale, and with an awèd face,
Among his brothers of the mountain chase.
In midst of all, the venerable priest
Eyed them with joy from greatest to the least,
And, after lifting up his agèd hands,
Thus spake he: 'Men of Latmos! shepherd bands!
Whose care it is to guard a thousand flocks:
Whether descended from beneath the rocks
That overtop your mountains; whether come
200   From valleys where the pipe is never dumb;
Or from your swelling downs, where sweet air stirs
Blue hare-bells lightly, and where prickly furze

Buds lavish gold; or ye, whose precious charge
Nibble their fill at ocean's very marge,
Whose mellow reeds are touched with sounds forlorn
By the dim echoes of old Triton's horn;
Mothers and wives! who day by day prepare
The scrip, with needments, for the mountain air;
And all ye gentle girls who foster up
Udderless lambs, and in a little cup   210
Will put choice honey for a favoured youth –
Yea, every one attend! for in good truth
Our vows are wanting to our great god Pan.
Are not our lowing heifers sleeker than
Night-swollen mushrooms? Are not our wide plains
Speckled with countless fleeces? Have not rains
Greened over April's lap? No howling sad
Sickens our fearful ewes; and we have had
Great bounty from Endymion our lord.
The earth is glad: the merry lark has poured   220
His early song against yon breezy sky,
That spreads so clear o'er our solemnity.'

   Thus ending, on the shrine he heaped a spire
Of teeming sweets, enkindling sacred fire;
Anon he stained the thick and spongy sod
With wine, in honour of the shepherd-god.
Now while the earth was drinking it, and while
Bay leaves were crackling in the fragrant pile,
And gummy frankincense was sparkling bright
'Neath smothering parsley, and a hazy light   230
Spread greyly eastward, thus a chorus sang:

   'O thou, whose mighty palace roof doth hang
From jagged trunks, and overshadoweth
Eternal whispers, glooms, the birth, life, death
Of unseen flowers in heavy peacefulness;
Who lov'st to see the hamadryads dress

Their ruffled locks where meeting hazels darken;
And through whole solemn hours dost sit, and hearken
The dreary melody of bedded reeds
In desolate places, where dank moisture breeds
The pipy hemlock to strange overgrowth;
Bethinking thee, how melancholy loth
Thou wast to lose fair Syrinx – do thou now –
By thy love's milky brow! –
By all the trembling mazes that she ran –
Hear us, great Pan!

'O thou, for whose soul-soothing quiet, turtles
Passion their voices cooingly 'mong myrtles,
What time thou wanderest at eventide
Through sunny meadows, that outskirt the side
Of thine enmossèd realms: O thou, to whom
Broad-leavèd fig trees even now foredoom
Their ripened fruitage; yellow-girted bees
Their golden honeycombs; our village leas
Their fairest-blossomed beans and poppied corn;
The chuckling linnet its five young unborn
To sing for thee; low creeping strawberries
Their summer coolness; pent up butterflies
Their freckled wings; yea, the fresh budding year
All its completions – be quickly near,
By every wind that nods the mountain pine,
O forester divine!

'Thou, to whom every faun and satyr flies
For willing service; whether to surprise
The squatted hare while in half-sleeping fit;
Or upward ragged precipices flit
To save poor lambkins from the eagle's maw;
Or by mysterious enticement draw
Bewildered shepherds to their path again;
Or to tread breathless round the frothy main,
And gather up all fancifullest shells

For thee to tumble into Naiads' cells,
And, being hidden, laugh at their out-peeping;
Or to delight thee with fantastic leaping,
The while they pelt each other on the crown
With silvery oak apples, and fir cones brown –
By all the echoes that about thee ring,
Hear us, O satyr king!

'O Hearkener to the loud clapping shears
While ever and anon to his shorn peers   280
A ram goes bleating; Winder of the horn,
When snouted wild-boars routing tender corn
Anger our huntsmen; Breather round our farms,
To keep off mildews, and all weather harms;
Strange ministrant of undescrib̀ed sounds,
That come a-swooning over hollow grounds,
And wither drearily on barren moors;
Dread opener of the mysterious doors
Leading to universal knowledge – see,
Great son of Dryope,   290
The many that are come to pay their vows
With leaves about their brows!

'Be still the unimaginable lodge
For solitary thinkings; such as dodge
Conception to the very bourne of heaven,
Then leave the naked brain; be still the leaven,
That spreading in this dull and clodded earth
Gives it a touch ethereal – a new birth;
Be still a symbol of immensity;
A firmament reflected in a sea;   300
An element filling the space between,
An unknown – but no more! we humbly screen
With uplift hands our foreheads, lowly bending,
And giving out a shout most heaven rending,
Conjure thee to receive our humble paean,
Upon thy Mount Lycean!'

Even while they brought the burden to a close,
A shout from the whole multitude arose,
That lingered in the air like dying rolls
310·   Of abrupt thunder, when Ionian shoals
Of dolphins bob their noses through the brine.
Meantime, on shady levels, mossy fine,
Young companies nimbly began dancing
To the swift treble pipe, and humming string.
Ay, those fair living forms swam heavenly
To tunes forgotten – out of memory;
Fair creatures! whose young children's children bred
Thermopylae its heroes – not yet dead,
But in old marbles ever beautiful.
320   High genitors, unconscious did they cull
Time's sweet first-fruits – they danced to weariness,
And then in quiet circles did they press
The hillock turf, and caught the latter end
Of some strange history, potent to send
A young mind from its bodily tenement.
Or they might watch the quoit-pitchers, intent
On either side; pitying the sad death
Of Hyacinthus, when the cruel breath
Of Zephyr slew him – Zephyr penitent,
330   Who now, ere Phoebus mounts the firmament,
Fondles the flower amid the sobbing rain.
The archers too, upon a wider plain,
Beside the feathery whizzing of the shaft
And the dull twanging bowstring, and the raft
Branch down sweeping from a tall ash top,
Called up a thousand thoughts to envelop
Those who would watch. Perhaps, the trembling knee
And frantic gape of lonely Niobe –
Poor, lonely Niobe! – when her lovely young
340   Were dead and gone, and her caressing tongue
Lay a lost thing upon her paly lip,
And very, very deadliness did nip

Her motherly cheeks. Aroused from this sad mood
By one, who at a distance loud hallooed,
Uplifting his strong bow into the air,
Many might after brighter visions stare:
After the Argonauts, in blind amaze
Tossing about on Neptune's restless ways,
Until, from the horizon's vaulted side,
There shot a golden splendour far and wide,   350
Spangling those million poutings of the brine
With quivering ore – 'twas even an awful shine
From the exaltation of Apollo's bow;
A heavenly beacon in their dreary woe.
Who thus were ripe for high contemplating,
Might turn their steps towards the sober ring
Where sat Endymion and the agèd priest
'Mong shepherds gone in eld, whose looks increased
The silvery setting of their mortal star.
There they discoursed upon the fragile bar   360
That keeps us from our homes ethereal,
And what our duties there: to nightly call
Vesper, the beauty-crest of summer weather;
To summon all the downiest clouds together
For the sun's purple couch; to emulate
In ministering the potent rule of fate
With speed of fire-tailèd exhalations:
To tint her pallid cheek with bloom, who cons
Sweet poesy by moonlight: besides these,
A world of other unguessed offices.   370
Anon they wandered, by divine converse,
Into Elysium, vying to rehearse
Each one his own anticipated bliss.
One felt heart-certain that he could not miss
His quick-gone love, among fair blossomed boughs,
Where every zephyr-sigh pouts, and endows
Her lips with music for the welcoming.
Another wished, mid that eternal spring,

To meet his rosy child, with feathery sails,
380   Sweeping, eye-earnestly, through almond vales –
Who, suddenly, should stoop through the smooth wind,
And with the balmiest leaves his temples bind;
And, ever after, through those regions be
His messenger, his little Mercury.
Some were athirst in soul to see again
Their fellow huntsmen o'er the wide champaign
In times long past; to sit with them, and talk
Of all the chances in their earthly walk;
Comparing, joyfully, their plenteous stores
390   Of happiness, to when upon the moors,
Benighted, close they huddled from the cold,
And shared their famished scrips. Thus all out-told
Their fond imaginations – saving him
Whose eyelids curtained up their jewels dim,
Endymion: yet hourly had he striven
To hide the cankering venom, that had riven
His fainting recollections. Now indeed
His senses had swooned off; he did not heed
The sudden silence, or the whispers low,
400   Or the old eyes dissolving at his woe,
Or anxious calls, or close of trembling palms,
Or maiden's sigh, that grief itself embalms:
But in the self-same fixèd trance he kept,
Like one who on the earth had never stepped.
Ay, even as dead still as a marble man,
Frozen in that old tale Arabian.

Who whispers him so pantingly and close?
Peona, his sweet sister – of all those,
His friends, the dearest. Hushing signs she made,
410   And breathed a sister's sorrow to persuade
A yielding up, a cradling on her care.
Her eloquence did breathe away the curse:
She led him, like some midnight spirit-nurse

Of happy changes in emphatic dreams,
Along a path between two little streams –
Guarding his forehead, with her round elbow,
From low-grown branches, and his footsteps slow
From stumbling over stumps and hillocks small –
Until they came to where these streamlets fall,
With mingled bubblings and a gentle rush,   420
Into a river, clear, brimful, and flush
With crystal mocking of the trees and sky.
A little shallop, floating there hard by,
Pointed its beak over the fringèd bank;
And soon it lightly dipped, and rose, and sank,
And dipped again, with the young couple's weight –
Peona guiding, through the water straight,
Towards a bowery island opposite,
Which gaining presently, she steerèd light
Into a shady, fresh, and ripply cove,   430
Where nested was an arbour, overwove
By many a summer's silent fingering;
To whose cool bosom she was used to bring
Her playmates, with their needle broidery,
And minstrel memories of times gone by.

   So she was gently glad to see him laid
Under her favourite bower's quiet shade,
On her own couch, new made of flower leaves,
Dried carefully on the cooler side of sheaves
When last the sun his autumn tresses shook,   440
And the tanned harvesters rich armfuls took.
Soon was he quieted to slumbrous rest:
But, ere it crept upon him, he had pressed
Peona's busy hand against his lips,
And still, a-sleeping, held her finger-tips
In tender pressure. And as a willow keeps
A patient watch over the stream that creeps
Windingly by it, so the quiet maid

Held her in peace: so that a whispering blade
Of grass, a wailful gnat, a bee bustling
Down in the blue-bells, or a wren light rustling
Among sere leaves and twigs, might all be heard.

O magic sleep! O comfortable bird,
That broodest o'er the troubled sea of the mind
Till it is hushed and smooth! O unconfined
Restraint! imprisoned liberty! great key
To golden palaces, strange minstrelsy,
Fountains grotesque, new trees, bespangled caves,
Echoing grottoes, full of tumbling waves
And moonlight; ay, to all the mazy world
Of silvery enchantment! Who, upfurled
Beneath thy drowsy wing a triple hour,
But renovates and lives? – Thus, in the bower,
Endymion was calmed to life again.
Opening his eyelids with a healthier brain,
He said: 'I feel this thine endearing love
All through my bosom: thou art as a dove
Trembling its closèd eyes and sleekèd wings
About me; and the pearliest dew not brings
Such morning incense from the fields of May,
As do those brighter drops that twinkling stray
From those kind eyes – the very home and haunt
Of sisterly affection. Can I want
Aught else, aught nearer heaven, than such tears?
Yet dry them up, in bidding hence all fears
That, any longer, I will pass my days
Alone and sad. No, I will once more raise
My voice upon the mountain-heights; once more
Make my horn parley from their foreheads hoar;
Again my trooping hounds their tongues shall loll
Around the breathèd boar; again I'll poll
The fair-grown yew tree for a chosen bow;
And, when the pleasant sun is getting low,

Again I'll linger in a sloping mead
To hear the speckled thrushes, and see feed
Our idle sheep. So be thou cheerèd, sweet,
And, if thy lute is here, softly entreat
My soul to keep in its resolvèd course.'

   Hereat Peona, in their silver source,
Shut her pure sorrow-drops with glad exclaim,   490
And took a lute, from which there pulsing came
A lively prelude, fashioning the way
In which her voice should wander. 'Twas a lay
More subtle cadenced, more forest wild
Than Dryope's lone lulling of her child;
And nothing since has floated in the air
So mournful strange. Surely some influence rare
Went, spiritual, through the damsel's hand;
For still, with Delphic emphasis, she spanned
The quick invisible strings, even though she saw   500
Endymion's spirit melt away and thaw
Before the deep intoxication.
But soon she came, with sudden burst, upon
Her self-possession – swung the lute aside,
And earnestly said: 'Brother, 'tis vain to hide
That thou dost know of things mysterious,
Immortal, starry; such alone could thus
Weigh down thy nature. Hast thou sinned in aught
Offensive to the heavenly powers? Caught
A Paphian dove upon a message sent?   510
Thy deathful bow against some deer-head bent
Sacred to Dian? Haply, thou hast seen
Her naked limbs among the alders green –
And that, alas! is death. No, I can trace
Something more high-perplexing in thy face!'

   Endymion looked at her, and pressed her hand,
And said, 'Art thou so pale, who wast so bland
And merry in our meadows? How is this?

Tell me thine ailment – tell me all amiss!
Ah! thou hast been unhappy at the change
Wrought suddenly in me. What indeed more strange?
Or more complete to overwhelm surmise?
Ambition is no sluggard: 'tis no prize,
That toiling years would put within my grasp,
That I have sighed for; with so deadly gasp
No man e'er panted for a mortal love.
So all have set my heavier grief above
These things which happen. Rightly have they done:
I, who still saw the horizontal sun
Heave his broad shoulder o'er the edge of the world,
Out-facing Lucifer, and then had hurled
My spear aloft, as signal for the chase –
I, who, for very sport of heart, would race
With my own steed from Araby; pluck down
A vulture from his towery perching; frown
A lion into growling, loth retire –
To lose, at once, all my toil-breeding fire,
And sink thus low! but I will ease my breast
Of secret grief, here in this bowery nest.

'This river does not see the naked sky,
Till it begins to progress silverly
Around the western border of the wood,
Whence, from a certain spot, its winding flood
Seems at the distance like a crescent moon:
And in that nook, the very pride of June,
Had I been used to pass my weary eves;
The rather for the sun unwilling leaves
So dear a picture of his sovereign power,
And I could witness his most kingly hour,
When he doth tighten up the golden reins,
And paces leisurely down amber plains
His snorting four. Now when his chariot last
Its beams against the zodiac-lion cast,

There blossomed suddenly a magic bed
Of sacred ditamy, and poppies red:
At which I wondered greatly, knowing well
That but one night had wrought this flowery spell;
And, sitting down close by, began to muse
What it might mean. Perhaps, thought I, Morpheus,
In passing here, his owlet pinions shook;   560
Or, it may be, ere matron Night uptook
Her ebon urn, young Mercury, by stealth,
Had dipped his rod in it: such garland wealth
Came not by common growth. Thus on I thought,
Until my head was dizzy and distraught.
Moreover, through the dancing poppies stole
A breeze, most softly lulling to my soul,
And shaping visions all about my sight
Of colours, wings, and bursts of spangly light;
The which became more strange, and strange, and dim,   570
And then were gulfed in a tumultuous swim –
And then I fell asleep. Ah, can I tell
The enchantment that afterwards befell?
Yet it was but a dream: yet such a dream
That never tongue, although it overteem
With mellow utterance, like a cavern spring,
Could figure out and to conception bring
All I beheld and felt. Methought I lay
Watching the zenith, where the milky way
Among the stars in virgin splendour pours;   580
And travelling my eye, until the doors
Of heaven appeared to open for my flight,
I became loth and fearful to alight
From such high soaring by a downward glance:
So kept me steadfast in that airy trance,
Spreading imaginary pinions wide.
When, presently, the stars began to glide,
And faint away, before my eager view:
At which I sighed that I could not pursue,

590   And dropped my vision to the horizon's verge –
And lo! from opening clouds, I saw emerge
The loveliest moon, that ever silvered o'er
A shell for Neptune's goblet: she did soar
So passionately bright, my dazzled soul
Commingling with her argent spheres did roll
Through clear and cloudy, even when she went
At last into a dark and vapoury tent –
Whereat, methought, the lidless-eyèd train
Of planets all were in the blue again.

600   To commune with those orbs, once more I raised
My sight right upward: but it was quite dazed
By a bright something, sailing down apace,
Making me quickly veil my eyes and face:
Again I looked, and, O ye deities,
Who from Olympus watch our destinies!
Whence that completed form of all completeness?
Whence came that high perfection of all sweetness?
Speak, stubborn earth, and tell me where, O where
Hast thou a symbol of her golden hair?

610   Not oat-sheaves drooping in the western sun;
Not – thy soft hand, fair sister! let me shun
Such follying before thee – yet she had,
Indeed, locks bright enough to make me mad;
And they were simply gordianed up and braided,
Leaving, in naked comeliness, unshaded,
Her pearl-round ears, white neck, and orbèd brow;
The which were blended in, I know not how,
With such a paradise of lips and eyes,
Blush-tinted cheeks, half smiles, and faintest sighs,

620   That, when I think thereon, my spirit clings
And plays about its fancy, till the stings
Of human neighbourhood envenom all.
Unto what awful power shall I call?
To what high fane? – Ah! see her hovering feet,
More bluely veined, more soft, more whitely sweet

Than those of sea-born Venus, when she rose
From out her cradle shell. The wind out-blows
Her scarf into a fluttering pavilion;
'Tis blue, and over-spangled with a million
Of little eyes, as though thou wert to shed,   630
Over the darkest, lushest blue-bell bed,
Handfuls of daisies.' – 'Endymion, how strange!
Dream within dream!' – 'She took an airy range,
And then, towards me, like a very maid,
Came blushing, waning, willing, and afraid,
And pressed me by the hand: Ah! 'twas too much;
Methought I fainted at the charmèd touch,
Yet held my recollection, even as one
Who dives three fathoms where the waters run
Gurgling in beds of coral: for anon,   640
I felt up-mounted in that region
Where falling stars dart their artillery forth,
And eagles struggle with the buffeting north
That balances the heavy meteor-stone –
Felt too, I was not fearful, nor alone,
But lapped and lulled along the dangerous sky.
Soon, as it seemed, we left our journeying high,
And straightway into frightful eddies swooped,
Such as aye muster where grey time has scooped
Huge dens and caverns in a mountain's side: 650
There hollow sounds aroused me, and I sighed
To faint once more by looking on my bliss –
I was distracted; madly did I kiss
The wooing arms which held me, and did give
My eyes at once to death – but 'twas to live,
To take in draughts of life from the gold fount
Of kind and passionate looks; to count, and count
The moments, by some greedy help that seemed
A second self, that each might be redeemed
And plundered of its load of blessedness.   660
Ah, desperate mortal! I e'en dared to press

Her very cheek against my crownèd lip,
And, at that moment, felt my body dip
Into a warmer air – a moment more,
Our feet were soft in flowers. There was store
Of newest joys upon that alp. Sometimes
A scent of violets, and blossoming limes,
Loitered around us; then of honey cells,
Made delicate from all white-flower bells;
670   And once, above the edges of our nest,
An arch face peeped – an Oread as I guessed.

'Why did I dream that sleep o'er-powered me
In midst of all this heaven? Why not see,
Far off, the shadows of his pinions dark,
And stare them from me? But no, like a spark
That needs must die, although its little beam
Reflects upon a diamond, my sweet dream
Fell into nothing – into stupid sleep.
And so it was, until a gentle creep,
680   A careful moving caught my waking ears,
And up I started. Ah! my sighs, my tears,
My clenchèd hands – for lo! the poppies hung
Dew-dabbled on their stalks, the ouzel sung
A heavy ditty, and the sullen day
Had chidden herald Hesperus away,
With leaden looks: the solitary breeze
Blustered, and slept, and its wild self did tease
With wayward melancholy; and I thought,
Mark me, Peona! that sometimes it brought
690   Faint fare-thee-wells, and sigh-shrillèd adieus! –
Away I wandered – all the pleasant hues
Of heaven and earth had faded: deepest shades
Were deepest dungeons; heaths and sunny glades
Were full of pestilent light; our taintless rills
Seemed sooty, and o'er-spread with upturned gills
Of dying fish; the vermeil rose had blown

In frightful scarlet, and its thorns out-grown
Like spiked aloe. If an innocent bird
Before my heedless footsteps stirred and stirred
In little journeys, I beheld in it   700
A disguised demon, missionèd to knit
My soul with under-darkness, to entice
My stumblings down some monstrous precipice:
Therefore I eager followed, and did curse
The disappointment. Time, that agèd nurse,
Rocked me to patience. Now, thank gentle heaven!
These things, with all their comfortings, are given
To my down-sunken hours, and with thee,
Sweet sister, help to stem the ebbing sea
Of weary life.'   710

       Thus ended he, and both
Sat silent: for the maid was very loth
To answer; feeling well that breathèd words
Would all be lost, unheard, and vain as swords
Against the enchasèd crocodile, or leaps
Of grasshoppers against the sun. She weeps,
And wonders; struggles to devise some blame;
To put on such a look as would say, *Shame
On this poor weakness!* but, for all her strife,
She could as soon have crushed away the life
From a sick dove. At length, to break the pause,   720
She said with trembling chance: 'Is this the cause?
This all? Yet it is strange, and sad, alas!
That one who through this middle earth should pass
Most like a sojourning demi-god, and leave
His name upon the harp-string, should achieve
No higher bard than simple maidenhood,
Singing alone – and fearfully – how the blood
Left his young cheek; and how he used to stray
He knew not where; and how he would say, *nay*,
If any said 'twas love – and yet 'twas love;   730

What could it be but love? How a ring-dove
Let fall a sprig of yew tree in his path;
And how he died; and then, that love doth scathe
The gentle heart, as northern blasts do roses;
And then the ballad of his sad life closes
With sighs, and an 'alas'! – Endymion!
Be rather in the trumpet's mouth – anon
Among the winds at large, that all may hearken!
Although, before the crystal heavens darken,
I watch and dote upon the silver lakes
Pictured in western cloudiness, that takes
The semblance of gold rocks and bright gold sands,
Islands, and creeks, and amber-fretted strands
With horses prancing o'er them, palaces
And towers of amethyst – would I so tease
My pleasant days, because I could not mount
Into those regions? The Morphean fount
Of that fine element that visions, dreams,
And fitful whims of sleep are made of, streams
Into its airy channels with so subtle,
So thin a breathing, not the spider's shuttle,
Circled a million times within the space
Of a swallow's nest-door, could delay a trace,
A tinting of its quality: how light
Must dreams themselves be, seeing they're more slight
Than the mere nothing that engenders them!
Then wherefore sully the entrusted gem
Of high and noble life with thoughts so sick?
Why pierce high-fronted honour to the quick
For nothing but a dream?' Hereat the youth
Looked up: a conflicting of shame and ruth
Was in his plaited brow: yet, his eyelids
Widened a little, as when Zephyr bids
A little breeze to creep between the fans
Of careless butterflies. Amid his pains
He seemed to taste a drop of manna-dew,

740

750

760

Full palatable; and a colour grew
Upon his cheek, while thus he lifeful spake.

  'Peona! ever have I longed to slake
My thirst for the world's praises: nothing base,   770
No merely slumbrous phantasm, could unlace
The stubborn canvas for my voyage prepared –
Though now 'tis tattered, leaving my bark bared
And sullenly drifting: yet my higher hope
Is of too wide, too rainbow-large a scope,
To fret at myriads of earthly wrecks.
Wherein lies happiness? In that which becks
Our ready minds to fellowship divine,
A fellowship with essence; till we shine,
Full alchemized, and free of space. Behold   780
The clear religion of heaven! Fold
A rose leaf round thy finger's taperness,
And soothe thy lips; hist, when the airy stress
Of music's kiss impregnates the free winds,
And with a sympathetic touch unbinds
Aeolian magic from their lucid wombs;
Then old songs waken from enclouded tombs;
Old ditties sigh above their father's grave;
Ghosts of melodious prophesyings rave
Round every spot where trod Apollo's foot;   790
Bronze clarions awake, and faintly bruit,
Where long ago a giant battle was;
And, from the turf, a lullaby doth pass
In every place where infant Orpheus slept.
Feel we these things? – that moment have we stepped
Into a sort of oneness, and our state
Is like a floating spirit's. But there are
Richer entanglements, enthralments far
More self-destroying, leading, by degrees,
To the chief intensity: the crown of these   800
Is made of love and friendship, and sits high

Upon the forehead of humanity.
All its more ponderous and bulky worth
Is friendship, whence there ever issues forth
A steady splendour; but at the tip-top,
There hangs by unseen film, an orbèd drop
Of light, and that is love: its influence,
Thrown in our eyes, genders a novel sense,
At which we start and fret; till in the end,
810   Melting into its radiance, we blend,
Mingle, and so become a part of it –
Nor with aught else can our souls interknit
So wingedly. When we combine therewith,
Life's self is nourished by its proper pith,
And we are nurtured like a pelican brood.
Ay, so delicious is the unsating food,
That men, who might have towered in the van
Of all the congregated world, to fan
And winnow from the coming step of time
820   All chaff of custom, wipe away all slime
Left by men-slugs and human serpentry,
Have been content to let occasion die,
Whilst they did sleep in love's elysium.
And, truly, I would rather be struck dumb,
Than speak against this ardent listlessness:
For I have ever thought that it might bless
The world with benefits unknowingly,
As does the nightingale, up-perchèd high,
And cloistered among cool and bunchèd leaves –
830   She sings but to her love, nor e'er conceives
How tip-toe Night holds back her dark-grey hood.
Just so may love, although 'tis understood
The mere commingling of passionate breath,
Produce more than our searching witnesseth –
What I know not: but who, of men, can tell
That flowers would bloom, or that green fruit would swell
To melting pulp, that fish would have bright mail,

The earth its dower of river, wood, and vale,
The meadows runnels, runnels pebble-stones,
The seed its harvest, or the lute its tones,   840
Tones ravishment, or ravishment its sweet,
If human souls did never kiss and greet?

　'Now, if this earthly love has power to make
Men's being mortal, immortal; to shake
Ambition from their memories, and brim
Their measure of content; what merest whim,
Seems all this poor endeavour after fame,
To one, who keeps within his steadfast aim
A love immortal, an immortal too.
Look not so wildered; for these things are true,   850
And never can be born of atomies
That buzz about our slumbers, like brain-flies,
Leaving us fancy-sick. No, no, I'm sure,
My restless spirit never could endure
To brood so long upon one luxury,
Unless it did, though fearfully, espy
A hope beyond the shadow of a dream.
My sayings will the less obscurèd seem,
When I have told thee how my waking sight
Has made me scruple whether that same night   860
Was passed in dreaming. Hearken, sweet Peona!
Beyond the matron-temple of Latona,
Which we should see but for these darkening boughs,
Lies a deep hollow, from whose ragged brows
Bushes and trees do lean all round athwart
And meet so nearly, that with wings outraught,
And spreaded tail, a vulture could not glide
Past them, but he must brush on every side.
Some mouldered steps lead into this cool cell,
Far as the slabbèd margin of a well,   870
Whose patient level peeps its crystal eye
Right upward, through the bushes, to the sky.

Oft have I brought thee flowers, on their stalks set
Like vestal primroses, but dark velvet
Edges them round, and they have golden pits:
'Twas there I got them, from the gaps and slits
In a mossy stone, that sometimes was my seat,
When all above was faint with midday heat.
And there in strife no burning thoughts to heed,
880   I'd bubble up the water through a reed;
So reaching back to boyhood; make me ships
Of moulted feathers, touchwood, alder chips,
With leaves stuck in them; and the Neptune be
Of their petty ocean. Oftener, heavily,
When love-lorn hours had left me less a child,
I sat contemplating the figures wild
Of o'er-head clouds melting the mirror through.
Upon a day, while thus I watched, by flew
A cloudy Cupid, with his bow and quiver,
890   So plainly charactered, no breeze would shiver
The happy chance: so happy, I was fain
To follow it upon the open plain,
And, therefore, was just going, when, behold!
A wonder, fair as any I have told –
The same bright face I tasted in my sleep,
Smiling in the clear well. My heart did leap
Through the cool depth. – It moved as if to flee –
I started up – when lo! refreshfully,
There came upon my face in plenteous showers,
900   Dew-drops, and dewy buds, and leaves, and flowers,
Wrapping all objects from my smothered sight,
Bathing my spirit in a new delight.
Ay, such a breathless honey-feel of bliss
Alone preserved me from the drear abyss
Of death, for the fair form had gone again.
Pleasure is oft a visitant; but pain
Clings cruelly to us, like the gnawing sloth
On the deer's tender haunches: late, and loth,

'Tis scared away by slow returning pleasure.
How sickening, how dark the dreadful leisure   910
Of weary days, made deeper exquisite,
By a fore-knowledge of unslumbrous night!
Like sorrow came upon me, heavier still,
Than when I wandered from the poppy hill:
And a whole age of lingering moments crept
Sluggishly by, ere more contentment swept
Away at once the deadly yellow spleen.
Yes, thrice have I this fair enchantment seen;
Once more been tortured with renewèd life.
When last the wintry gusts gave over strife   920
With the conquering sun of spring, and left the skies
Warm and serene, but yet with moistened eyes
In pity of the shattered infant buds –
That time thou didst adorn, with amber studs,
My hunting cap, because I laughed and smiled,
Chatted with thee, and many days exiled
All torment from my breast – 'twas even then,
Straying about, yet, cooped up in the den
Of helpless discontent, hurling my lance
From place to place, and following at chance,   930
At last, by hap, through some young trees it struck,
And, plashing among bedded pebbles, stuck
In the middle of a brook, whose silver ramble
Down twenty little falls, through reeds and bramble,
Tracing along, it brought me to a cave,
Whence it ran brightly forth, and white did lave
The nether sides of mossy stones and rock –
'Mong which it gurgled blythe adieus, to mock
Its own sweet grief at parting. Overhead,
Hung a lush screen of drooping weeds, and spread   940
Thick, as to curtain up some wood-nymph's home.
"Ah! impious mortal, whither do I roam?"
Said I, low voiced: "Ah, whither! 'Tis the grot
 Of Proserpine, when Hell, obscure and hot,

Doth her resign, and where her tender hands
She dabbles, on the cool and sluicy sands;
Or 'tis the cell of Echo, where she sits,
And babbles thorough silence, till her wits
Are gone in tender madness, and anon,
Faints into sleep, with many a dying tone
Of sadness. O that she would take my vows,
And breathe them sighingly among the boughs,
To sue her gentle ears for whose fair head,
Daily, I pluck sweet flowerets from their bed,
And weave them dyingly – send honey-whispers
Round every leaf, that all those gentle lispers
May sigh my love unto her pitying!
O charitable Echo! hear, and sing
This ditty to her! Tell her –" So I stayed
My foolish tongue, and listening, half afraid,
Stood stupefied with my own empty folly,
And blushing for the freaks of melancholy.
Salt tears were coming, when I heard my name
Most fondly lipped, and then these accents came:
"Endymion! the cave is secreter
Than the isle of Delos. Echo hence shall stir
No sighs but sigh-warm kisses, or light noise
Of thy combing hand, the while it travelling cloys
And trembles through my labyrinthine hair."
At that oppressed I hurried in. Ah! where
Are those swift moments? Whither are they fled?
I'll smile no more, Peona; nor will wed
Sorrow the way to death; but patiently
Bear up against it – so farewell, sad sigh;
And come instead demurest meditation,
To occupy me wholly, and to fashion
My pilgrimage for the world's dusky brink.
No more will I count over, link by link,
My chain of grief: no longer strive to find
A half-forgetfulness in mountain wind

950

960

970

980

Blustering about my ears. Ay, thou shalt see,
Dearest of sisters, what my life shall be;
What a calm round of hours shall make my days.
There is a paly flame of hope that plays
Where'er I look; but yet, I'll say 'tis naught –
And here I bid it die. Have not I caught,
Already, a more healthy countenance?
By this the sun is setting; we may chance
Meet some of our near-dwellers with my car.'

    This said, he rose, faint-smiling like a star   990
Through autumn mists, and took Peona's hand:
They stepped into the boat, and launched from land.

BOOK II
O sovereign power of love! O grief! O balm!
All records, saving thine, come cool, and calm,
And shadowy, through the mist of passèd years:
For others, good or bad, hatred and tears
Have become indolent, but touching thine,
One sigh doth echo, one poor sob doth pine,
One kiss brings honey-dew from buried days.
The woes of Troy, towers smothering o'er their blaze,
Stiff-holden shields, far-piercing spears, keen blades,
Struggling, and blood, and shrieks – all dimly fades   10
Into some backward corner of the brain:
Yet, in our very souls, we feel amain
The close of Troilus and Cressid sweet.
Hence, pageant history! hence, gilded cheat!
Swart planet in the universe of deeds!
Wide sea, that one continuous murmur breeds
Along the pebbled shore of memory!
Many old rotten-timbered boats there be
Upon thy vaporous bosom, magnified
To goodly vessels; many a sail of pride,   20
And golden keeled, is left unlaunched and dry.

But wherefore this? What care, though owl did fly
About the great Athenian admiral's mast?
What care, though striding Alexander passed
The Indus with his Macedonian numbers?
Though old Ulysses tortured from his slumbers
The glutted Cyclops, what care? – Juliet leaning
Amid her window-flowers, sighing, weaning
Tenderly her fancy from its maiden snow,
30   Doth more avail than these. The silver flow
Of Hero's tears, the swoon of Imogen,
Fair Pastorella in the bandit's den,
Are things to brood on with more ardency
Than the death-day of empires. Fearfully
Must such conviction come upon his head,
Who, thus far, discontent, has dared to tread,
Without one muse's smile, or kind behest,
The path of love and poesy. But rest,
In chafing restlessness, is yet more drear
40   Than to be crushed in striving to uprear
Love's standard on the battlements of song.
So once more days and nights aid me along,
Like legioned soldiers.

[*Venus and Adonis*]
        After a thousand mazes overgone,
At last, with sudden step, he came upon
A chamber, myrtle walled, embowered high,
390   Full of light, incense, tender minstrelsy,
And more of beautiful and strange beside:
For on a silken couch of rosy pride,
In midst of all, there lay a sleeping youth
Of fondest beauty; fonder, in fair sooth,
Than sighs could fathom, or contentment reach:
And coverlids gold-tinted like the peach,
Or ripe October faded marigolds,
Fell sleek about him in a thousand folds –

Not hiding up an Apollonian curve
Of neck and shoulder, nor the tenting swerve   400
Of knee from knee, nor ankles pointing light;
But rather, giving them to the fillèd sight
Officiously. Sideway his face reposed
On one white arm, and tenderly unclosed,
By tenderest pressure, a faint damask mouth
To slumbery pout; just as the morning south
Disparts a dew-lipped rose. Above his head,
Four lily stalks did their white honours wed
To make a coronal; and round him grew
All tendrils green, of every bloom and hue,   410
Together intertwined and trammelled fresh:
The vine of glossy sprout; the ivy mesh,
Shading its Ethiope berries; and woodbine,
Of velvet leaves and bugle-blooms divine;
Convolvulus in streakèd vases flush;
The creeper, mellowing for an autumn blush;
And virgin's bower, trailing airily;
With others of the sisterhood. Hard by,
Stood serene Cupids watching silently.
One, kneeling to a lyre, touched the strings,   420
Muffling to death the pathos with his wings;
And, ever and anon, uprose to look
At the youth's slumber; while another took
A willow-bough, distilling odorous dew,
And shook it on his hair; another flew
In through the woven roof, and fluttering-wise
Rained violets upon his sleeping eyes.

At these enchantments, and yet many more,
The breathless Latmian wondered o'er and o'er;
Until, impatient in embarrassment,   430
He forthright passed, and lightly treading went
To that same feathered lyrist, who straightway,
Smiling, thus whispered: 'Though from upper day

Thou art a wanderer, and thy presence here
Might seem unholy, be of happy cheer!
For 'tis the nicest touch of human honour,
When some ethereal and high-favouring donor
Presents immortal bowers to mortal sense –
As now 'tis done to thee, Endymion. Hence
440 Was I in no wise startled. So recline
Upon these living flowers. Here is wine,
Alive with sparkles – never, I aver,
Since Ariadne was a vintager,
So cool a purple: taste these juicy pears,
Sent me by sad Vertumnus, when his fears
Were high about Pomona: here is cream,
Deepening to richness from a snowy gleam;
Sweeter than that nurse Amalthea skimmed
For the boy Jupiter: and here, undimmed
450 By any touch, a bunch of blooming plums
Ready to melt between an infant's gums:
And here is manna picked from Syrian trees,
In starlight, by the three Hesperides.
Feast on, and meanwhile I will let thee know
Of all these things around us.' He did so,
Still brooding o'er the cadence of his lyre;
And thus: 'I need not any hearing tire
By telling how the sea-born goddess pined
For a mortal youth, and how she strove to bind
460 Him all in all unto her doting self.
Who would not be so prisoned? but, fond elf,
He was content to let her amorous plea
Faint through his careless arms; content to see
An unseized heaven dying at his feet;
Content, O fool! to make a cold retreat,
When on the pleasant grass such love, lovelorn,
Lay sorrowing; when every tear was born
Of diverse passion; when her lips and eyes
Were closed in sullen moisture, and quick sighs

Came vexed and pettish through her nostrils small.   470
Hush! no exclaim – yet, justly mightest thou call
Curses upon his head. – I was half glad,
But my poor mistress went distract and mad,
When the boar tusked him: so away she flew
To Jove's high throne, and by her plainings drew
Immortal tear-drops down the thunderer's beard;
Whereon, it was decreed he should be reared
Each summer-time to life. Lo! this is he,
That same Adonis, safe in the privacy
Of this still region all his winter-sleep.   480
Ay, sleep; for when our love-sick queen did weep
Over his wanèd corse, the tremulous shower
Healed up the wound, and, with a balmy power,
Medicined death to a lengthened drowsiness:
The which she fills with visions, and doth dress
In all this quiet luxury; and hath set
Us young immortals, without any let,
To watch his slumber through. 'Tis well nigh passed,
Even to a moment's filling up, and fast
She scuds with summer breezes, to pant through   490
The first long kiss, warm firstling, to renew
Embowered sports in Cytherea's isle.
Look! how those wingèd listeners all this while
Stand anxious! See! behold!' – This clamant word
Broke through the careful silence; for they heard
A rustling noise of leaves, and out there fluttered
Pigeons and doves: Adonis something muttered
The while one hand, that erst upon his thigh
Lay dormant, moved convulsed and gradually
Up to his forehead. Then there was a hum   500
Of sudden voices, echoing, 'Come! come!
Arise! awake! Clear summer has forth walked
Unto the clover-sward, and she has talked
Full soothingly to every nested finch:
Rise, Cupids! or we'll give the blue-bell pinch

To your dimpled arms. Once more sweet life begin!'
At this, from every side they hurried in,
Rubbing their sleepy eyes with lazy wrists,
And doubling over head their little fists
510   In backward yawns. But all were soon alive:
For as delicious wine doth, sparkling, dive
In nectared clouds and curls through water fair,
So from the arbour roof down swelled an air
Odorous and enlivening; making all
To laugh, and play, and sing, and loudly call
For their sweet queen – when lo! the wreathèd green
Disparted, and far upward could be seen
Blue heaven, and a silver car, air-borne,
Whose silent wheels, fresh wet from clouds of morn,
520   Spun off a drizzling dew, which falling chill
On soft Adonis' shoulders, made him still
Nestle and turn uneasily about.
Soon were the white doves plain, with necks stretched out,
And silken traces tightened in descent;
And soon, returning from love's banishment,
Queen Venus leaning downward open-armed.
Her shadow fell upon his breast, and charmed
A tumult to his heart, and a new life
Into his eyes. Ah, miserable strife,
530   But for her comforting! unhappy sight,
But meeting her blue orbs! Who, who can write
Of these first minutes? The unchariest muse
To embracements warm as theirs makes coy excuse.

     O it has ruffled every spirit there,
Saving Love's self, who stands superb to share
The general gladness. Awfully he stands;
A sovereign quell is in his waving hands;
No sight can bear the lightning of his bow;
His quiver is mysterious, none can know
540   What themselves think of it; from forth his eyes

There darts strange light of varied hues and dyes;
A scowl is sometimes on his brow, but who
Look full upon it feel anon the blue
Of his fair eyes run liquid through their souls.
Endymion feels it, and no more controls
The burning prayer within him; so, bent low,
He had begun a plaining of his woe.
But Venus, bending forward, said: 'My child,
Favour this gentle youth; his days are wild
With love – he – but alas! too well I see   550
Thou know'st the deepness of his misery.
Ah, smile not so, my son: I tell thee true,
That when through heavy hours I used to rue,
The endless sleep of this new-born Adon',
This stranger aye I pitied. For upon
A dreary morning once I fled away
Into the breezy clouds, to weep and pray
For this my love, for vexing Mars had teased
Me even to tears. Thence, when a little eased,
Down-looking, vacant, through a hazy wood,   560
I saw this youth as he despairing stood:
Those same dark curls blown vagrant in the wind;
Those same full-fringèd lids a constant blind
Over his sullen eyes. I saw him throw
Himself on withered leaves, even as though
Death had come sudden; for no jot he moved,
Yet muttered wildly. I could hear he loved
Some fair immortal, and that his embrace
Had zoned her through the night. There is no trace
Of this in heaven: I have marked each cheek,   570
And find it is the vainest thing to seek;
And that of all things 'tis kept secretest.
Endymion! one day thou wilt be blest:
So still obey the guiding hand that fends
Thee safely through these wonders for sweet ends.
'Tis a concealment needful in extreme,

And if I guessed not so, the sunny beam
Thou shouldst mount up to with me. Now adieu!
Here must we leave thee.' – At these words up-flew
The impatient doves, uprose the floating car,
Up went the hum celestial. High afar
The Latmian saw them minish into naught;
And, when all were clear vanished, still he caught
A vivid lightning from that dreadful bow.
When all was darkened, with Aetnean throe
The earth closed – gave a solitary moan –
And left him once again in twilight lone.

[*End of Book II*]

                       Ye who have yearned
With too much passion, will here stay and pity
For the mere sake of truth, as 'tis a ditty
Not of these days, but long ago 'twas told
By a cavern wind unto a forest old;
And then the forest told it in a dream
To a sleeping lake, whose cool and level gleam
A poet caught as he was journeying
To Phoebus' shrine; and in it he did fling
His weary limbs, bathing an hour's space,
And after, straight in that inspirèd place
He sang the story up into the air,
Giving it universal freedom. There
Has it been ever sounding for those ears
Whose tips are glowing hot. The legend cheers
Yon sentinel stars; and he who listens to it
Must surely be self-doomed or he will rue it:
For quenchless burnings come upon the heart,
Made fiercer by a fear lest any part
Should be engulfèd in the eddying wind.
As much as here is penned doth always find
A resting place, thus much comes clear and plain.
Anon the strange voice is upon the wane –

And 'tis but echoed from departing sound, 850
That the fair visitant at last unwound
Her gentle limbs, and left the youth asleep. –
Thus the tradition of the gusty deep.

Now turn we to our former chroniclers. –
Endymion awoke, that grief of hers
Sweet-paining on his ear: he sickly guessed
How lone he was once more, and sadly pressed
His empty arms together, hung his head,
And most forlorn upon that widowed bed
Sat silently. Love's madness he had known: 860
Often with more than tortured lion's groan
Moanings had burst from him; but now that rage
Had passed away. No longer did he wage
A rough-voiced war against the dooming stars.
No, he had felt too much for such harsh jars.
The lyre of his soul Aeolian-tuned
Forgot all violence, and but communed
With melancholy thought. O he had swooned
Drunken from Pleasure's nipple; and his love
Henceforth was dove-like. Loth was he to move 870
From the imprinted couch, and when he did,
'Twas with slow, languid paces, and face hid
In muffling hands. So tempered, out he strayed
Half seeing visions that might have dismayed
Alecto's serpents; ravishments more keen
Than Hermes' pipe, when anxious he did lean
Over eclipsing eyes; and at the last
It was a sounding grotto, vaulted vast,
O'er-studded with a thousand, thousand pearls,
And crimson-mouthèd shells with stubborn curls, 880
Of every shape and size, even to the bulk
In which whales arbour close, to brood and sulk
Against an endless storm. Moreover too,
Fish-semblances, of green and azure hue,

Ready to snort their streams. In this cool wonder
Endymion sat down, and 'gan to ponder
On all his life: his youth, up to the day
When 'mid acclaim, and feasts, and garlands gay,
He stepped upon his shepherd throne; the look
890 Of his white palace in wild forest nook,
And all the revels he had lorded there;
Each tender maiden whom he once thought fair,
With every friend and fellow-woodlander –
Passed like a dream before him. Then the spur
Of the old bards to mighty deeds; his plans
To nurse the golden age 'mong shepherd clans;
That wondrous night; the great Pan-festival;
His sister's sorrow; and his wanderings all,
Until into the earth's deep maw he rushed;
900 Then all its buried magic, till it flushed
High with excessive love. 'And now', thought he,
'How long must I remain in jeopardy
Of blank amazements that amaze no more?
Now I have tasted her sweet soul to the core
All other depths are shallow: essences,
Once spiritual, are like muddy lees,
Meant but to fertilize my earthly root,
And make my branches lift a golden fruit
Into the bloom of heaven. Other light,
910 Though it be quick and sharp enough to blight
The Olympian eagle's vision, is dark,
Dark as the parentage of chaos. Hark!
My silent thoughts are echoing from these shells;
Or they are but the ghosts, the dying swells
Of noises far away? – list!' – Hereupon
He kept an anxious ear. The humming tone
Came louder, and behold, there as he lay,
On either side out-gushed, with misty spray,
A copious spring; and both together dashed
920 Swift, mad, fantastic round the rocks and lashed

Among the conches and shells of the lofty grot,
Leaving a trickling dew. At last they shot
Down from the ceiling's height, pouring a noise
As of some breathless racers whose hopes poise
Upon the last few steps, and with spent force
Along the ground they took a winding course.
Endymion followed – for it seemed that one
Ever pursued, the other strove to shun –
Followed their languid mazes, till well nigh
He had left thinking of the mystery,   930
And was now rapt in tender hoverings
Over the vanished bliss. Ah! what is it sings
His dream away? What melodies are these?
They sound as through the whispering of trees,
Not native in such barren vaults. Give ear!

   'O Arethusa, peerless nymph! why fear
Such tenderness as mine? Great Dian, why,
Why didst thou hear her prayer? O that I
Were rippling round her dainty fairness now,
Circling about her waist, and striving how   940
To entice her to a dive! then stealing in
Between her luscious lips and eyelids thin!
O that her shining hair was in the sun,
And I distilling from it thence to run
In amorous rillets down her shrinking form!
To linger on her lily shoulders, warm
Between her kissing breasts, and every charm
Touch-raptured! – See how painfully I flow;
Fair maid, be pitiful to my great woe.
Stay, stay thy weary course, and let me lead,   950
A happy wooer, to the flowery mead
Where all that beauty snared me.' – 'Cruel god,
Desist! or my offended mistress' nod
Will stagnate all thy fountains – tease me not
With siren words – Ah, have I really got

Such power to madden thee? And is it true –
Away, away, or I shall dearly rue
My very thoughts: in mercy then away,
Kindest Alpheus, for should I obey
960   My own dear will, 'twould be a deadly bane.
O, Oread-Queen! would that thou hadst a pain
Like this of mine, then would I fearless turn
And be a criminal. Alas, I burn,
I shudder – gentle river, get thee hence.
Alpheus! thou enchanter! every sense
Of mine was once made perfect in these woods.
Fresh breezes, bowery lawns, and innocent floods,
Ripe fruits, and lonely couch, contentment gave;
But ever since I heedlessly did lave
970   In thy deceitful stream, a panting glow
Grew strong within me: wherefore serve me so,
And call it love? Alas, 'twas cruelty.
Not once more did I close my happy eye
Amid the thrushes' song. Away! Avaunt!
O 'twas a cruel thing.' – 'Now thou dost taunt
So softly, Arethusa, that I think
If thou wast playing on my shady brink,
Thou wouldst bathe once again. Innocent maid!
Stifle thine heart no more; nor be afraid
980   Of angry powers – there are deities
Will shade us with their wings. Those fitful sighs
'Tis almost death to hear. O let me pour
A dewy balm upon them! – fear no more,
Sweet Arethusa! Dian's self must feel
Sometimes these very pangs. Dear maiden, steal
Blushing into my soul, and let us fly
These dreary caverns for the open sky.
I will delight thee all my winding course,
From the green sea up to my hidden source
990   About Arcadian forests; and will show
The channels where my coolest waters flow

Through mossy rocks; where, 'mid exuberant green,
I roam in pleasant darkness, more unseen
Than Saturn in his exile; where I brim
Round flowery islands, and take thence a skim
Of mealy sweets, which myriads of bees
Buzz from their honeyed wings: and thou shouldst please
Thyself to choose the richest, where we might
Be incense-pillowed every summer night.
Doff all sad fears, thou white deliciousness,   1000
And let us be thus comforted; unless
Thou couldst rejoice to see my hopeless stream
Hurry distracted from Sol's temperate beam,
And pour to death along some hungry sands.' –
'What can I do, Alpheus? Dian stands
Severe before me. Persecuting fate!
Unhappy Arethusa! thou wast late
A huntress free in –' At this, sudden fell
Those two sad streams adown a fearful dell.
The Latmian listened, but he heard no more,   1010
Save echo, faint repeating o'er and o'er
The name of Arethusa. On the verge
Of that dark gulf he wept, and said: 'I urge
Thee, gentle Goddess of my pilgrimage,
By our eternal hopes, to soothe, to assuage,
If thou art powerful, these lovers' pains;
And make them happy in some happy plains.'

    He turned – there was a whelming sound – he stepped –
There was a cooler light; and so he kept
Towards it by a sandy path, and lo!   1020
More suddenly than doth a moment go,
The visions of the earth were gone and fled –
He saw the giant sea above his head.

BOOK III
There are who lord it o'er their fellow-men
With most prevailing tinsel: who unpen

Their baaing vanities, to browse away
The comfortable green and juicy hay
From human pastures; or – O torturing fact! –
Who, through an idiot blink, will see unpacked
Fire-branded foxes to sear up and singe
Our gold and ripe-eared hopes. With not one tinge
Of sanctuary splendour, not a sight
Able to face an owl's, they still are dight
By the blear-eyed nations in empurpled vests,
And crowns, and turbans. With unladen breasts,
Save of blown self-applause, they proudly mount
To their spirit's perch, their being's high account,
Their tip-top nothings, their dull skies, their thrones –
Amid the fierce intoxicating tones
Of trumpets, shoutings, and belaboured drums,
And sudden cannon. Ah! how all this hums,
In wakeful ears, like uproar passed and gone –
Like thunder clouds that spake to Babylon,
And set those old Chaldeans to their tasks. –
Are then regalities all gilded masks?
No, there are thronèd seats unscalable
But by a patient wing, a constant spell,
Or by ethereal things that, unconfined,
Can make a ladder of the eternal wind,
And poise about in cloudy thunder-tents
To watch the abysm-birth of elements.
Ay, 'bove the withering of old-lipped Fate
A thousand Powers keep religious state,
In water, fiery realm, and airy bourne,
And, silent as a consecrated urn,
Hold sphery sessions for a season due.
Yet few of these far majesties – ah, few! –
Have bared their operations to this globe –
Few, who with gorgeous pageantry enrobe
Our piece of heaven – whose benevolence
Shakes hand with our own Ceres, every sense

Filling with spiritual sweets to plenitude,
As bees gorge full their cells. And, by the feud   40
'Twixt Nothing and Creation, I here swear,
Eterne Apollo! that thy Sister fair
Is of all these the gentlier-mightiest.
When thy gold breath is misting in the west,
She unobservèd steals unto her throne,
And there she sits most meek and most alone;
As if she had not pomp subservient;
As if thine eye, high Poet, was not bent
Towards her with the Muses in thine heart;
As if the ministering stars kept not apart,   50
Waiting for silver-footed messages.
O Moon! the oldest shades 'mong oldest trees
Feel palpitations when thou lookest in:
O Moon! old boughs lisp forth a holier din
The while they feel thine airy fellowship
Thou dost bless everywhere, with silver lip
Kissing dead things to life. The sleeping kine,
Couched in thy brightness, dream of fields divine:
Innumerable mountains rise, and rise,
Ambitious for the hallowing of thine eyes;   60
And yet thy benediction passeth not
One obscure hiding-place, one little spot
Where pleasure may be sent. The nested wren
Has thy fair face within its tranquil ken,
And from beneath a sheltering ivy leaf
Takes glimpses of thee; thou art a relief
To the poor patient oyster, where it sleeps
Within its pearly house. The mighty deeps,
The monstrous sea is thine – the myriad sea!
O Moon! far-spooming Ocean bows to thee,   70
And Tellus feels his forehead's cumbrous load.

[*Glaucus's Story*]
                                        'My soul stands
Now past the midway from mortality,
And so I can prepare without a sigh
To tell thee briefly all my joy and pain.
I was a fisher once, upon this main,
And my boat danced in every creek and bay.
Rough billows were my home by night and day –
The sea-gulls not more constant – for I had
No housing from the storm and tempests mad,
But hollow rocks – and they were palaces
Of silent happiness, of slumbrous ease.
Long years of misery have told me so.
Ay, thus it was one thousand years ago.
One thousand years! – Is it then possible
To look so plainly through them? to dispel
A thousand years with backward glance sublime?
To breathe away as 'twere all scummy slime
From off a crystal pool, to see its deep,
And one's own image from the bottom peep?
Yes: now I am no longer wretched thrall,
My long captivity and moanings all
Are but a slime, a thin-pervading scum,
The which I breathe away, and thronging come
Like things of yesterday my youthful pleasures.

   'I touched no lute, I sang not, trod no measures:
I was a lonely youth on desert shores.
My sports were lonely, 'mid continuous roars,
And craggy isles, and sea-mew's plaintive cry
Plaining discrepant between sea and sky.
Dolphins were still my playmates; shapes unseen
Would let me feel their scales of gold and green,
Nor be my desolation; and, full oft,
When a dread waterspout had reared aloft
Its hungry hugeness, seeming ready-ripe

320

330

340

To burst with hoarsest thunderings, and wipe
My life away like a vast sponge of fate,
Some friendly monster, pitying my sad state,   350
Has dived to its foundations, gulfed it down,
And left me tossing safely. But the crown
Of all my life was utmost quietude:
More did I love to lie in cavern rude,
Keeping in wait whole days for Neptune's voice,
And if it came at last, hark, and rejoice!
There blushed no summer eve but I would steer
My skiff along green shelving coasts, to hear
The shepherd's pipe come clear from aery steep,
Mingled with ceaseless bleatings of his sheep: 360
And never was a day of summer shine,
But I beheld its birth upon the brine,
For I would watch all night to see unfold
Heaven's gates, and Aethon snort his morning gold
Wide o'er the swelling streams: and constantly
At brim of day-tide, on some grassy lea,
My nets would be spread out, and I at rest.
The poor folk of the sea-country I blessed
With daily boon of fish most delicate:
They knew not whence this bounty, and elate   370
Would strew sweet flowers on a sterile beach.

'Why was I not contented? Wherefore reach
At things which, but for thee, O Latmian!
Had been my dreary death? Fool! I began
To feel distempered longings: to desire
The utmost privilege that ocean's sire
Could grant in benediction – to be free
Of all his kingdom. Long in misery
I wasted, ere in one extremest fit
I plunged for life or death. To interknit   380
One's senses with so dense a breathing stuff
Might seem a work of pain; so not enough

Can I admire how crystal-smooth it felt,
And buoyant round my limbs. At first I dwelt
Whole days and days in sheer astonishment,
Forgetful utterly of self-intent,
Moving but with the mighty ebb and flow,
Then, like a new-fledged bird that first doth show
His spreaded feathers to the morrow chill,
390   I tried in fear the pinions of my will.
'Twas freedom! and at once I visited
The ceaseless wonders of this ocean-bed.
No need to tell thee of them, for I see
That thou hast been a witness – it must be –
For these I know thou canst not feel a drouth,
By the melancholy corners of that mouth.
So I will in my story straightway pass
To more immediate matter. Woe, alas!
That love should be my bane! Ah, Scylla fair!
400   Why did poor Glaucus ever, ever dare

To sue thee to his heart? Kind stranger-youth!
I loved her to the very white of truth,
And she would not conceive it. Timid thing!
She fled me swift as sea-bird on the wing,
Round every isle, and point, and promontory,
From where large Hercules wound up his story
Far as Egyptian Nile. My passion grew
The more, the more I saw her dainty hue
Gleam delicately through the azure clear,
410   Until 'twas too fierce agony to bear;
And in that agony, across my grief
It flashed, that Circe might find some relief –
Cruel enchantress! So above the water
I reared my head, and looked for Phoebus' daughter.
Aeaea's isle was wondering at the moon: –
It seemed to whirl around me, and a swoon
Left me dead-drifting to that fatal power.

'When I awoke, 'twas in a twilight bower;
Just when the light of morn, with hum of bees,
Stole through its verdurous matting of fresh trees.   420
How sweet, and sweeter! for I heard a lyre,
And over it a sighing voice expire.
It ceased – I caught light footsteps; and anon
The fairest face that morn e'er looked upon
Pushed through a screen of roses. Starry Jove!
With tears, and smiles, and honey-words she wove
A net whose thraldom was more bliss than all
The range of flowered Elysium. Thus did fall
The dew of her rich speech: "Ah! Art awake?
O let me hear thee speak, for Cupid's sake!   430
I am so oppressed with joy! Why, I have shed
An urn of tears, as though thou wert cold-dead.
And now I find thee living, I will pour
From these devoted eyes their silver store,
Until exhausted of the latest drop,
So it will pleasure thee, and force thee stop
Here, that I too may live: but if beyond
Such cool and sorrowful offerings, thou art fond
Of soothing warmth, of dalliance supreme;
If thou art ripe to taste a long love-dream;   440
If smiles, if dimples, tongues for ardour mute,
Hang in thy vision like a tempting fruit,
O let me pluck it for thee." Thus she linked
Her charming syllables, till indistinct
Their music came to my o'er-sweetened soul;
And then she hovered over me, and stole
So near, that if no nearer it had been
This furrowed visage thou hadst never seen.

'Young man of Latmos! thus particular
Am I, that thou mayst plainly see how far   450
This fierce temptation went: and thou mayst not
Exclaim, "How then, was Scylla quite forgot?"

'Who could resist? Who in this universe?
She did so breathe ambrosia; so immerse
My fine existence in a golden clime.
She took me like a child of suckling time,
And cradled me in roses. Thus condemned,
The current of my former life was stemmed,
And to this arbitrary queen of sense
I bowed a trancèd vassal: nor would thence
Have moved, even though Amphion's harp had wooed
Me back to Scylla o'er the billows rude.
For as Apollo each eve doth devise
A new apparelling for western skies,
So every eve, nay, every spendthrift hour,
Shed balmy consciousness within that bower.
And I was free of haunts umbrageous;
Could wander in the mazy forest-house
Of squirrels, foxes shy, and antlered deer,
And birds from coverts innermost and drear
Warbling for very joy mellifluous sorrow –
To me new born delights!
                   'Now let me borrow,
For moments few, a temperament as stern
As Pluto's sceptre, that my words not burn
These uttering lips, while I in calm speech tell
How specious heaven was changed to real hell.

  'One morn she left me sleeping: half awake
I sought for her smooth arms and lips, to slake
My greedy thirst with nectarous camel-draughts;
But she was gone. Whereat the barbèd shafts
Of disappointment stuck in me so sore,
That out I ran and searched the forest o'er.
Wandering about in pine and cedar gloom
Damp awe assailed me; for there 'gan to boom
A sound of moan, an agony of sound,
Sepulchral from the distance all around.

Then came a conquering earth-thunder, and rumbled
That fierce complain to silence, while I stumbled
Down a precipitous path, as if impelled.
I came to a dark valley. – Groanings swelled   490
Poisonous about my ears, and louder grew,
The nearer I approached a flame's gaunt blue,
That glared before me through a thorny brake.
This fire, like the eye of gordian snake,
Bewitched me towards, and I soon was near
A sight too fearful for the feel of fear:
In thicket hid I cursed the haggard scene –
The banquet of my arms, my arbour queen,
Seated upon an up-torn forest root;
And all around her shapes, wizard and brute,   500
Laughing, and wailing, grovelling, serpenting,
Showing tooth, tusk, and venom-bag, and sting!
O such deformities! Old Charon's self,
Should he give up awhile his penny pelf,
And take a dream 'mong rushes Stygian,
It could not be so phantasied. Fierce, wan,
And tyrannizing was the lady's look,
As over them a gnarlèd staff she shook.
Oft-times upon the sudden she laughed out,
And from a basket emptied to the rout   510
Clusters of grapes, the which they ravened quick
And roared for more; with many a hungry lick
About their shaggy jaws. Avenging, slow,
Anon she took a branch of mistletoe,
And emptied on't a black dull-gurgling phial –
Groaned one and all, as if some piercing trial
Was sharpening for their pitiable bones.
She lifted up the charm: appealing groans
From their poor breasts went sueing to her ear
In vain; remorseless as an infant's bier   520
She whisked against their eyes the sooty oil.
Whereat was heard a noise of painful toil,

Increasing gradual to a tempest rage,
Shrieks, yells, and groans of torture-pilgrimage;
Until their grievèd bodies 'gan to bloat
And puff from the tail's end to stiflèd throat.
Then was appalling silence: then a sight
More wildering than all that hoarse affright;
For the whole herd, as by a whirlwind writhen,
Went through the dismal air like one huge Python
Antagonizing Boreas – and so vanished.
Yet there was not a breath of wind: she banished
These phantoms with a nod. Lo! from the dark
Came waggish fauns, and nymphs, and satyrs stark,
With dancing and loud revelry – and went
Swifter than centaurs after rapine bent.
Sighing an elephant appeared and bowed
Before the fierce witch, speaking thus aloud
In human accent: "Potent goddess! chief
Of pains resistless! make my being brief,
Or let me from this heavy prison fly –
Or give me to the air, or let me die!
I sue not for my happy crown again;
I sue not for my phalanx on the plain;
I sue not for my lone, my widowed wife;
I sue not for my ruddy drops of life,
My children fair, my lovely girls and boys!
I will forget them; I will pass these joys;
Ask naught so heavenward, so too, too high:
Only I pray, as fairest boon, to die,
Or be delivered from this cumbrous flesh,
From this gross, detestable, filthy mesh,
And merely given to the cold bleak air.
Have mercy, Goddess! Circe, feel my prayer!"

    'That cursed magician's name fell icy numb
Upon my wild conjecturing: truth had come
Naked and sabre-like against my heart.

530

540

550

I saw a fury whetting a death-dart;
And my slain spirit, overwrought with fright,
Fainted away in that dark lair of night. 560
Think, my deliverer, how desolate
My waking must have been! disgust, and hate,
And terrors manifold divided me
A spoil amongst them. I prepared to flee
Into the dungeon core of that wild wood:
I fled three days – when lo! before me stood
Glaring the angry witch. O Dis! even now,
A clammy dew is beading on my brow,
At mere remembering her pale laugh, and curse.
"Ha! ha! Sir Dainty! there must be a nurse 570
Made of rose leaves and thistledown, express,
To cradle thee my sweet, and lull thee – yes,
I am too flinty-hard for thy nice touch:
My tenderest squeeze is but a giant's clutch.
So, fairy-thing, it shall have lullabies
Unheard of yet: and it shall still its cries
Upon some breast more lily-feminine.
Oh, no – it shall not pine, and pine, and pine
More than one pretty, trifling thousand years;
And then 'twere pity, but fate's gentle shears 580
Cut short its immortality. Sea-flirt!
Young dove of the waters! truly I'll not hurt
One hair of thine: see how I weep and sigh,
That our heart-broken parting is so nigh.
And must we part? Ah, yes, it must be so.
Yet ere thou leavest me in utter woe,
Let me sob over thee my last adieus,
And speak a blessing. Mark me! Thou hast thews
Immortal, for thou art of heavenly race:
But such a love is mine, that here I chase 590
Eternally away from thee all bloom
Of youth, and destine thee towards a tomb.
Hence shalt thou quickly to the watery vast;

And there, ere many days be overpassed,
Disabled age shall seize thee; and even then
Thou shalt not go the way of agèd men;
But live and wither, cripple and still breathe
Ten hundred years – which gone, I then bequeath
Thy fragile bones to unknown burial.
Adieu, sweet love, adieu!" – As shot stars fall,
She fled ere I could groan for mercy. Stung
And poisoned was my spirit; despair sung
A war-song of defiance 'gainst all hell.
A hand was at my shoulder to compel
My sullen steps; another 'fore my eyes
Moved on with pointed finger. In this guise
Enforcèd, at the last by ocean's foam
I found me – by my fresh, my native home.
Its tempering coolness, to my life akin,
Came salutary as I waded in;
And, with a blind voluptuous rage, I gave
Battle to the swollen billow-ridge, and drave
Large froth before me, while there yet remained
Hale strength, nor from my bones all marrow drained.

'Young lover, I must weep – such hellish spite
With dry cheek who can tell? While thus my might
Proving upon this element, dismayed,
Upon a dead thing's face my hand I laid.
I looked – 'twas Scylla! Cursèd, cursèd Circe!
O vulture-witch, hast never heard of mercy?
Could not thy harshest vengeance be content,
But thou must nip this tender innocent
Because I loved her? – Cold, O cold indeed
Were her fair limbs, and like a common weed
The sea-swell took her hair. Dead as she was
I clung about her waist, nor ceased to pass
Fleet as an arrow through unfathomed brine,
Until there shone a fabric crystalline,

600

610

620

Ribbed and inlaid with coral, pebble, and pearl.
Headlong I darted; at one eager swirl   630
Gained its bright portal, entered, and behold!
'Twas vast, and desolate, and icy-cold;
And all around – But wherefore this to thee
Who in few minutes more thyself shalt see? –
I left poor Scylla in a niche and fled.
My fevered parchings up, my scathing dread
Met palsy half-way: soon these limbs became
Gaunt, withered, sapless, feeble, cramped, and lame . . .'

BOOK IV

Muse of my native land! loftiest Muse!
O first-born on the mountains! by the hues
Of heaven on the spiritual air begot!
Long didst thou sit alone in northern grot,
While yet our England was a wolfish den;
Before our forests heard the talk of men;
Before the first of Druids was a child,
Long didst thou sit amid our regions wild
Rapt in a deep prophetic solitude.
There came an eastern voice of solemn mood –   10
Yet wast thou patient. Then sang forth the Nine,
Apollo's garland – yet didst thou divine
Such home-bred glory, that they cried in vain,
'Come hither, Sister of the Island!' Plain
Spake fair Ausonia; and once more she spake
A higher summons – still didst thou betake
Thee to thy native hopes. O thou hast won
A full accomplishment! The thing is done,
Which undone, these our latter days had risen
On barren souls. Great Muse, thou know'st what prison,   20
Of flesh and bone, curbs, and confines, and frets
Our spirit's wings. Despondency besets
Our pillows, and the fresh tomorrow morn
Seems to give forth its light in very scorn

Of our dull, uninspired, snail-pacèd lives.
Long have I said, how happy he who shrives
To thee! But then I thought on poets gone,
And could not pray – nor could I now – so on
I move to the end in lowliness of heart.

[*Indian Maid's Roundelay*]
                                    Then she,
Sitting beneath the midmost forest tree,
For pity sang this roundelay:

  'O Sorrow,
  Why dost borrow
The natural hue of health, from vermeil lips? –
   To give maiden blushes
   To the white rose bushes?
Or is't thy dewy hand the daisy tips?

  'O Sorrow
  Why dost borrow
The lustrous passion from a falcon-eye? –
   To give the glow-worm light?
   Or, on a moonless night,
To tinge, on syren shores, the salt sea-spry?

  'O Sorrow,
  Why dost borrow
The mellow ditties from a mourning tongue? –
   To give at evening pale
   Unto the nightingale,
That thou mayst listen the cold dews among?

  'O Sorrow,
  Why dost borrow
Heart's lightness from the merriment of May? –
   A lover would not tread
   A cowslip on the head,
Though he should dance from eve till peep of day –

    Nor any drooping flower   170
    Held sacred for thy bower,
Wherever he may sport himself and play.

    'To Sorrow,
    I bade good-morrow,
And thought to leave her far away behind.
    But cheerly, cheerly,
    She loves me dearly;
She is so constant to me, and so kind:
    I would deceive her
    And so leave her,   180
But ah! she is so constant and so kind.

'Beneath my palm trees, by the river side,
I sat a-weeping: in the whole world wide
There was no one to ask me why I wept –
    And so I kept
Brimming the water-lily cups with tears
    Cold as my fears.

'Beneath my palm trees, by the river side,
I sat a-weeping: what enamoured bride,
Cheated by shadowy wooer from the clouds,   190
    But hides and shrouds
Beneath dark palm trees by a river-side?

'And as I sat, over the light blue hills
There came a noise of revellers: the rills
Into the wide stream came of purple hue –
    'Twas Bacchus and his crew!
The earnest trumpet spake, and silver thrills
From kissing cymbals made a merry din –
    'Twas Bacchus and his kin!
Like to a moving vintage down they came,   200
Crowned with green leaves, and faces all on flame –
All madly dancing through the pleasant valley,
    To scare thee, Melancholy!

O then, O then, thou wast a simple name!
And I forgot thee, as the berried holly
By shepherds is forgotten, when, in June,
Tall chestnuts keep away the sun and moon –
    I rushed into the folly!

'Within his car, aloft, young Bacchus stood,
Trifling his ivy-dart, in dancing mood,
    With sidelong laughing;
And little rills of crimson wine imbrued
His plump white arms, and shoulders, enough white
    For Venus' pearly bite;
And near him rode Silenus on his ass,
Pelted with flowers as he on did pass
    Tipsily quaffing.

'Whence came ye, merry Damsels! whence came ye!
So many, and so many, and such glee?
Why have ye left your bowers desolate,
    Your lutes and gentler fate? –
"We follow Bacchus! Bacchus on the wing,
    A-conquering!
Bacchus, young Bacchus! good or ill betide,
We dance before him thorough kingdoms wide –
Come hither, lady fair, and joinèd be
    To our wild minstrelsy!"

'Whence came ye, jolly Satyrs! whence came ye!
So many, and so many, and such glee?
Why have ye left your forest haunts, why left
    Your nuts in oak-tree cleft? –
"For wine, for wine we left our kernel tree;
For wine we left our heath, and yellow brooms,
    And cold mushrooms;
For wine we follow Bacchus through the earth –
Great God of breathless cups and chirping mirth! –
Come hither, lady fair, and joinèd be
    To our mad minstrelsy!"

210

220

230

'Over wide streams and mountains great we went,
And, save when Bacchus kept his ivy tent,   240
Onward the tiger and the leopard pants,
     With Asian elephants:
Onward these myriads – with song and dance,
With zebras striped, and sleek Arabians' prance,
Web-footed alligators, crocodiles,
Bearing upon their scaly backs, in files,
Plump infant laughers mimicking the coil
Of seamen, and stout galley-rowers' toil –
With toying oars and silken sails they glide,
     Nor care for wind and tide.   250

'Mounted on panthers' furs and lions' manes,
From rear to van they scour about the plains;
A three days' journey in a moment done:
And always, at the rising of the sun,
About the wilds they hunt with spear and horn,
     On spleenful unicorn.

'I saw Osirian Egypt kneel adown
     Before the vine-wreath crown!
I saw parched Abyssinia rouse and sing
     To the silver cymbals' ring!   260
I saw the whelming vintage hotly pierce
     Old Tartary the fierce!
The kings of Ind their jewel-sceptres vail,
And from their treasures scatter pearlèd hail.
Great Brahma from his mystic heaven groans,
     And all his priesthood moans;
Before young Bacchus' eye-wink turning pale. –
Into these regions came I following him,
Sick hearted, weary – so I took a whim
To stray away into these forests drear   270
     Alone, without a peer:
And I have told thee all thou mayest hear.

'Young stranger!
    I've been a ranger
In search of pleasure throughout every clime:
    Alas, 'tis not for me!
    Bewitched I sure must be,
To lose in grieving all my maiden prime.

'Come then, Sorrow!
280   Sweetest Sorrow!
Like an own babe I nurse thee on my breast:
    I thought to leave thee
    And deceive thee,
But now of all the world I love thee best.

    'There is not one,
    No, no, not one
But thee to comfort a poor lonely maid:
    Thou art her mother,
    And her brother,
290 Her playmate, and her wooer in the shade.'

[*Conclusion*]

                                    . . . At the last
900 Endymion said: 'Are not our fates all cast?
Why stand we here? Adieu, ye tender pair!
Adieu!' Whereat those maidens, with wild stare,
Walked dizzily away. Painèd and hot
His eyes went after them, until they got
Near to a cypress grove, whose deadly maw,
In one swift moment, would what then he saw
Engulf for ever. 'Stay!' he cried, 'ah, stay!
Turn, damsels! hist! one word I have to say.
910 Sweet Indian, I would see thee once again.
It is a thing I dote on: so I'd fain,
Peona, ye should hand in hand repair
Into those holy groves, that silent are
Behind great Dian's temple. I'll be yon,

At Vesper's earliest twinkle – they are gone –
But once, once, once again –' At this he pressed
His hands against his face, and then did rest
His head upon a mossy hillock green,
And so remained as he a corpse had been
All the long day, save when he scantly lifted   920
His eyes abroad, to see how shadows shifted
With the slow move of time – sluggish and weary
Until the poplar tops, in journey dreary,
Had reached the river's brim. Then up he rose,
And, slowly as that very river flows,
Walked towards the temple grove with this lament:
'Why such a golden eve? The breeze is sent
Careful and soft, that not a leaf may fall
Before the serene father of them all
Bows down his summer head below the west.   930
Now am I of breath, speech, and speed possessed,
But at the setting I must bid adieu
To her for the last time. Night will strew
On the damp grass myriads of lingering leaves,
And with them shall I die; nor much it grieves
To die, when summer dies on the cold sward.
Why, I have been a butterfly, a lord
Of flowers, garlands, love-knots, silly posies,
Groves, meadows, melodies, and arbour roses.
My kingdom's at its death, and just it is   940
That I should die with it: so in all this
We miscall grief, bale, sorrow, heartbreak, woe,
What is there to plain of? By Titan's foe
I am but rightly served.' So saying, he
Tripped lightly on, in sort of deathful glee,
Laughing at the clear stream and setting sun,
As though they jests had been: nor had he done
His laugh at nature's holy countenance,
Until that grove appeared, as if perchance,
And then his tongue with sober seemlihed   950

Gave utterance as he entered: 'Ha! I said,
"King of the butterflies", but by this gloom,
And by old Rhadamanthus' tongue of doom,
This dusk religion, pomp of solitude,
And the Promethean clay by thief endued,
By old Saturnus' forelock, by his head
Shook with eternal palsy, I did wed
Myself to things of light from infancy;
And thus to be cast out, thus lorn to die,
Is sure enough to make a mortal man
Grow impious.' So he inwardly began
On things for which no wording can be found,
Deeper and deeper sinking, until drowned
Beyond the reach of music: for the choir
Of Cynthia he heard not, though rough briar
Nor muffling thicket interposed to dull
The vesper hymn, far swollen, soft and full,
Through the dark pillars of those sylvan aisles.
He saw not the two maidens, nor their smiles,
Wan as primroses gathered at midnight
By chilly-fingered spring. 'Unhappy wight!
Endymion!' said Peona, 'we are here!
What wouldst thou ere we all are laid on bier?'
Then he embraced her, and his lady's hand
Pressed, saying: 'Sister, I would have command,
If it were heaven's will, on our sad fate.'
At which that dark-eyed stranger stood elate
And said, in a new voice, but sweet as love,
To Endymion's amaze: 'By Cupid's dove,
And so thou shalt! and by the lily truth
Of my own breast thou shalt, belovèd youth!'
And as she spake, into her face there came
Light, as reflected from a silver flame:
Her long black hair swelled ampler, in display
Full golden; in her eyes a brighter day
Dawned blue and full of love. Ay, he beheld

960

970

980

Phoebe, his passion! Joyous she upheld
Her lucid bow, continuing thus: 'Drear, drear
Has our delaying been; but foolish fear
Withheld me first; and then decrees of fate;   990
And then 'twas fit that from this mortal state
Thou shouldst, my love, by some unlooked for change
Be spiritualized. Peona, we shall range
These forests, and to thee they safe shall be
As was thy cradle; hither shalt thou flee
To meet us many a time.' Next Cynthia bright
Peona kissed, and blessed with fair good-night:
Her brother kissed her too, and knelt adown
Before his goddess, in a blissful swoon.
She gave her fair hands to him, and behold,   1000
Before three swiftest kisses he had told,
They vanished far away! – Peona went
Home through the gloomy wood in wonderment.

═══

Nebuchadnezzar's Dream

Before he went to live with owls and bats
    Nebuchadnezzar had an ugly dream,
    Worse than a housewife's when she thinks her cream
Made a naumachia for mice and rats.
So scared, he sent for that 'Good King of Cats',
    Young Daniel, who straightway did pluck the beam
    From out his eye, and said 'I do not deem
Your sceptre worth a straw – your cushion old door-mats'.
A horrid nightmare similar somewhat
    Of late has haunted a most valiant crew   10
        Of loggerheads and chapmen – we are told
That any Daniel though he be a sot
    Can make their lying lips turn pale of hue
        By drawling out, 'Ye are that head of Gold.'
                                    (Not published by Keats)

To Mrs Reynolds's Cat

Cat! who hast passed thy grand climacteric,
　　How many mice and rats hast in thy days
　　Destroyed? How many tit-bits stolen? Gaze
With those bright languid segments green, and prick
Those velvet ears – but prithee do not stick
　　Thy latent talons in me, and up-raise
　　Thy gentle mew, and tell me all thy frays
Of fish and mice, and rats and tender chick.
Nay, look not down, nor lick thy dainty wrists –
　　For all the wheezy asthma, and for all
Thy tail's tip is nicked off, and though the fists
　　Of many a maid have given thee many a maul,
Still is that fur as soft as when the lists
　　In youth thou enteredst on glass-bottled wall.

(Not published by Keats)

On Sitting Down to Read King Lear Once Again

O golden-tongued Romance, with serene lute!
　　Fair plumèd Syren, Queen of far-away!
　　Leave melodizing on this wintry day,
Shut up thine olden pages, and be mute:
Adieu! for, once again, the fierce dispute
　　Betwixt damnation and impassioned clay
　　Must I burn through, once more humbly assay
The bitter-sweet of this Shakespearian fruit:
Chief Poet! and ye clouds of Albion,
　　Begetters of our deep eternal theme!
When through the old oak forest I am gone,
　　Let me not wander in a barren dream,

But, when I am consumèd in the fire,
Give me new Phoenix wings to fly at my desire.

(Not published by Keats)

'When I have fears that I may cease to be'

When I have fears that I may cease to be
  Before my pen has gleaned my teeming brain,
Before high-pilèd books, in charactery,
  Hold like rich garners the full-ripened grain;
When I behold, upon the night's starred face,
  Huge cloudy symbols of a high romance,
And think that I may never live to trace
  Their shadows, with the magic hand of chance;
And when I feel, fair creature of an hour!
  That I shall never look upon thee more,
Never have relish in the faery power
  Of unreflecting love! – then on the shore
Of the wide world I stand alone, and think
Till love and fame to nothingness do sink.

(Not published by Keats)

To —*

Time's sea hath been five years at its slow ebb,
  Long hours have to and fro let creep the sand,
Since I was tangled in thy beauty's web,
  And snared by the ungloving of thy hand.
And yet I never look on midnight sky,
  But I behold thine eyes' well memoried light;
I cannot look upon the rose's dye,

* A lady whom he saw for some few moments at Vauxhall.

But to thy cheek my soul doth take its flight;
I cannot look on any budding flower,
But my fond ear, in fancy at thy lips,
And hearkening for a love-sound, doth devour
Its sweets in the wrong sense: – Thou dost eclipse
Every delight with sweet remembering,
And grief unto my darling joys dost bring.

(Not published by Keats)

=====

'O thou whose face hath felt the Winter's wind'

['. . . I had no Idea but of the Morning and the Thrush said I was
right – seeming to say . . .'
(letter to J. H. Reynolds, 19 February 1816)]

'O thou whose face hath felt the Winter's wind,
Whose eye has seen the snow-clouds hung in mist,
And the black elm tops, 'mong the freezing stars,
To thee the spring will be a harvest-time.
O thou, whose only book has been the light
Of supreme darkness which thou feddest on
Night after night when Phoebus was away,
To thee the Spring shall be a triple morn.
O fret not after knowledge – I have none,
And yet my song comes native with the warmth.
O fret not after knowledge – I have none,
And yet the Evening listens. He who saddens
At thought of idleness cannot be idle,
And he's awake who thinks himself asleep.'

(Not published by Keats)

To J. H. Reynolds, Esq.

Dear Reynolds, as last night I lay in bed,
There came before my eyes that wonted thread
Of shapes, and shadows, and remembrances,
That every other minute vex and please:
Things all disjointed come from North and South –
Two witch's eyes above a cherub's mouth,
Voltaire with casque and shield and habergeon,
And Alexander with his nightcap on,
Old Socrates a-tying his cravat,
And Hazlitt playing with Miss Edgeworth's cat,   10
And Junius Brutus, pretty well so so,
Making the best of's way towards Soho.

   Few are there who escape these visitings –
Perhaps one or two whose lives have patient wings,
And through whose curtains peeps no hellish nose,
No wild-boar tushes, and no mermaid's toes;
But flowers bursting out with lusty pride,
And young Aeolian harps personified,
Some, Titian colours touched into real life –
The sacrifice goes on; the pontiff knife   20
Gloams in the sun, the milk-white heifer lows,
The pipes go shrilly, the libation flows;
A white sail shows above the green-head cliff,
Moves round the point, and throws her anchor stiff.
The mariners join hymn with those on land.

   You know the Enchanted Castle – it doth stand
Upon a rock, on the border of a lake,
Nested in trees, which all do seem to shake
From some old magic-like Urganda's sword.
O Phoebus! that I had thy sacred word   30

To show this castle, in fair dreaming wise,
Unto my friend, while sick and ill he lies!

You know it well enough, where it doth seem
A mossy place, a Merlin's Hall, a dream.
You know the clear lake, and the little isles,
The mountains blue, and cold near-neighbour rills,
All which elsewhere are but half animate;
Here do they look alive to love and hate,
To smiles and frowns; they seem a lifted mound
40   Above some giant, pulsing underground.

Part of the building was a chosen see,
Built by a banished santon of Chaldee;
The other part, two thousand years from him,
Was built by Cuthbert de Saint Aldebrim;
Then there's a little wing, far from the sun,
Built by a Lapland witch turned maudlin nun;
And many other juts of agèd stone
Founded with many a mason-devil's groan.

The doors all look as if they oped themselves,
50   The windows as if latched by fays and elves,
And from them comes a silver flash of light,
As from the westward of a summer's night;
Or like a beauteous woman's large blue eyes
Gone mad through olden songs and poesies –

See! what is coming from the distance dim!
A golden galley all in silken trim!
Three rows of oars are lightening, moment-whiles,
Into the verdurous bosoms of those isles.
Towards the shade, under the castle wall,
60   It comes in silence – now 'tis hidden all.
The clarion sounds, and from a postern-grate
An echo of sweet music doth create
A fear in the poor herdsman, who doth bring
His beasts to trouble the enchanted spring.

He tells of the sweet music, and the spot,
To all his friends – and they believe him not.

O that our dreamings all, of sleep or wake,
Would all their colours from the sunset take,
From something of material sublime,
Rather than shadow our own soul's daytime   70
In the dark void of night. For in the world
We jostle – but my flag is not unfurled
On the admiral staff – and to philosophize
I dare not yet! O, never will the prize,
High reason, and the lore of good and ill,
Be my award! Things cannot to the will
Be settled, but they tease us out of thought.
Or is it that imagination brought
Beyond its proper bound, yet still confined,
Lost in a sort of purgatory blind,   80
Cannot refer to any standard law
Of either earth or heaven? It is a flaw
In happiness, to see beyond our bourne –
It forces us in summer skies to mourn;
It spoils the singing of the nightingale.

Dear Reynolds, I have a mysterious tale,
And cannot speak it. The first page I read
Upon a lampit rock of green seaweed
Among the breakers. 'Twas a quiet eve;
The rocks were silent, the wide sea did weave   90
An untumultuous fringe of silver foam
Along the flat brown sand. I was at home
And should have been most happy – but I saw
Too far into the sea, where every maw
The greater on the less feeds evermore. –
But I saw too distinct into the core
Of an eternal fierce destruction,
And so from happiness I far was gone.
Still am I sick of it; and though, today,

100 I've gathered young spring-leaves, and flowers gay
       Of periwinkle and wild strawberry,
       Still do I that most fierce destruction see –
       The shark at savage prey, the hawk at pounce,
       The gentle robin, like a pard or ounce,
       Ravening a worm. – Away, ye horrid moods!
       Moods of one's mind! You know I hate them well,
       You know I'd sooner be a clapping bell
       To some Kamchatkan missionary church,
       Than with these horrid moods be left in lurch.
110 Do you get health – and Tom the same – I'll dance,
       And from detested moods in new romance
       Take refuge. Of bad lines a centaine dose
       Is sure enough – and so 'here follows prose' . . .

(Not published by Keats)

════

Isabella; or, The Pot of Basil

I

Fair Isabel, poor simple Isabel! ~~pilgram (wearing palms~~
    Lorenzo, a young palmer in Love's eye!
They could not in the self-same mansion dwell
    Without some stir of heart, some malady;
They could not sit at meals but feel how well
    It soothed each to be the other by;
They could not, sure, beneath the same roof sleep
But to each other dream, and nightly weep.

II

With every morn their love grew tenderer,
10   With every eve deeper and tenderer still;
He might not in house, field, or garden stir,
    But her full shape would all his seeing fill;
And his continual voice was pleasanter
    To her than noise of trees or hidden rill;

Her lute-string gave an echo of his name,
She spoilt her half-done broidery with the same.

III

He knew whose gentle hand was at the latch
    Before the door had given her to his eyes;
And from her chamber-window he would catch
    Her beauty farther than the falcon spies;
And constant as her vespers would he watch,   20
    Because her face was turned to the same skies;
And with sick longing all the night outwear,
To hear her morning-step upon the stair.

IV

A whole long month of May in this sad plight
    Made their cheeks paler by the break of June:
'To-morrow will I bow to my delight,
    To-morrow will I ask my lady's boon.'
'O may I never see another night,
    Lorenzo, if thy lips breathe not love's tune.'   30
So spake they to their pillows; but, alas,
Honeyless days and days did he let pass –

V

Until sweet Isabella's untouched cheek
    Fell sick within the rose's just domain,
Fell thin as a young mother's, who doth seek
    By every lull to cool her infant's pain:
'How ill she is,' said he, 'I may not speak,
    And yet I will, and tell my love all plain:
If looks speak love-laws, I will drink her tears,
And at the least 'twill startle off her cares.'   40

VI

So said he one fair morning, and all day
    His heart beat awfully against his side;
And to his heart he inwardly did pray

For power to speak; but still the ruddy tide
Stifled his voice, and pulsed resolve away –
   Fevered his high conceit of such a bride,
Yet brought him to the meekness of a child:
Alas! when passion is both meek and wild!

VII

So once more he had waked and anguishèd
   A dreary night of love and misery,
If Isabel's quick eye had not been wed
   To every symbol on his forehead high.
She saw it waxing very pale and dead,
   And straight all flushed; so, lispèd tenderly,
'Lorenzo!' – here she ceased her timid quest,
But in her tone and look he read the rest.

VIII

'O Isabella, I can half-perceive
   That I may speak my grief into thine ear.
If thou didst ever anything believe,
   Believe how I love thee, believe how near
My soul is to its doom: I would not grieve
   Thy hand by unwelcome pressing, would not fear
Thine eyes by gazing; but I cannot live
Another night, and not my passion shrive.

IX

'Love! thou art leading me from wintry cold,
   Lady! thou leadest me to summer clime,
And I must taste the blossoms that unfold
   In its ripe warmth this gracious morning time.'
So said, his erewhile timid lips grew bold,
   And poesied with hers in dewy rhyme:
Great bliss was with them, and great happiness
Grew, like a lusty flower, in June's caress.

X

Parting they seemed to tread upon the air,
    Twin roses by the zephyr blown apart
Only to meet again more close, and share
    The inward fragrance of each other's heart.
She, to her chamber gone, a ditty fair
    Sang, of delicious love and honeyed dart;
He with light steps went up a western hill,
And bade the sun farewell, and joyed his fill.   80

XI

All close they met again, before the dusk
    Had taken from the stars its pleasant veil,
All close they met, all eves, before the dusk
    Had taken from the stars its pleasant veil,
Close in a bower of hyacinth and musk,
    Unknown of any, free from whispering tale.
Ah! better had it been for ever so,
Than idle ears should pleasure in their woe.

XII

Were they unhappy then? – It cannot be –
    Too many tears for lovers have been shed,   90
Too many sighs give we to them in fee,
    Too much of pity after they are dead,
Too many doleful stories do we see,
    Whose matter in bright gold were best be read;
Except in such a page where Theseus' spouse
Over the pathless waves towards him bows.

XIII

But, for the general award of love,
    The little sweet doth kill much bitterness;
Though Dido silent is in under-grove,
    And Isabella's was a great distress,   100
Though young Lorenzo in warm Indian clove
    Was not embalmed, this truth is not the less –

Even bees, the little almsmen of spring-bowers,
Know there is richest juice in poison-flowers.

XIV

With her two brothers this fair lady dwelt,
   Enrichèd from ancestral merchandise,
And for them many a weary hand did swelt
   In torchèd mines and noisy factories,
And many once proud-quivered loins did melt
   In blood from stinging whip – with hollow eyes
Many all day in dazzling river stood,
To take the rich-ored driftings of the flood.

XV

For them the Ceylon diver held his breath,
   And went all naked to the hungry shark;
For them his ears gushed blood; for them in death
   The seal on the cold ice with piteous bark
Lay full of darts; for them alone did seethe
   A thousand men in troubles wide and dark:
Half-ignorant, they turned an easy wheel,
That set sharp racks at work to pinch and peel.

XVI

Why were they proud? Because their marble founts
   Gushed with more pride than do a wretch's tears? –
Why were they proud? Because fair orange-mounts
   Were of more soft ascent than lazar stairs? –
Why were they proud? Because red-lined accounts
   Were richer than the songs of Grecian years? –
Why were they proud? again we ask aloud,
Why in the name of Glory were they proud?

XVII

Yet were these Florentines as self-retired
   In hungry pride and gainful cowardice,
As two close Hebrews in that land inspired,

Paled in and vineyarded from beggar-spies –
The hawks of ship-mast forests – the untired
   And panniered mules for ducats and old lies –
Quick cat's-paws on the generous stray-away –
Great wits in Spanish, Tuscan, and Malay.

XVIII

How was it these same ledger-men could spy
   Fair Isabella in her downy nest?
How could they find out in Lorenzo's eye
   A straying from his toil? Hot Egypt's pest   140
Into their vision covetous and sly!
   How could these money-bags see east and west? –
Yet so they did – and every dealer fair
Must see behind, as doth the hunted hare.

XIX

O eloquent and famed Boccaccio!
   Of thee we now should ask forgiving boon,
And of thy spicy myrtles as they blow,
   And of thy roses amorous of the moon,
And of thy lilies, that do paler grow
   Now they can no more hear thy gittern's tune.   150
For venturing syllables that ill beseem
The quiet glooms of such a piteous theme.

XX

Grant thou a pardon here, and then the tale
   Shall move on soberly, as it is meet;
There is no other crime, no mad assail
   To make old prose in modern rhyme more sweet:
But it is done – succeed the verse or fail –
   To honour thee, and thy gone spirit greet,
To stead thee as a verse in English tongue,
An echo of thee in the north wind sung.   160

XXI

These brethren having found by many signs
     What love Lorenzo for their sister had,
And how she loved him too, each unconfines
     His bitter thoughts to other, well nigh mad
That he, the servant of their trade designs,
     Should in their sister's love be blithe and glad,
When 'twas their plan to coax her by degrees
To some high noble and his olive-trees.

XXII

And many a jealous conference had they,
170   And many times they bit their lips alone,
Before they fixed upon a surest way
     To make the youngster for his crime atone;
And at the last, these men of cruel clay
     Cut Mercy with a sharp knife to the bone,
For they resolvèd in some forest dim
To kill Lorenzo, and there bury him.

XXIII

So on a pleasant morning, as he leant
     Into the sunrise, o'er the balustrade
Of the garden-terrace, towards him they bent
180   Their footing through the dews; and to him said,
'You seem there in the quiet of content,
     Lorenzo, and we are most loth to invade
Calm speculation; but if you are wise,
     Bestride your steed while cold is in the skies.

XXIV

'To-day we purpose, ay, this hour we mount
     To spur three leagues towards the Apennine;
Come down, we pray thee, ere the hot sun count
     His dewy rosary on the eglantine.'
Lorenzo, courteously as he was wont,
190   Bowed a fair greeting to these serpents' whine;

And went in haste, to get in readiness,
With belt, and spur, and bracing huntsman's dress.

XXV

And as he to the court-yard passed along,
   Each third step did he pause, and listened oft
If he could hear his lady's matin-song,
   Or the light whisper of her footstep soft;
And as he thus over his passion hung,
   He heard a laugh full musical aloft,
When, looking up, he saw her features bright
Smile through an in-door lattice, all delight.   200

XXVI

'Love, Isabel!' said he, 'I was in pain
   Lest I should miss to bid thee a good morrow:
Ah! what if I should lose thee, when so fain
   I am to stifle all the heavy sorrow
Of a poor three hours' absence? but we'll gain
   Out of the amorous dark what day doth borrow.
Good bye! I'll soon be back.' 'Good bye!' said she –
And as he went she chanted merrily.

XXVII

So the two brothers and their murdered man
   Rode past fair Florence, to where Arno's stream   210
Gurgles through straitened banks, and still doth fan
   Itself with dancing bulrush, and the bream
Keeps head against the freshets. Sick and wan
   The brothers' faces in the ford did seem,
Lorenzo's flush with love. – They passed the water
Into a forest quiet for the slaughter.

XXVIII

There was Lorenzo slain and buried in,
   There in that forest did his great love cease.
Ah! when a soul doth thus its freedom win,
   It aches in loneliness – is ill at peace   220

As the break-covert blood-hounds of such sin.
  They dipped their swords in the water, and did tease
Their horses homeward, with convulsèd spur,
Each richer by his being a murderer.

XXIX

They told their sister how, with sudden speed,
  Lorenzo had ta'en ship for foreign lands,
Because of some great urgency and need
  In their affairs, requiring trusty hands.
Poor girl! put on thy stifling widow's weed,
230 And 'scape at once from Hope's accursèd bands;
To-day thou wilt not see him, nor to-morrow,
And the next day will be a day of sorrow.

XXX

She weeps alone for pleasures not to be;
  Sorely she wept until the night came on,
And then, instead of love, O misery!
  She brooded o'er the luxury alone:
His image in the dusk she seemed to see,
  And to the silence made a gentle moan,
Spreading her perfect arms upon the air,
240 And on her couch low murmuring 'Where? O where?'

XXXI

But Selfishness, Love's cousin, held not long
  Its fiery vigil in her single breast.
She fretted for the golden hour, and hung
  Upon the time with feverish unrest –
Not long – for soon into her heart a throng
  Of higher occupants, a richer zest,
Came tragic – passion not to be subdued,
And sorrow for her love in travels rude.

XXXII

In the mid days of autumn, on their eves
    The breath of Winter comes from far away,   250
And the sick west continually bereaves
    Of some gold tinge, and plays a roundelay
Of death among the bushes and the leaves,
    To make all bare before he dares to stray
From his north cavern. So sweet Isabel
By gradual decay from beauty fell,

XXXIII

Because Lorenzo came not. Oftentimes
    She asked her brothers, with an eye all pale,
Striving to be itself, what dungeon climes
    Could keep him off so long? They spake a tale   260
Time after time, to quiet her. Their crimes
    Came on them, like a smoke from Hinnom's vale;
And every night in dreams they groaned aloud,
To see their sister in her snowy shroud.

XXXIV

And she had died in drowsy ignorance,
    But for a thing more deadly dark than all.
It came like a fierce potion, drunk by chance,
    Which saves a sick man from the feathered pall
For some few gasping moments; like a lance,
    Waking an Indian from his cloudy hall   270
With cruel pierce, and bringing him again
Sense of the gnawing fire at heart and brain.

XXXV

It was a vision. – In the drowsy gloom,
    The dull of midnight, at her couch's foot
Lorenzo stood, and wept: the forest tomb
    Had marred his glossy hair which once could shoot
Lustre into the sun, and put cold doom
    Upon his lips, and taken the soft lute

From his lorn voice, and past his loamèd ears
280   Had made a miry channel for his tears.

XXXVI

Strange sound it was, when the pale shadow spake;
    For there was striving, in its piteous tongue,
To speak as when on earth it was awake,
    And Isabella on its music hung.
Languor there was in it, and tremulous shake,
    As in a palsied Druid's harp unstrung;
And through it moaned a ghostly under-song,
Like hoarse night-gusts sepulchral briars among.

XXXVII

Its eyes, though wild, were still all dewy bright
290   With love, and kept all phantom fear aloof
From the poor girl by magic of their light,
    The while it did unthread the horrid woof
Of the late darkened time – the murderous spite
    Of pride and avarice, the dark pine roof
In the forest, and the sodden turfèd dell,
Where, without any word, from stabs he fell.

XXXVIII

Saying moreover, 'Isabel, my sweet!
    Red whortle-berries droop above my head,
And a large flint-stone weighs upon my feet;
300   Around me beeches and high chestnuts shed
Their leaves and prickly nuts; a sheep-fold bleat
    Comes from beyond the river to my bed:
Go, shed one tear upon my heather-bloom,
And it shall comfort me within the tomb.

XXXIX

'I am a shadow now, alas! alas!
    Upon the skirts of human-nature dwelling
Alone. I chant alone the holy mass,
    While little sounds of life are round me knelling,

And glossy bees at noon do fieldward pass,
    And many a chapel bell the hour is telling, 310
Paining me through: those sounds grow strange to me,
And thou art distant in humanity.

XL

'I know what was, I feel full well what is,
    And I should rage, if spirits could go mad;
Though I forget the taste of earthly bliss,
    That paleness warms my grave, as though I had
A eraph chosen from the bright abyss
    To be my spouse: thy paleness makes me glad;
Thy beauty grows upon me, and I feel
A greater love through all my essence steal.' 320

XLI

The Spirit mourn'd 'Adieu!' – dissolved and left
    The atom darkness in a slow turmoil;
As when of healthful midnight sleep bereft,
    Thinking on rugged hours and fruitless toil,
We put our eyes into a pillowy cleft,
    And see the spangly gloom froth up and boil:
It made sad Isabella's eyelids ache,
And in the dawn she started up awake –

XLII

'Ha! ha!' said she, 'I knew not this hard life,
    I thought the worst was simple misery; 330
I thought some Fate with pleasure or with strife
    Portioned us – happy days, or else to die;
But there is crime – a brother's bloody knife!
    Sweet Spirit, thou hast schooled my infancy:
I'll visit thee for this, and kiss thine eyes,
And greet thee morn and even in the skies.'

XLIII

When the full morning came, she had devised
    How she might secret to the forest hie;

How she might find the clay, so dearly prized,
340   And sing to it one latest lullaby;
How her short absence might be unsurmised,
    While she the inmost of the dream would try.
Resolved, she took with her an agèd nurse,
And went into that dismal forest-hearse.

XLIV

See, as they creep along the river side,
    How she doth whisper to that agèd dame,
And, after looking round the champaign wide,
    Shows her a knife. – 'What feverous hectic flame
Burns in thee, child? – What good can thee betide,
350   That thou shouldst smile again?' The evening came,
And they had found Lorenzo's earthy bed –
The flint was there, the berries at his head.

XLV

Who hath not loitered in a green church-yard,
    And let his spirit, like a demon-mole,
Work through the clayey soil and gravel hard,
    To see skull, coffined bones, and funeral stole;
Pitying each form that hungry Death hath marred
    And filling it once more with human soul?
Ah! this is holiday to what was felt
360   When Isabella by Lorenzo knelt.

XLVI

She gazed into the fresh-thrown mould, as though
    One glance did fully all its secrets tell;
Clearly she saw, as other eyes would know
    Pale limbs at bottom of a crystal well;
Upon the murderous spot she seemed to grow,
    Like to a native lily of the dell –
Then with her knife, all sudden, she began
To dig more fervently than misers can.

XLVII

Soon she turned up a soilèd glove, whereon
   Her silk had played in purple phantasies,   370
She kissed it with a lip more chill than stone,
   And put it in her bosom, where it dries
And freezes utterly unto the bone
   Those dainties made to still an infant's cries:
Then 'gan she work again, nor stayed her care,
But to throw back at times her veiling hair.

XLVIII

That old nurse stood beside her wondering,
   Until her heart felt pity to the core
At sight of such a dismal labouring,
   And so she kneelèd, with her locks all hoar,   380
And put her lean hands to the horrid thing.
   Three hours they laboured at this travail sore –
At last they felt the kernel of the grave,
And Isabella did not stamp and rave.

XLIX

Ah! wherefore all this wormy circumstance?
   Why linger at the yawning tomb so long?
O for the gentleness of old Romance,
   The simple plaining of a minstrel's song!
Fair reader, at the old tale take a glance,
   For here, in truth, it doth not well belong   390
To speak – O turn thee to the very tale,
And taste the music of that vision pale.

L

With duller steel than the Persèan sword
   They cut away no formless monster's head,
But one, whose gentleness did well accord
   With death, as life. The ancient harps have said,
Love never dies, but lives, immortal Lord:
   If Love impersonate was ever dead,

Pale Isabella kissed it, and low moaned.
400   'Twas Love – cold, dead indeed, but not dethroned.

LI

In anxious secrecy they took it home,
    And then the prize was all for Isabel.
She calmed its wild hair with a golden comb,
    And all around each eye's sepulchral cell
Pointed each fringèd lash; the smeared loam
    With tears, as chilly as a dripping well,
She drenched away – and still she combed, and kept
Sighing all day – and still she kissed, and wept.

LII

Then in a silken scarf – sweet with the dews
410   Of precious flowers plucked in Araby,
And divine liquids come with odorous ooze
    Through the cold serpent-pipe refreshfully –
She wrapped it up; and for its tomb did choose
    A garden-pot, wherein she laid it by,
And covered it with mould, and o'er it set
Sweet basil, which her tears kept ever wet.

LIII

And she forgot the stars, the moon, and sun,
    And she forgot the blue above the trees,
And she forgot the dells where waters run,
420   And she forgot the chilly autumn breeze;
She had no knowledge when the day was done,
    And the new morn she saw not, but in peace
Hung over her sweet basil evermore,
And moistened it with tears unto the core.

LIV

And so she ever fed it with thin tears,
    Whence thick, and green, and beautiful it grew,
So that it smelt more balmy than its peers
    Of basil-tufts in Florence; for it drew

Nurture besides, and life, from human fears,
    From the fast mouldering head there shut from view: 430
So that the jewel, safely casketed,
Came forth, and in perfumèd leafits spread.

LV

O Melancholy, linger here awhile!
    O Music, Music, breathe despondingly!
O Echo, Echo, from some sombre isle,
    Unknown, Lethean, sigh to us – O sigh!
Spirits in grief, lift up your heads, and smile.
    Lift up your heads, sweet Spirits, heavily,
And make a pale light in your cypress glooms,
Tinting with silver wan your marble tombs.   440

LVI

Moan hither, all ye syllables of woe,
    From the deep throat of sad Melpomene!
Through bronzèd lyre in tragic order go,
    And touch the strings into a mystery;
Sound mournfully upon the winds and low;
    For simple Isabel is soon to be
Among the dead. She withers, like a palm
Cut by an Indian for its juicy balm.

LVII

O leave the palm to wither by itself;
    Let not quick Winter chill its dying hour! –   450
It may not be – those Baälites of pelf,
    Her brethren, noted the continual shower
From her dead eyes; and many a curious elf,
    Among her kindred, wondered that such dower
Of youth and beauty should be thrown aside
By one marked out to be a Noble's bride.

LVIII

And, furthermore, her brethren wondered much
    Why she sat drooping by the basil green,

And why it flourished, as by magic touch.
460   Greatly they wondered what the thing might mean:
They could not surely give belief, that such
    A very nothing would have power to wean
Her from her own fair youth, and pleasures gay,
And even remembrance of her love's delay.

LIX

Therefore they watched a time when they might sift
    This hidden whim; and long they watched in vain:
For seldom did she go to chapel-shrift,
    And seldom felt she any hunger-pain;
And when she left, she hurried back, as swift
470   As bird on wing to breast its eggs again;
And, patient as a hen-bird, sat her there
Beside her basil, weeping through her hair.

LX

Yet they contrived to steal the basil-pot,
    And to examine it in secret place.
The thing was vile with green and livid spot,
    And yet they knew it was Lorenzo's face:
The guerdon of their murder they had got,
    And so left Florence in a moment's space,
Never to turn again. Away they went,
480   With blood upon their heads, to banishment.

LXI

O Melancholy, turn thine eyes away!
    O Music, Music, breathe despondingly!
O Echo, Echo, on some other day,
    From isles Lethean, sigh to us – O sigh!
Spirits of grief, sing not your 'Well-a-way!'
    For Isabel, sweet Isabel, will die –
Will die a death too lone and incomplete,
Now they have ta'en away her basil sweet.

LXII

Piteous she looked on dead and senseless things,
    Asking for her lost basil amorously;   490
And with melodious chuckle in the strings
    Of her lorn voice, she oftentimes would cry
After the pilgrim in his wanderings,
    To ask him where her basil was, and why
'Twas hid from her: 'For cruel 'tis,' said she,
'To steal my basil-pot away from me.'

LXIII

And so she pined, and so she died forlorn,
    Imploring for her basil to the last.
No heart was there in Florence but did mourn
    In pity of her love, so overcast.   500
And a sad ditty on this story born
    From mouth to mouth through all the country passed:
Still is the burthen sung – 'O cruelty,
To steal my basil-pot away from me!'

———

On Visiting the Tomb of Burns

The town, the churchyard, and the setting sun,
    The clouds, the trees, the rounded hills all seem,
        Though beautiful, cold – strange – as in a dream
I dreamèd long ago. Now new begun
The short-lived, paly summer is but won
    From winter's ague, for one hour's gleam;
        Through sapphire-warm, their stars do never beam –
All is cold Beauty; pain is never done
For who has mind to relish, Minos-wise,
    The real of Beauty, free from that dead hue   10
        Fickly imagination and sick pride
    Cast wan upon it! Burns! with honour due

I have oft honoured thee. Great shadow, hide
Thy face! I sin against thy native skies.

(Not published by Keats)

A Song about Myself

1

There was a naughty boy,
　A naughty boy was he,
He would not stop at home,
　He could not quiet be –
　　He took
　　In his knapsack
　　A book
　　Full of vowels
　　And a shirt
10　　With some towels –
　　A slight cap
　　For night-cap –
　　A hair brush,
　　Comb ditto,
　　New stockings,
　　For old ones
　　Would split O!
　　This knapsack
　　Tight at's back
20　　He rivetted close
And followed his nose
　　To the North,
　　To the North,
And followed his nose
　　To the North.

II
There was a naughty boy
  And a naughty boy was he,
For nothing would he do
  But scribble poetry –
    He took   30
    An inkstand
    In his hand
    And a pen
    Big as ten
    In the other
    And away
    In a pother
    He ran
    To the mountains
    And fountains   40
    And ghostès
    And postès
    And witches
    And ditches,
    And wrote
    In his coat
    When the weather
    Was cool –
    Fear of gout –
    And without   50
    When the weather
    Was warm.
    Och, the charm
    When we choose
To follow one's nose
  To the North,
  To the North,
To follow one's nose
  To the North!

III

60   There was a naughty boy
        And a naughty boy was he,
     He kept little fishes
        In washing tubs three
            In spite
            Of the might
            Of the maid,
            Nor afraid
            Of his granny-good,
            He often would
70   Hurly burly
            Get up early
            And go,
            By hook or crook,
            To the brook
            And bring home
            Miller's thumb,
            Tittlebat
            Not over fat,
            Minnows small
80   As the stall
            Of a glove,
            Not above
            The size
            Of a nice
            Little baby's
            Little finger –
            O he made
            ('Twas his trade)
     Of fish a pretty kettle,
90   A kettle –
            A kettle,
     Of fish a pretty kettle,
            A kettle!

IV
There was a naughty boy,
   And a naughty boy was he,
He ran away to Scotland
   The people for to see –
     There he found
     That the ground
     Was as hard,   100
     That a yard
     Was as long,
     That a song
     Was as merry,
     That a cherry
     Was as red,
     That lead
     Was as weighty,
     That fourscore
     Was as eighty,   110
     That a door
     Was as wooden
     As in England –
So he stood in his shoes
   And he wondered,
   He wondered,
He stood in his
   Shoes and he wondered.
     (Not published by Keats)

———

From *Fragment of the 'Castle Builder'*

Sir, Convent Garden is a monstrous beast:
From morning, four o'clock, to twelve at noon,
It swallows cabbages without a spoon,
And then, from twelve till two, this Eden made is
A promenade for cooks and ancient ladies;

And then for supper, 'stead of soup and poaches,
It swallows chairmen, damns, and Hackney coaches.
In short, Sir, 'tis a very place for monks,
For it containeth twenty thousand punks,
Which any man may number for his sport,
By following fat elbows up a court . . .

(Not published by Keats)

===

'And what is love? It is a doll dressed up'

And what is love? It is a doll dressed up
For idleness to cosset, nurse, and dandle;
A thing of soft misnomers, so divine
That silly youth doth think to make itself
Divine by loving, and so goes on
Yawning and doting a whole summer long,
Till Miss's comb is made a pearl tiara,
And common Wellingtons turn Romeo boots;
Till Cleopatra lives at Number Seven,
And Antony resides in Brunswick Square.
Fools! if some passions high have warmed the world,
If queens and soldiers have played deep for hearts,
It is no reason why such agonies
Should be more common than the growth of weeds.
Fools! make me whole again that weighty pearl
The queen of Egypt melted, and I'll say
That ye may love in spite of beaver hats.

(Not published by Keats)

Hyperion. A Fragment

BOOK I

Deep in the shady sadness of a vale
Far sunken from the healthy breath of morn,
Far from the fiery noon, and eve's one star,
Sat grey-haired Saturn, quiet as a stone,
Still as the silence round about his lair;
Forest on forest hung above his head
Like cloud on cloud. No stir of air was there,
Not so much life as on a summer's day
Robs not one light seed from the feathered grass,
But where the dead leaf fell, there did it rest.   10
A stream went voiceless by, still deadened more
By reason of his fallen divinity
Spreading a shade: the Naiad 'mid her reeds
Pressed her cold finger closer to her lips.

  Along the margin-sand large foot-marks went,
No further than to where his feet had strayed,
And slept there since. Upon the sodden ground
His old right hand lay nerveless, listless, dead,
Unsceptred; and his realmless eyes were closed;
While his bowed head seemed listening to the Earth,   20
His ancient mother, for some comfort yet.

  It seemed no force could wake him from his place;
But there came one, who with a kindred hand
Touched his wide shoulders, after bending low
With reverence, though to one who knew it not.
She was a Goddess of the infant world;
By her in stature the tall Amazon
Had stood a pigmy's height: she would have ta'en
Achilles by the hair and bent his neck;
Or with a finger stayed Ixion's wheel.   30

Her face was large as that of Memphian sphinx,
Pedestalled haply in a palace court,
When sages looked to Egypt for their lore.
But O! how unlike marble was that face,
How beautiful, if sorrow had not made
Sorrow more beautiful than Beauty's self.
There was a listening fear in her regard,
As if calamity had but begun;
As if the vanward clouds of evil days
40   Had spent their malice, and the sullen rear
Was with its storèd thunder labouring up.
One hand she pressed upon that aching spot
Where beats the human heart, as if just there,
Though an immortal, she felt cruel pain;
The other upon Saturn's bended neck
She laid, and to the level of his ear
Leaning with parted lips, some words she spake
In solemn tenor and deep organ tone –
Some mourning words, which in our feeble tongue
50   Would come in these like accents (O how frail
To that large utterance of the early Gods!)
'Saturn, look up! – though wherefore, poor old King?
I have no comfort for thee, no, not one:
I cannot say, "O wherefore sleepest thou?"
For heaven is parted from thee, and the earth
Knows thee not, thus afflicted, for a God;
And ocean too, with all its solemn noise,
Has from thy sceptre passed; and all the air
Is emptied of thine hoary majesty.
60   Thy thunder, conscious of the new command,
Rumbles reluctant o'er our fallen house;
And thy sharp lightning in unpractised hands
Scorches and burns our once serene domain.
O aching time! O moments big as years!
All as ye pass swell out the monstrous truth,
And press it so upon our weary griefs

That unbelief has not a space to breathe.
Saturn, sleep on – O thoughtless, why did I
Thus violate thy slumbrous solitude?
Why should I ope thy melancholy eyes?   70
Saturn, sleep on, while at thy feet I weep!'

    As when, upon a trancèd summer-night,
Those green-robed senators of mighty woods,
Tall oaks, branch-charmèd by the earnest stars,
Dream, and so dream all night without a stir,
Save from one gradual solitary gust
Which comes upon the silence, and dies off,
As if the ebbing air had but one wave;
So came these words and went; the while in tears
She touched her fair large forehead to the ground,   80
Just where her falling hair might be outspread
A soft and silken mat for Saturn's feet.
One moon, with alteration slow, had shed
Her silver seasons four upon the night,
And still these two were postured motionless,
Like natural sculpture in cathedral cavern;
The frozen God still couchant on the earth,
And the sad Goddess weeping at his feet:
Until at length old Saturn lifted up
His faded eyes, and saw his kingdom gone,   90
And all the gloom and sorrow of the place,
And that fair kneeling Goddess; and then spake,
As with a palsied tongue, and while his beard
Shook horrid with such aspen-malady:
'O tender spouse of gold Hyperion,
Thea, I feel thee ere I see thy face;
Look up, and let me see our doom in it;
Look up, and tell me if this feeble shape
Is Saturn's; tell me, if thou hear'st the voice
Of Saturn; tell me, if this wrinkling brow,   100
Naked and bare of its great diadem,

Peers like the front of Saturn. Who had power
To make me desolate? whence came the strength?
How was it nurtured to such bursting forth,
While Fate seemed strangled in my nervous grasp?
But it is so; and I am smothered up,
And buried from all godlike exercise
Of influence benign on planets pale,
Of admonitions to the winds and seas,
Of peaceful sway above man's harvesting,
And all those acts which Deity supreme
Doth ease its heart of love in. – I am gone
Away from my own bosom; I have left
My strong identity, my real self,
Somewhere between the throne and where I sit
Here on this spot of earth. Search, Thea, search!
Open thine eyes eterne, and sphere them round
Upon all space – space starred, and lorn of light;
Space regioned with life-air; and barren void;
Spaces of fire, and all the yawn of hell.
Search, Thea, search! and tell me, if thou seest
A certain shape or shadow, making way
With wings or chariot fierce to repossess
A heaven he lost erewhile: it must – it must
Be of ripe progress: Saturn must be King.
Yes, there must be a golden victory;
There must be Gods thrown down, and trumpets blown
Of triumph calm, and hymns of festival
Upon the gold clouds metropolitan,
Voices of soft proclaim, and silver stir
Of strings in hollow shells; and there shall be
Beautiful things made new, for the surprise
Of the sky-children. I will give command:
Thea! Thea! Thea! where is Saturn?'

    This passion lifted him upon his feet,
And made his hands to struggle in the air,

His Druid locks to shake and ooze with sweat,
His eyes to fever out, his voice to cease.
He stood, and heard not Thea's sobbing deep;
A little time, and then again he snatched
Utterance thus: 'But cannot I create?   140
Cannot I form? Cannot I fashion forth
Another world, another universe,
To overbear and crumble this to naught?
Where is another Chaos? Where?' – That word
Found way unto Olympus, and made quake
The rebel three. Thea was startled up,
And in her bearing was a sort of hope,
As thus she quick-voiced spake, yet full of awe.

'This cheers our fallen house: come to our friends,   150
O Saturn! come away, and give them heart.
I know the covert, for thence came I hither.'
Thus brief; then with beseeching eyes she went
With backward footing through the shade a space:
He followed, and she turned to lead the way
Through agèd boughs, that yielded like the mist
Which eagles cleave up-mounting from their nest.

Meanwhile in other realms big tears were shed,
More sorrow like to this, and such like woe,
Too huge for mortal tongue or pen of scribe.   160
The Titans fierce, self-hid, or prison-bound,
Groaned for the old allegiance once more,
And listened in sharp pain for Saturn's voice.
But one of the whole mammoth-brood still kept
His sovereignty, and rule, and majesty –
Blazing Hyperion on his orbèd fire
Still sat, still snuffed the incense, teeming up
From man to the sun's God – yet unsecure:
For as among us mortals omens drear
Fright and perplex, so also shuddered he –   170
Not at dog's howl, or gloom-bird's hated screech,

Or the familiar visiting of one
Upon the first toll of his passing-bell,
Or prophesyings of the midnight lamp;
But horrors, portioned to a giant nerve,
Oft made Hyperion ache. His palace bright
Bastioned with pyramids of glowing gold,
And touched with shade of bronzèd obelisks,
Glared a blood-red through all its thousand courts,
180   Arches, and domes, and fiery galleries;
And all its curtains of Aurorian clouds
Flushed angerly, while sometimes eagle's wings,
Unseen before by Gods or wondering men,
Darkened the place, and neighing steeds were heard,
Not heard before by Gods or wondering men.
Also, when he would taste the spicy wreaths
Of incense, breathed aloft from sacred hills,
Instead of sweets, his ample palate took
Savour of poisonous brass and metal sick:
190   And so, when harboured in the sleepy west,
After the full completion of fair day,
For rest divine upon exalted couch
And slumber in the arms of melody,
He paced away the pleasant hours of ease
With stride colossal, on from hall to hall;
While far within each aisle and deep recess,
His wingèd minions in close clusters stood,
Amazed and full of fear; like anxious men
Who on wide plains gather in panting troops,
200   When earthquakes jar their battlements and towers.
Even now, while Saturn, roused from icy trance,
Went step for step with Thea through the woods,
Hyperion, leaving twilight in the rear,
Came slope upon the threshold of the west;
Then, as was wont, his palace-door flew ope
In smoothest silence, save what solemn tubes,
Blown by the serious Zephyrs, gave of sweet

And wandering sounds, slow-breathèd melodies –
And like a rose in vermeil tint and shape,
In fragrance soft, and coolness to the eye,   210
That inlet to severe magnificence
Stood full blown, for the God to enter in.

  He entered, but he entered full of wrath;
His flaming robes streamed out beyond his heels,
And gave a roar, as if of earthly fire,
That scared away the meek ethereal Hours
And made their dove-wings tremble. On he flared,
From stately nave to nave, from vault to vault,
Through bowers of fragrant and enwreathèd light,
And diamond-pavèd lustrous long arcades,   220
Until he reached the great main cupola.
There standing fierce beneath, he stamped his foot,
And from the basement deep to the high towers
Jarred his own golden region; and before
The quavering thunder thereupon had ceased,
His voice leapt out, despite of god-like curb,
To this result: 'O dreams of day and night!
O monstrous forms! O effigies of pain!
O spectres busy in a cold, cold gloom!
O lank-eared Phantoms of black-weeded pools!   230
Why do I know ye? Why have I seen ye? Why
Is my eternal essence thus distraught
To see and to behold these horrors new?
Saturn is fallen, am I too to fall?
Am I to leave this haven of my rest,
This cradle of my glory, this soft clime,
This calm luxuriance of blissful light,
These crystalline pavilions, and pure fanes,
Of all my lucent empire? It is left
Deserted, void, nor any haunt of mine.   240
The blaze, the splendour, and the symmetry,
I cannot see – but darkness, death and darkness.

Even here, into my centre of repose,
The shady visions come to domineer,
Insult, and blind, and stifle up my pomp. –
Fall! – No, by Tellus and her briny robes!
Over the fiery frontier of my realms
I will advance a terrible right arm
Shall scare that infant thunderer, rebel Jove,
250   And bid old Saturn take his throne again.' –
He spake, and ceased, the while a heavier threat
Held struggle with his throat but came not forth;
For as in theatres of crowded men
Hubbub increases more they call out 'Hush!',
So at Hyperion's words the Phantoms pale
Bestirred themselves, thrice horrible and cold;
And from the mirrored level where he stood
A mist arose, as from a scummy marsh.
At this, through all his bulk an agony
260   Crept gradual, from the feet unto the crown,
Like a lithe serpent vast and muscular
Making slow way, with head and neck convulsed
From over-strainèd might. Released, he fled
To the eastern gates, and full six dewy hours
Before the dawn in season due should blush,
He breathed fierce breath against the sleepy portals,
Cleared them of heavy vapours, burst them wide
Suddenly on the ocean's chilly streams.
The planet orb of fire, whereon he rode
270   Each day from east to west the heavens through,
Spun round in sable curtaining of clouds;
Not therefore veilèd quite, blindfold, and hid,
But ever and anon the glancing spheres,
Circles, and arcs, and broad-belting colure,
Glowed through, and wrought upon the muffling dark
Sweet-shapèd lightnings from the nadir deep
Up to the zenith – hieroglyphics old
Which sages and keen-eyed astrologers

Then living on the earth, with labouring thought
Won from the gaze of many centuries –   280
Now lost, save what we find on remnants huge
Of stone, or marble swart, their import gone,
Their wisdom long since fled. Two wings this orb
Possessed for glory, two fair argent wings,
Ever exalted at the God's approach:
And now, from forth the gloom their plumes immense
Rose, one by one, till all outspreaded were;
While still the dazzling globe maintained eclipse,
Awaiting for Hyperion's command.
Fain would he have commanded, fain took throne   290
And bid the day begin, if but for change.
He might not. – No, though a primeval God:
The sacred seasons might not be disturbed.
Therefore the operations of the dawn
Stayed in their birth, even as here 'tis told.
Those silver wings expanded sisterly,
Eager to sail their orb; the porches wide
Opened upon the dusk demesnes of night;
And the bright Titan, frenzied with new woes,
Unused to bend, by hard compulsion bent   300
His spirit to the sorrow of the time;
And all along a dismal rack of clouds,
Upon the boundaries of day and night,
He stretched himself in grief and radiance faint.
There as he lay, the Heaven with its stars
Looked down on him with pity, and the voice
Of Coelus, from the universal space,
Thus whispered low and solemn in his ear:
'O brightest of my children dear, earth-born
And sky-engendered, Son of Mysteries   310
All unrevealèd even to the powers
Which met at thy creating; at whose joys
And palpitations sweet, and pleasures soft,
I, Coelus, wonder how they came and whence;

And at the fruits thereof what shapes they be,
Distinct, and visible – symbols divine,
Manifestations of that beauteous life
Diffused unseen throughout eternal space:
Of these new-formed art thou, O brightest child!
320   Of these, thy brethren and the Goddesses!
There is sad feud among ye, and rebellion
Of son against his sire. I saw him fall,
I saw my first-born tumbled from his throne!
To me his arms were spread, to me his voice
Found way from forth the thunders round his head!
Pale wox I, and in vapours hid my face.
Art thou, too, near such doom? Vague fear there is:
For I have seen my sons most unlike Gods.
Divine ye were created, and divine
330   In sad demeanour, solemn, undisturbed,
Unrufflèd, like high Gods, ye lived and ruled:
Now I behold in you fear, hope, and wrath;
Actions of rage and passion – even as
I see them, on the mortal world beneath,
In men who die. This is the grief, O Son!
Sad sign of ruin, sudden dismay, and fall!
Yet do thou strive; as thou art capable,
As thou canst move about, an evident God;
And canst oppose to each malignant hour
340   Ethereal presence. I am but a voice;
My life is but the life of winds and tides,
No more than winds and tides can I avail. –
But thou canst. – Be thou therefore in the van
Of circumstance; yea, seize the arrow's barb
Before the tense string murmur. – To the earth!
For there thou wilt find Saturn, and his woes.
Meantime I will keep watch on thy bright sun,
And of thy seasons be a careful nurse.' –
Ere half this region-whisper had come down,
350   Hyperion arose, and on the stars

Lifted his curvèd lids, and kept them wide
Until it ceased; and still he kept them wide;
And still they were the same bright, patient stars.
Then with a slow incline of his broad breast,
Like to a diver in the pearly seas,
Forward he stooped over the airy shore,
And plunged all noiseless into the deep night.

BOOK II
Just at the self-same beat of Time's wide wings,
Hyperion slid into the rustled air
And Saturn gained with Thea that sad place
Where Cybele and the bruised Titans mourned.
It was a den where no insulting light
Could glimmer on their tears; where their own groans
They felt, but heard not, for the solid roar
Of thunderous waterfalls and torrents hoarse,
Pouring a constant bulk, uncertain where.
Crag jutting forth to crag, and rocks that seemed   10
Ever as if just rising from a sleep,
Forehead to forehead held their monstrous horns;
And thus in thousand hugest fantasies
Made a fit roofing to this nest of woe.
Instead of thrones, hard flint they sat upon,
Couches of rugged stone, and slaty ridge
Stubborned with iron. All were not assembled:
Some chained in torture, and some wandering.
Coeus, and Gyges, and Briareüs,
Typhon, and Dolor, and Porphyrion,   20
With many more, the brawniest in assault,
Were pent in regions of laborious breath;
Dungeoned in opaque element, to keep
Their clenchèd teeth still clenched, and all their limbs
Locked up like veins of metal, cramped and screwed;
Without a motion, save of their big hearts
Heaving in pain, and horribly convulsed

With sanguine fev'rous boiling gurge of pulse.
Mnemosyne was straying in the world;
Far from her moon had Phoebe wanderèd;
And many else were free to roam abroad,
But for the main, here found they covert drear.
Scarce images of life, one here, one there,
Lay vast and edgeways; like a dismal cirque
Of Druid stones, upon a forlorn moor,
When the chill rain begins at shut of eve,
In dull November, and their chancel vault,
The Heaven itself, is blinded throughout night.
Each one kept shroud, nor to his neighbour gave
Or word, or look, or action of despair.
Creüs was one; his ponderous iron mace
Lay by him, and a shattered rib of rock
Told of his rage, ere he thus sank and pined.
Iäpetus another; in his grasp,
A serpent's plashy neck; its barbèd tongue
Squeezed from the gorge, and all its uncurled length
Dead – and because the creature could not spit
Its poison in the eyes of conquering Jove.
Next Cottus; prone he lay, chin uppermost,
As though in pain, for still upon the flint
He ground severe his skull, with open mouth
And eyes at horrid working. Nearest him
Asia, born of most enormous Caf,
Who cost her mother Tellus keener pangs,
Though feminine, than any of her sons:
More thought than woe was in her dusky face,
For she was prophesying of her glory;
And in her wide imagination stood
Palm-shaded temples, and high rival fanes,
By Oxus or in Ganges' sacred isles.
Even as Hope upon her anchor leans,
So leant she, not so fair, upon a tusk
Shed from the broadest of her elephants.

Above her, on a crag's uneasy shelve,
Upon his elbow raised, all prostrate else,
Shadowed Enceladus – once tame and mild
As grazing ox unworried in the meads;
Now tiger-passioned, lion-thoughted, wroth,
He meditated, plotted, and even now
Was hurling mountains in that second war,   70
Not long delayed, that scared the younger Gods
To hide themselves in forms of beast and bird.
Not far hence Atlas; and beside him prone
Phorcus, the sire of Gorgons. Neighboured close
Oceanus, and Tethys, in whose lap
Sobbed Clymene among her tangled hair.
In midst of all lay Themis, at the feet
Of Ops the queen all clouded round from sight;
No shape distinguishable, more than when
Thick night confounds the pine-tops with the clouds –   80
And many else whose names may not be told.
For when the Muse's wings are air-ward spread,
Who shall delay her flight? And she must chant
Of Saturn, and his guide, who now had climbed
With damp and slippery footing from a depth
More horrid still. Above a sombre cliff
Their heads appeared, and up their stature grew
Till on the level height their steps found ease:
Then Thea spread abroad her trembling arms
Upon the precincts of this nest of pain,   90
And sidelong fixed her eye on Saturn's face.
There saw she direst strife – the supreme God
At war with all the frailty of grief,
Of rage, of fear, anxiety, revenge,
Remorse, spleen, hope, but most of all despair.
Against these plagues he strove in vain; for Fate
Had poured a mortal oil upon his head,
A disanointing poison, so that Thea,

Affrighted, kept her still, and let him pass
100   First onwards in, among the fallen tribe.

      As with us mortal men, the laden heart
Is persecuted more, and fevered more,
When it is nighing to the mournful house
Where other hearts are sick of the same bruise;
So Saturn, as he walked into the midst,
Felt faint, and would have sunk among the rest,
But that he met Enceladus's eye,
Whose mightiness, and awe of him, at once
Came like an inspiration; and he shouted,
110   'Titans, behold your God!' At which some groaned;
Some started on their feet; some also shouted;
Some wept, some wailed, all bowed with reverence;
And Ops, uplifting her black folded veil,
Showed her pale cheeks, and all her forehead wan,
Her eye-brows thin and jet, and hollow eyes.
There is a roaring in the bleak-grown pines
When Winter lifts his voice; there is a noise
Among immortals when a God gives sign,
With hushing finger, how he means to load
120   His tongue with the full weight of utterless thought,
With thunder, and with music, and with pomp:
Such noise is like the roar of bleak-grown pines,
Which, when it ceases in this mountained world,
No other sound succeeds; but ceasing here,
Among these fallen, Saturn's voice therefrom
Grew up like organ, that begins anew
Its strain, when other harmonies, stopped short,
Leave the dinned air vibrating silverly.
Thus grew it up: 'Not in my own sad breast,
130   Which is its own great judge and searcher-out,
Can I find reason why ye should be thus:
Not in the legends of the first of days,
Studied from that old spirit-leavèd book

Which starry Uranus with finger bright
Saved from the shores of darkness, when the waves
Low-ebbed still hid it up in shallow gloom –
And the which book ye know I ever kept
For my firm-basèd footstool – Ah, infirm!
Not there, nor in sign, symbol, or portent
Of element, earth, water, air, and fire –   140
At war, at peace, or inter-quarrelling
One against one, or two, or three, or all
Each several one against the other three,
As fire with air loud warring when rain-floods
Drown both, and press them both against earth's face,
Where, finding sulphur, a quadruple wrath
Unhinges the poor world – not in that strife,
Wherefrom I take strange lore, and read it deep,
Can I find reason why ye should be thus –
No, nowhere can unriddle, though I search,   150
And pore on Nature's universal scroll
Even to swooning, why ye, Divinities,
The first-born of all shaped and palpable Gods,
Should cower beneath what, in comparison,
Is untremendous might. Yet ye are here,
O'erwhelmed, and spurned, and battered, ye are here!
O Titans, shall I say, "Arise!"? – Ye groan:
Shall I say "Crouch!"? – Ye groan. What can I then?
O Heaven wide! O unseen parent dear!
What can I? Tell me, all ye brethren Gods,   160
How we can war, how engine our great wrath!
O speak your counsel now, for Saturn's ear
Is all a-hungered. Thou, Oceanus,
Ponderest high and deep, and in thy face
I see, astonied, that severe content
Which comes of thought and musing. Give us help!'

So ended Saturn; and the God of the Sea,
Sophist and sage from no Athenian grove,

But cogitation in his watery shades,
170 Arose, with locks not oozy, and began,
In murmurs which his first-endeavouring tongue
Caught infant-like from the far-foamèd sands.
'O ye, whom wrath consumes! who, passion-stung,
Writhe at defeat, and nurse your agonies!
Shut up your senses, stifle up your ears,
My voice is not a bellows unto ire.
Yet listen, ye who will, whilst I bring proof
How ye, perforce, must be content to stoop;
And in the proof much comfort will I give,
180 If ye will take that comfort in its truth.
We fall by course of Nature's law, not force
Of thunder, or of Jove. Great Saturn, thou
Hast sifted well the atom-universe;
But for this reason, that thou art the King,
And only blind from sheer supremacy,
One avenue was shaded from thine eyes,
Through which I wandered to eternal truth.
And first, as thou wast not the first of powers,
So art thou not the last; it cannot be:
190 Thou art not the beginning nor the end.
From Chaos and parental Darkness came
Light, the first fruits of that intestine broil,
That sullen ferment, which for wondrous ends
Was ripening in itself. The ripe hour came,
And with it Light, and Light, engendering
Upon its own producer, forthwith touched
The whole enormous matter into life.
Upon that very hour, our parentage,
The Heavens, and the Earth, were manifest:
200 Then thou first born, and we the giant race,
Found ourselves ruling new and beauteous realms.
Now comes the pain of truth, to whom 'tis pain –
O folly! for to bear all naked truths,
And to envisage circumstance, all calm,

That is the top of sovereignty. Mark well!
As Heaven and Earth are fairer, fairer far
Than Chaos and blank Darkness, though once chiefs;
And as we show beyond that Heaven and Earth
In form and shape compact and beautiful,
In will, in action free, companionship,   210
And thousand other signs of purer life;
So on our heels a fresh perfection treads,
A power more strong in beauty, born of us
And fated to excel us, as we pass
In glory that old Darkness: nor are we
Thereby more conquered, than by us the rule
Of shapeless Chaos. Say, doth the dull soil
Quarrel with the proud forests it hath fed,
And feedeth still, more comely than itself?
Can it deny the chiefdom of green groves?   220
Or shall the tree be envious of the dove
Because it cooeth, and hath snowy wings
To wander wherewithal and find its joys?
We are such forest-trees, and our fair boughs
Have bred forth, not pale solitary doves,
But eagles golden-feathered, who do tower
Above us in their beauty, and must reign
In right thereof. For 'tis the eternal law
That first in beauty should be first in might.
Yea, by that law, another race may drive   230
Our conquerors to mourn as we do now.
Have ye beheld the young God of the Seas,
My dispossessor? Have ye seen his face?
Have ye beheld his chariot, foamed along
By noble wingèd creatures he hath made?
I saw him on the calmèd waters scud,
With such a glow of beauty in his eyes,
That it enforced me to bid sad farewell
To all my empire: farewell sad I took,
And hither came, to see how dolorous fate   240

Had wrought upon ye; and how I might best
Give consolation in this woe extreme.
Receive the truth, and let it be your balm.'

Whether through posed conviction, or disdain,
They guarded silence, when Oceanus
Left murmuring, what deepest thought can tell?
But so it was; none answered for a space,
Save one whom none regarded, Clymene;
And yet she answered not, only complained,
250   With hectic lips, and eyes up-looking mild,
Thus wording timidly among the fierce:
'O Father, I am here the simplest voice,
And all my knowledge is that joy is gone,
And this thing woe crept in among our hearts,
There to remain for ever, as I fear.
I would not bode of evil, if I thought
So weak a creature could turn off the help
Which by just right should come of mighty Gods;
Yet let me tell my sorrow, let me tell
260   Of what I heard, and how it made me weep,
And know that we had parted from all hope.
I stood upon a shore, a pleasant shore,
Where a sweet clime was breathèd from a land
Of fragrance, quietness, and trees, and flowers.
Full of calm joy it was, as I of grief;
Too full of joy and soft delicious warmth;
So that I felt a movement in my heart
To chide, and to reproach that solitude
With songs of misery, music of our woes;
270   And sat me down, and took a mouthèd shell
And murmured into it, and made melody –
O melody no more! for while I sang,
And with poor skill let pass into the breeze
The dull shell's echo, from a bowery strand
Just opposite, an island of the sea,

There came enchantment with the shifting wind,
That did both drown and keep alive my ears.
I threw my shell away upon the sand,
And a wave filled it, as my sense was filled
With that new blissful golden melody. 280
A living death was in each gush of sounds,
Each family of rapturous hurried notes,
That fell, one after one, yet all at once,
Like pearl beads dropping sudden from their string;
And then another, then another strain,
Each like a dove leaving its olive perch,
With music winged instead of silent plumes,
To hover round my head, and make me sick
Of joy and grief at once. Grief overcame,
And I was stopping up my frantic ears, 290
When, past all hindrance of my trembling hands,
A voice came sweeter, sweeter than all tune,
And still it cried, "Apollo! young Apollo!
The morning-bright Apollo! young Apollo!"
I fled, it followed me, and cried "Apollo!"
O Father, and O Brethren, had ye felt
Those pains of mine – O Saturn, hadst thou felt,
Ye would not call this too indulgèd tongue
Presumptuous, in thus venturing to be heard.'

So far her voice flowed on, like timorous brook 300
That, lingering along a pebbled coast,
Doth fear to meet the sea: but sea it met,
And shuddered; for the overwhelming voice
Of huge Enceladus swallowed it in wrath:
The ponderous syllables, like sullen waves
In the half-glutted hollows of reef-rocks,
Came booming thus, while still upon his arm
He leaned – not rising, from supreme contempt:
'Or shall we listen to the over-wise,
Or to the over-foolish, Giant-Gods? 310

Not thunderbolt on thunderbolt, till all
That rebel Jove's whole armoury were spent,
Not world on world upon these shoulders piled
Could agonize me more than baby-words
In midst of this dethronement horrible.
Speak! Roar! Shout! Yell! ye sleepy Titans all.
Do ye forget the blows, the buffets vile?
Are ye not smitten by a youngling arm?
Dost thou forget, sham Monarch of the Waves,
320   Thy scalding in the seas? What, have I roused
Your spleens with so few simple words as these?
O joy! for now I see ye are not lost:
O joy! for now I see a thousand eyes
Wide-glaring for revenge!' – As this he said,
He lifted up his stature vast, and stood,
Still without intermission speaking thus:
'Now ye are flames, I'll tell you how to burn,
And purge the ether of our enemies;
How to feed fierce the crooked stings of fire,
330   And singe away the swollen clouds of Jove,
Stifling that puny essence in its tent.
O let him feel the evil he hath done;
For though I scorn Oceanus's lore,
Much pain have I for more than loss of realms:
The days of peace and slumbrous calm are fled;
Those days, all innocent of scathing war,
When all the fair Existences of heaven
Came open-eyed to guess what we would speak –
That was before our brows were taught to frown,
340   Before our lips knew else but solemn sounds;
That was before we knew the wingèd thing,
Victory, might be lost, or might be won.
And be ye mindful that Hyperion,
Our brightest brother, still is undisgraced –
Hyperion, lo! his radiance is here!'

All eyes were on Enceladus's face,
And they beheld, while still Hyperion's name
Flew from his lips up to the vaulted rocks,
A pallid gleam across his features stern –
Not savage, for he saw full many a God   350
Wroth as himself. He looked upon them all,
And in each face he saw a gleam of light,
But splendider in Saturn's, whose hoar locks
Shone like the bubbling foam about a keel
When the prow sweeps into a midnight cove.
In pale and silver silence they remained,
Till suddenly a splendour, like the morn,
Pervaded all the beetling gloomy steeps,
All the sad spaces of oblivion,
And every gulf, and every chasm old,   360
And every height, and every sullen depth,
Voiceless, or hoarse with loud tormented streams;
And all the everlasting cataracts,
And all the headlong torrents far and near,
Mantled before in darkness and huge shade,
Now saw the light and made it terrible.
It was Hyperion: a granite peak
His bright feet touched, and there he stayed to view
The misery his brilliance had betrayed
To the most hateful seeing of itself.   370
Golden his hair of short Numidian curl,
Regal his shape majestic, a vast shade
In midst of his own brightness, like the bulk
Of Memnon's image at the set of sun
To one who travels from the dusking East:
Sighs, too, as mournful as that Memnon's harp,
He uttered, while his hands contemplative
He pressed together, and in silence stood.
Despondence seized again the fallen Gods
At sight of the dejected King of Day,   380
And many hid their faces from the light:

But fierce Enceladus sent forth his eyes
Among the brotherhood; and, at their glare,
Uprose Iäpetus, and Creüs too,
And Phorcus, sea-born, and together strode
To where he towered on his eminence.
There those four shouted forth old Saturn's name;
Hyperion from the peak loud answered, 'Saturn!'
Saturn sat near the Mother of the Gods,
390   In whose face was no joy, though all the Gods
Gave from their hollow throats the name of 'Saturn!'

BOOK III

Thus in alternate uproar and sad peace,
Amazèd were those Titans utterly.
O leave them, Muse! O leave them to their woes;
For thou art weak to sing such tumults dire:
A solitary sorrow best befits
Thy lips, and antheming a lonely grief.
Leave them, O Muse! for thou anon wilt find
Many a fallen old Divinity
Wandering in vain about bewildered shores.
10   Meantime touch piously the Delphic harp,
And not a wind of heaven but will breathe
In aid soft warble from the Dorian flute;
For lo! 'tis for the Father of all verse.
Flush every thing that hath a vermeil hue,
Let the rose glow intense and warm the air,
And let the clouds of even and of morn
Float in voluptuous fleeces o'er the hills;
Let the red wine within the goblet boil,
Cold as a bubbling well; let faint-lipped shells,
20   On sands, or in great deeps, vermilion turn
Through all their labyrinths; and let the maid
Blush keenly, as with some warm kiss surprised.
Chief isle of the embowered Cyclades,
Rejoice, O Delos, with thine olives green,

And poplars, and lawn-shading palms, and beech,
In which the Zephyr breathes the loudest song,
And hazels thick, dark-stemmed beneath the shade:
Apollo is once more the golden theme!
Where was he, when the Giant of the Sun
Stood bright, amid the sorrow of his peers?   30
Together had he left his mother fair
And his twin-sister sleeping in their bower,
And in the morning twilight wandered forth
Beside the osiers of a rivulet,
Full ankle-deep in lilies of the vale.
The nightingale had ceased, and a few stars
Were lingering in the heavens, while the thrush
Began calm-throated. Throughout all the isle
There was no covert, no retirèd cave
Unhaunted by the murmurous noise of waves,   40
Though scarcely heard in many a green recess.
He listened, and he wept, and his bright tears
Went trickling down the golden bow he held.
Thus with half-shut suffusèd eyes he stood,
While from beneath some cumbrous boughs hard by
With solemn step an awful Goddess came,
And there was purport in her looks for him,
Which he with eager guess began to read
Perplexed, the while melodiously he said:
'How cam'st thou over the unfooted sea?   50
Or hath that antique mien and robèd form
Moved in these vales invisible till now?
Sure I have heard those vestments sweeping o'er
The fallen leaves, when I have sat alone
In cool mid-forest. Surely I have traced
The rustle of those ample skirts about
These grassy solitudes, and seen the flowers
Lift up their heads, as still the whisper passed.
Goddess! I have beheld those eyes before,
And their eternal calm, and all that face,   60

Or I have dreamed.' – 'Yes,' said the supreme shape,
Thou hast dreamed of me; and awaking up
Didst find a lyre all golden by thy side,
Whose strings touched by thy fingers, all the vast
Unwearied ear of the whole universe
Listened in pain and pleasure at the birth
Of such new tuneful wonder. Is't not strange
That thou shouldst weep, so gifted? Tell me, youth,
What sorrow thou canst feel; for I am sad
70   When thou dost shed a tear. Explain thy griefs
To one who in this lonely isle hath been
The watcher of thy sleep and hours of life,
From the young day when first thy infant hand
Plucked witless the weak flowers, till thine arm
Could bend that bow heroic to all times.
Show thy heart's secret to an ancient Power
Who hath forsaken old and sacred thrones
For prophecies of thee, and for the sake
Of loveliness new born.' – Apollo then,
80   With sudden scrutiny and gloomless eyes,
Thus answered, while his white melodious throat
Throbbed with the syllables: 'Mnemosyne!
Thy name is on my tongue, I know not how;
Why should I tell thee what thou so well seest?
Why should I strive to show what from thy lips
Would come no mystery? For me, dark, dark,
And painful vile oblivion seals my eyes:
I strive to search wherefore I am so sad,
Until a melancholy numbs my limbs;
90   And then upon the grass I sit, and moan,
Like one who once had wings. O why should I
Feel cursed and thwarted, when the liegeless air
Yields to my step aspirant? Why should I
Spurn the green turf as hateful to my feet?
Goddess benign, point forth some unknown thing:
Are there not other regions than this isle?

What are the stars? There is the sun, the sun!
And the most patient brilliance of the moon!
And stars by thousands! Point me out the way
To any one particular beauteous star,   100
And I will flit into it with my lyre,
And make its silvery splendour pant with bliss.
I have heard the cloudy thunder: Where is power?
Whose hand, whose essence, what Divinity
Makes this alarum in the elements,
While I here idle listen on the shores
In fearless yet in aching ignorance?
O tell me, lonely Goddess, by thy harp,
That waileth every morn and eventide,
Tell me why thus I rave, about these groves!   110
Mute thou remainest – mute! yet I can read
A wondrous lesson in thy silent face:
Knowledge enormous makes a God of me.
Names, deeds, grey legends, dire events, rebellions,
Majesties, sovran voices, agonies,
Creations and destroyings, all at once
Pour into the wide hollows of my brain,
And deify me, as if some blithe wine
Or bright elixir peerless I had drunk,
And so become immortal.' – Thus the God,   120
While his enkindlèd eyes, with level glance
Beneath his white soft temples, steadfast kept
Trembling with light upon Mnemosyne.
Soon wild commotions shook him, and made flush
All the immortal fairness of his limbs –
Most like the struggle at the gate of death;
Or liker still to one who should take leave
Of pale immortal death, and with a pang
As hot as death's is chill, with fierce convulse
Die into life: so young Apollo anguished.   130
His very hair, his golden tresses famed
Kept undulation round his eager neck.

During the pain Mnemosyne upheld
Her arms as one who prophesied. – At length
Apollo shrieked – and lo! from all his limbs
Celestial . . .

———

The Eve of St Agnes

I

St Agnes' Eve – Ah, bitter chill it was!
The owl, for all his feathers, was a-cold;
The hare limped trembling through the frozen grass,
And silent was the flock in woolly fold:
Numb were the Beadsman's fingers, while he told
His rosary, and while his frosted breath,
Like pious incense from a censer old,
　Seemed taking flight for heaven, without a death,
Past the sweet Virgin's picture, while his prayer he saith.

II

His prayer he saith, this patient, holy man;
Then takes his lamp, and riseth from his knees,
And back returneth, meagre, barefoot, wan,
Along the chapel aisle by slow degrees:
The sculptured dead, on each side, seem to freeze,
Emprisoned in black, purgatorial rails;
Knights, ladies, praying in dumb orat'ries,
　He passeth by; and his weak spirit fails
To think how they may ache in icy hoods and mails.

III

Northward he turneth through a little door,
And scarce three steps, ere Music's golden tongue
Flattered to tears this agèd man and poor;
But no – already had his deathbell rung:
The joys of all his life were said and sung:
His was harsh penance on St Agnes' Eve.

Another way he went, and soon among
    Rough ashes sat he for his soul's reprieve,
And all night kept awake, for sinners' sake to grieve.

IV

    That ancient Beadsman heard the prelude soft;
    And so it chanced, for many a door was wide,
    From hurry to and fro. Soon, up aloft,
    The silver, snarling trumpets 'gan to chide:
    The level chambers, ready with their pride,
    Were glowing to receive a thousand guests:
    The carvèd angels, ever eager-eyed,
    Stared, where upon their heads the cornice rests,
With hair blown back, and wings put cross-wise on their breasts.

V

    At length burst in the argent revelry,
    With plume, tiara, and all rich array,
    Numerous as shadows haunting faerily
    The brain, new-stuffed, in youth, with triumphs gay
    Of old romance. These let us wish away,
    And turn, sole-thoughted, to one Lady there,
    Whose heart had brooded, all that wintry day,
    On love, and winged St Agnes' saintly care,
As she had heard old dames full many times declare.

VI

    They told her how, upon St Agnes' Eve,
    Young virgins might have visions of delight,
    And soft adorings from their loves receive
    Upon the honeyed middle of the night,
    If ceremonies due they did aright;
    As, supperless to bed they must retire,
    And couch supine their beauties, lily white;
    Nor look behind, nor sideways, but require
Of Heaven with upward eyes for all that they desire.

VII

Full of this whim was thoughtful Madeline:
The music, yearning like a God in pain,
She scarcely heard: her maiden eyes divine,
Fixed on the floor, saw many a sweeping train
Pass by – she heeded not at all: in vain
Came many a tip-toe, amorous cavalier,
And back retired – not cooled by high disdain,
But she saw not: her heart was otherwhere.
She sighed for Agnes' dreams, the sweetest of the year.

VIII

She danced along with vague, regardless eyes,
Anxious her lips, her breathing quick and short:
The hallowed hour was near at hand: she sighs
Amid the timbrels, and the thronged resort
Of whisperers in anger, or in sport;
'Mid looks of love, defiance, hate, and scorn,
Hoodwinked with faery fancy – all amort,
Save to St Agnes and her lambs unshorn,
And all the bliss to be before to-morrow morn.

IX

So, purposing each moment to retire,
She lingered still. Meantime, across the moors,
Had come young Porphyro, with heart on fire
For Madeline. Beside the portal doors,
Buttressed from moonlight, stands he, and implores
All saints to give him sight of Madeline
But for one moment in the tedious hours,
That he might gaze and worship all unseen;
Perchance speak, kneel, touch, kiss – in sooth such things
    have been.

X

He ventures in – let no buzzed whisper tell,
All eyes be muffled, or a hundred swords

Will storm his heart, Love's fev'rous citadel:
For him, those chambers held barbarian hordes,
Hyena foemen, and hot-blooded lords,
Whose very dogs would execrations howl
Against his lineage: not one breast affords
Him any mercy, in that mansion foul,
Save one old beldame, weak in body and in soul.   90

XI

Ah, happy chance! the agèd creature came,
Shuffling along with ivory-headed wand,
To where he stood, hid from the torch's flame,
Behind a broad hall-pillar, far beyond
The sound of merriment and chorus bland:
He startled her; but soon she knew his face,
And grasped his fingers in her palsied hand,
Saying, 'Mercy, Porphyro! hie thee from this place:
They are all here to-night, the whole blood-thirsty race!

XII

'Get hence! get hence! there's dwarfish Hildebrand –   100
He had a fever late, and in the fit
He cursèd thee and thine, both house and land:
Then there's that old Lord Maurice, not a whit
More tame for his grey hairs – Alas me! flit!
Flit like a ghost away.' 'Ah, gossip dear,
We're safe enough; here in this arm-chair sit,
And tell me how –' 'Good Saints! not here, not here;
Follow me, child, or else these stones will be thy bier.'

XIII

He followed through a lowly archèd way,
Brushing the cobwebs with his lofty plume,   110
And as she muttered, 'Well-a – well-a-day!'
He found him in a little moonlight room,
Pale, latticed, chill, and silent as a tomb.
'Now tell me where is Madeline,' said he,

'O tell me, Angela, by the holy loom
Which none but secret sisterhood may see,
When they St Agnes' wool are weaving piously.'

XIV

'St Agnes? Ah! it is St Agnes' Eve –
Yet men will murder upon holy days:
Thou must hold water in a witch's sieve,
And be liege-lord of all the Elves and Fays,
To venture so: it fills me with amaze
To see thee, Porphyro! – St Agnes' Eve!
God's help! my lady fair the conjuror plays
This very night. Good angels her deceive!
But let me laugh awhile, I've mickle time to grieve.'

XV

Feebly she laugheth in the languid moon,
While Porphyro upon her face doth look,
Like puzzled urchin on an agèd crone
Who keepeth closed a wondrous riddle-book,
As spectacled she sits in chimney nook.
But soon his eyes grew brilliant, when she told
His lady's purpose; and he scarce could brook
Tears, at the thought of those enchantments cold,
And Madeline asleep in lap of legends old.

XVI

Sudden a thought came like a full-blown rose,
Flushing his brow, and in his painèd heart
Made purple riot; then doth he propose
A stratagem, that makes the beldame start:
'A cruel man and impious thou art:
Sweet lady, let her pray, and sleep, and dream
Alone with her good angels, far apart
From wicked men like thee. Go, go! – I deem
Thou canst not surely be the same that thou didst seem.'

XVII

   'I will not harm her, by all saints I swear,'
   Quoth Porphyro: 'O may I ne'er find grace
   When my weak voice shall whisper its last prayer,
   If one of her soft ringlets I displace,
   Or look with ruffian passion in her face:
   Good Angela, believe me by these tears,   150
   Or I will, even in a moment's space,
   Awake, with horrid shout, my foeman's ears,
And beard them, though they be more fanged than wolves
     and bears.'

XVIII

   'Ah! why wilt thou affright a feeble soul?
   A poor, weak, palsy-stricken, churchyard thing,
   Whose passing-bell may ere the midnight toll;
   Whose prayers for thee, each morn and evening,
   Were never missed.' – Thus plaining, doth she bring
   A gentler speech from burning Porphyro,
   So woeful, and of such deep sorrowing,   160
   That Angela gives promise she will do
Whatever he shall wish, betide her weal or woe.

XIX

   Which was, to lead him, in close secrecy,
   Even to Madeline's chamber, and there hide
   Him in a closet, of such privacy
   That he might see her beauty unespied,
   And win perhaps that night a peerless bride,
   While legioned faeries paced the coverlet,
   And pale enchantment held her sleepy-eyed.
   Never on such a night have lovers met,   170
Since Merlin paid his Demon all the monstrous debt.

XX

   'It shall be as thou wishest,' said the Dame:
   'All cates and dainties shall be storèd there

Quickly on this feast-night; by the tambour frame
Her own lute thou wilt see. No time to spare,
For I am slow and feeble, and scarce dare
On such a catering trust my dizzy head.
Wait here, my child, with patience; kneel in prayer
The while. Ah! thou must needs the lady wed,
180   Or may I never leave my grave among the dead.'

XXI

So saying, she hobbled off with busy fear.
The lover's endless minutes slowly passed;
The dame returned, and whispered in his ear
To follow her; with agèd eyes aghast
From fright of dim espial. Safe at last,
Through many a dusky gallery, they gain
The maiden's chamber, silken, hushed, and chaste;
Where Porphyro took covert, pleased amain.
His poor guide hurried back with agues in her brain.

XXII

190   Her faltering hand upon the balustrade,
Old Angela was feeling for the stair,
When Madeline, St Agnes' charmèd maid,
Rose, like a missioned spirit, unaware:
With silver taper's light, and pious care,
She turned, and down the agèd gossip led
To a safe level matting. Now prepare,
Young Porphyro, for gazing on that bed –
She comes, she comes again, like ring-dove frayed and fled.

XXIII

Out went the taper as she hurried in;
200   Its little smoke, in pallid moonshine, died:
She closed the door, she panted, all akin
To spirits of the air, and visions wide –
No uttered syllable, or, woe betide!

But to her heart, her heart was voluble,
Paining with eloquence her balmy side;
As though a tongueless nightingale should swell
Her throat in vain, and die, heart-stiflèd, in her dell.

XXIV

A casement high and triple-arched there was,
All garlanded with carven imag'ries
Of fruits, and flowers, and bunches of knot-grass,
And diamonded with panes of quaint device,   210
Innumerable of stains and splendid dyes,
As are the tiger-moth's deep-damasked wings;
And in the midst, 'mong thousand heraldries,
And twilight saints, and dim emblazonings,
A shielded scutcheon blushed with blood of queens and kings.

XXV

Full on this casement shone the wintry moon,
And threw warm gules on Madeline's fair breast,
As down she knelt for heaven's grace and boon;
Rose-bloom fell on her hands, together pressed,   220
And on her silver cross soft amethyst,
And on her hair a glory, like a saint:
She seemed a splendid angel, newly dressed,
Save wings, for Heaven – Porphyro grew faint;
She knelt, so pure a thing, so free from mortal taint.

XXVI

Anon his heart revives; her vespers done,
Of all its wreathèd pearls her hair she frees;
Unclasps her warmèd jewels one by one;
Loosens her fragrant bodice; by degrees
Her rich attire creeps rustling to her knees: 230
Half-hidden, like a mermaid in sea-weed,
Pensive awhile she dreams awake, and sees,
In fancy, fair St Agnes in her bed,
But dares not look behind, or all the charm is fled.

XXVII

Soon, trembling in her soft and chilly nest,
    In sort of wakeful swoon, perplexed she lay,
Until the poppied warmth of sleep oppressed
    Her soothèd limbs, and soul fatigued away –
Flown, like a thought, until the morrow-day;
    Blissfully havened both from joy and pain;
Clasped like a missal where swart Paynims pray;
    Blinded alike from sunshine and from rain,
As though a rose should shut, and be a bud again.

XXVIII

Stolen to this paradise, and so entranced,
    Porphyro gazed upon her empty dress,
And listened to her breathing, if it chanced
    To wake into a slumbrous tenderness;
Which when he heard, that minute did he bless,
    And breathed himself: then from the closet crept,
Noiseless as fear in a wide wilderness,
    And over the hushed carpet, silent, stepped,
And 'tween the curtains peeped, where, lo! – how fast she slept.

XXIX

Then by the bed-side, where the faded moon
    Made a dim, silver twilight, soft he set
A table, and, half anguished, threw thereon
    A cloth of woven crimson, gold, and jet –
O for some drowsy Morphean amulet!
    The boisterous, midnight, festive clarion,
The kettle-drum, and far-heard clarinet,
    Affray his ears, though but in dying tone; –
The hall door shuts again, and all the noise is gone.

XXX

And still she slept an azure-lidded sleep,
    In blanchèd linen, smooth, and lavendered,
While he from forth the closet brought a heap

Of candied apple, quince, and plum, and gourd,
With jellies soother than the creamy curd,
And lucent syrups, tinct with cinnamon;
Manna and dates, in argosy transferred
From Fez; and spicèd dainties, every one,
From silken Samarkand to cedared Lebanon.   270

XXXI

These delicates he heaped with glowing hand
On golden dishes and in baskets bright
Of wreathèd silver; sumptuous they stand
In the retirèd quiet of the night,
Filling the chilly room with perfume light.
'And now, my love, my seraph fair, awake!
Thou art my heaven, and I thine eremite:
Open thine eyes, for meek St Agnes' sake,
Or I shall drowse beside thee, so my soul doth ache.'

XXXII

Thus whispering, his warm, unnervèd arm   280
Sank in her pillow. Shaded was her dream
By the dusk curtains – 'twas a midnight charm
Impossible to melt as iced stream:
The lustrous salvers in the moonlight gleam;
Broad golden fringe upon the carpet lies.
It seemed he never, never could redeem
From such a steadfast spell his lady's eyes;
So mused awhile, entoiled in woofèd fantasies.

XXXIII

Awakening up, he took her hollow lute,
Tumultuous, and, in chords that tenderest be,   290
He played an ancient ditty, long since mute,
In Provence called, 'La belle dame sans mercy',
Close to her ear touching the melody –
Wherewith disturbed, she uttered a soft moan:
He ceased – she panted quick – and suddenly

Her blue affrayèd eyes wide open shone.
Upon his knees he sank, pale as smooth-sculptured stone.

XXXIV

Her eyes were open, but she still beheld,
Now wide awake, the vision of her sleep –
There was a painful change, that nigh expelled
The blisses of her dream so pure and deep.
At which fair Madeline began to weep,
And moan forth witless words with many a sigh,
While still her gaze on Porphyro would keep;
Who knelt, with joinèd hands and piteous eye,
Fearing to move or speak, she looked so dreamingly.

XXXV

'Ah, Porphyro!' said she, 'but even now
Thy voice was at sweet tremble in mine ear,
Made tuneable with every sweetest vow,
And those sad eyes were spiritual and clear:
How changed thou art! How pallid, chill, and drear!
Give me that voice again, my Porphyro,
Those looks immortal, those complainings dear!
O leave me not in this eternal woe,
For if thou diest, my Love, I know not where to go.'

XXXVI

Beyond a mortal man impassioned far
At these voluptuous accents, he arose,
Ethereal, flushed, and like a throbbing star
Seen mid the sapphire heaven's deep repose;
Into her dream he melted, as the rose
Blendeth its odour with the violet –
Solution sweet. Meantime the frost-wind blows
Like Love's alarum pattering the sharp sleet
Against the window-panes; St Agnes' moon hath set.

XXXVII

'Tis dark: quick pattereth the flaw-blown sleet.
'This is no dream, my bride, my Madeline!'
'Tis dark: the icèd gusts still rave and beat.
'No dream, alas! alas! and woe is mine!
Porphyro will leave me here to fade and pine. –
Cruel! what traitor could thee hither bring?   330
I curse not, for my heart is lost in thine,
Though thou forsakest a deceivèd thing –
A dove forlorn and lost with sick unprunèd wing.'

XXXVIII

'My Madeline! sweet dreamer! lovely bride!
Say, may I be for aye thy vassal blessed?
Thy beauty's shield, heart-shaped and vermeil dyed?
Ah, silver shrine, here will I take my rest
After so many hours of toil and quest,
A famished pilgrim – saved by miracle.
Though I have found, I will not rob thy nest   340
Saving of thy sweet self; if thou think'st well
To trust, fair Madeline, to no rude infidel.

XXXIX

Hark! 'tis an elfin-storm from faery land,
Of haggard seeming, but a boon indeed:
Arise – arise! the morning is at hand.
The bloated wassaillers will never heed –
Let us away, my love, with happy speed –
There are no ears to hear, or eyes to see,
Drowned all in Rhenish and the sleepy mead;
Awake! arise! my love, and fearless be,   350
For o'er the southern moors I have a home for thee.'

XL

She hurried at his words, beset with fears,
For there were sleeping dragons all around,
At glaring watch, perhaps, with ready spears –
Down the wide stairs a darkling way they found.

In all the house was heard no human sound.
A chain-drooped lamp was flickering by each door;
The arras, rich with horseman, hawk, and hound,
Fluttered in the besieging wind's uproar;
360   And the long carpets rose along the gusty floor.

XLI

They glide, like phantoms, into the wide hall;
Like phantoms, to the iron porch, they glide;
Where lay the Porter, in uneasy sprawl,
With a huge empty flaggon by his side:
The wakeful bloodhound rose, and shook his hide,
But his sagacious eye an inmate owns.
By one, and one, the bolts full easy slide –
The chains lie silent on the footworn stones –
The key turns, and the door upon its hinges groans.

XLII

370   And they are gone – ay, ages long ago
These lovers fled away into the storm.
That night the Baron dreamt of many a woe,
And all his warrior-guests, with shade and form
Of witch, and demon, and large coffin-worm,
Were long be-nightmared. Angela the old
Died palsy-twitched, with meagre face deform;
The Beadsman, after thousand aves told,
For aye unsought for slept among his ashes cold.

=====

The Eve of St Mark

Upon a Sabbath-day it fell;
Twice holy was the Sabbath bell,
That called the folk to evening prayer;
The city streets were clean and fair
From wholesome drench of April rains;
And, on the western window panes,

The chilly sunset faintly told
Of unmatured green valleys cold,
Of the green thorny bloomless hedge,
Of rivers new with spring-tide sedge,   10
Of primroses by sheltered rills,
And daisies on the aguish hills.
Twice holy was the Sabbath bell:
The silent streets were crowded well
With staid and pious companies,
Warm from their fireside orat'ries,
And moving, with demurest air,
To even-song, and vesper prayer.
Each archèd porch, and entry low,
Was filled with patient folk and slow,   20
With whispers hush, and shuffling feet,
While played the organs loud and sweet.

The bells had ceased, the prayers begun,
And Bertha had not yet half done
A curious volume, patched and torn,
That all day long, from earliest morn,
Had taken captive her two eyes,
Among its golden broideries;
Perplexed her with a thousand things –
The stars of Heaven, and angels' wings,   30
Martyrs in a fiery blaze,
Azure saints 'mid silver rays,
Aaron's breastplate, and the seven
Candlesticks John saw in Heaven,
The wingèd Lion of Saint Mark,
And the Covenantal Ark,
With its many mysteries,
Cherubim and golden mice.

Bertha was a maiden fair,
Dwelling in the old Minster Square;   40
From her fireside she could see,

Sidelong, its rich antiquity,
Far as the Bishop's garden-wall,
Where sycamores and elm-trees tall,
Full-leaved, the forest had outstripped,
By no sharp north-wind ever nipped,
So sheltered by the mighty pile.
Bertha arose, and read awhile,
With forehead 'gainst the window-pane.
50   Again she tried, and then again,
Until the dusk eve left her dark
Upon the legend of St Mark.
From pleated lawn-frill, fine and thin,
She lifted up her soft warm chin,
With aching neck and swimming eyes,
And dazed with saintly imageries.

All was gloom, and silent all,
Save now and then the still foot-fall
Of one returning townwards late,
60   Past the echoing Minster gate.
The clamorous daws, that all the day
Above tree-tops and towers play,
Pair by pair had gone to rest,
Each in its ancient belfry-nest,
Where asleep they fall betimes,
To music of the drowsy chimes.

All was silent, all was gloom,
Abroad and in the homely room:
Down she sat, poor cheated soul!
70   And struck a lamp from the dismal coal,
Leaned forward, with bright drooping hair,
And slant book full against the glare.
Her shadow, in uneasy guise,
Hovered about, a giant size,
On ceiling beam and old oak chair,
The parrot's cage, and panel square;

And the warm angled winter screen,
On which were many monsters seen,
Called doves of Siam, Lima mice,
And legless birds of Paradise,   80
Macaw, and tender Av'davat,
And silken-furred Angora cat.
Untired she read, her shadow still
Glowered about, as it would fill
The room with wildest forms and shades,
As though some ghostly Queen of Spades
Had come to mock behind her back,
And dance, and ruffle her garments black.
Untired she read the legend page,
Of holy Mark, from youth to age,   90
On land, on sea, in pagan chains,
Rejoicing for his many pains.
Sometimes the learned eremite,
With golden star, or dagger bright,
Referred to pious poesies
Written in smallest crow-quill size
Beneath the text; and thus the rhyme
Was parcelled out from time to time:
'– Als writith he of swevenis
Men han beforne they wake in bliss,   100
Whanne that hir friendès thinke hem bound
In crimpede shroude farre under grounde;
And how a litling child mote be
A saint er its nativitie,
Gif that the modre (God her blesse!)
Kepen in solitarinesse,
And kissen devoute the holy croce.
Of Goddis love, and Sathan's force,
He writith; and thinges many mo:
Of swichè thinges I may not show.   110
Bot I must tellen verilie
Somdel of Saintè Cicilie,

And chieflie what he auctorith
Of Saintè Markis life and death.'

At length her constant eyelids come
Upon the fervent martyrdom;
Then lastly to his holy shrine,
Exalt amid the tapers' shine
At Venice . . .
                    (Not published by Keats)

──────

'Why did I laugh tonight? . . .'

Why did I laugh tonight? No voice will tell:
    No God, no Demon of severe response,
Deigns to reply from Heaven or from Hell.
    Then to my human heart I turn at once –
Heart! thou and I are here sad and alone;
    Say, wherefore did I laugh! O mortal pain!
O Darkness! Darkness! ever must I moan,
    To question Heaven and Hell and Heart in vain.
Why did I laugh? I know this being's lease
    My fancy to its utmost blisses spreads;
Yet could I on this very midnight cease,
    And the world's gaudy ensigns see in shreds.
Verse, Fame, and Beauty are intense indeed,
    But Death intenser – Death is Life's high meed.
                    (Not published by Keats)

Character of Charles Brown

I

He is to weet a melancholy carle:
Thin in the waist, with bushy head of hair,
As hath the seeded thistle when in parle
It holds the Zephyr, ere it sendeth fair
Its light balloons into the summer air;
Thereto his beard had not begun to bloom,
No brush had touched his chin or razor sheer;
No care had touched his cheek with mortal doom,
But new he was and bright as scarf from Persian loom.

II

Ne cared he for wine, or half-and-half,   10
Ne cared he for fish or flesh or fowl,
And sauces held he worthless as the chaff;
He 'sdained the swine-herd at the wassail-bowl,
Ne with lewd ribbalds sat he cheek by jowl,
Ne with sly Lemans in the scorner's chair,
But after water-brooks this Pilgrim's soul
Panted, and all his food was woodland air
Though he would oft-times feast on gillyflowers rare.

III

The slang of cities in no wise he knew,
Tipping the wink to him was heathen Greek.   20
He sipped no olden Tom or ruin blue,
Or Nantz or cheery-brandy drank full meek
By many a damsel hoarse and rouge of cheek.
Nor did he know each agèd watchman's beat,
Nor in obscurèd purlieus would he seek
For curlèd Jewesses, with ankles neat,
Who as they walk abroad make tinkling with their feet.

                          (Not published by Keats)

A Dream, after reading Dante's Episode of Paolo and Francesca

As Hermes once took to his feathers light,
    When lullèd Argus, baffled, swooned and slept,
So on a Delphic reed, my idle spright
    So played, so charmed, so conquered, so bereft
The dragon-world of all its hundred eyes;
    And, seeing it asleep, so fled away –
Not to pure Ida with its snow-cold skies,
    Nor unto Tempe where Jove grieved that day;
But to that second circle of sad hell,
    Where in the gust, the whirlwind, and the flaw
Of rain and hail-stones, lovers need not tell
    Their sorrows. Pale were the sweet lips I saw,
Pale were the lips I kissed, and fair the form
I floated with, about that melancholy storm.

La Belle Dame sans Merci. A Ballad

I
O what can ail thee, knight-at-arms,
    Alone and palely loitering?
The sedge has withered from the lake,
    And no birds sing.

II
O what can ail thee, knight-at-arms,
    So haggard and so woe-begone?
The squirrel's granary is full,
    And the harvest's done.

III
I see a lily on thy brow,
    With anguish moist and fever-dew,
And on thy cheeks a fading rose
    Fast withereth too.

IV

I met a lady in the meads,
    Full beautiful – a faery's child,
Her hair was long, her foot was light,
    And her eyes were wild.

V

I made a garland for her head,
    And bracelets too, and fragrant zone;
She looked at me as she did love,
    And made sweet moan.   20

VI

I set her on my pacing steed,
    And nothing else saw all day long,
For sidelong would she bend, and sing
    A faery's song.

VII

She found me roots of relish sweet,
    And honey wild, and manna-dew,
And sure in language strange she said –
    'I love thee true'.

VIII

She took me to her elfin grot,
    And there she wept and sighed full sore,   30
And there I shut her wild wild eyes
    With kisses four.

IX

And there she lullèd me asleep
    And there I dreamed – Ah! woe betide! –
The latest dream I ever dreamt
    On the cold hill side.

X

I saw pale kings and princes too,
   Pale warriors, death-pale were they all;
They cried – 'La Belle Dame sans Merci
40   Thee hath in thrall!'

XI

I saw their starved lips in the gloam,
   With horrid warning gapèd wide,
And I awoke and found me here,
   On the cold hill's side.

XII

And this is why I sojourn here
   Alone and palely loitering,
Though the sedge is withered from the lake,
   And no birds sing.

To Sleep

O soft embalmer of the still midnight,
   Shutting, with careful fingers and benign,
Our gloom-pleased eyes, embowered from the light,
   Enshaded in forgetfulness divine:
O soothest Sleep! if so it please thee, close
   In midst of this thine hymn, my willing eyes,
Or wait the 'Amen', ere thy poppy throws
   Around my bed its lulling charities.
Then save me, or the passèd day will shine
10 Upon my pillow, breeding many woes;
   Save me from curious conscience, that still hoards
Its strength for darkness, burrowing like the mole;
   Turn the key deftly in the oilèd wards,
And seal the hushèd casket of my soul.

                                   (Not published by Keats)

'If by dull rhymes our English must be chained'

If by dull rhymes our English must be chained,
And, like Andromeda, the Sonnet sweet
Fettered, in spite of painèd loveliness,
Let us find out, if we must be constrained,
Sandals more interwoven and complete
To fit the naked foot of Poesy:
Let us inspect the lyre, and weigh the stress
Of every chord, and see what may be gained
By ear industrious, and attention meet;
Misers of sound and syllable, no less   10
Than Midas of his coinage, let us be
Jealous of dead leaves in the bay wreath crown;
So, if we may not let the Muse be free,
She will be bound with garlands of her own.

(Not published by Keats)

Ode to Psyche

O Goddess! hear these tuneless numbers, wrung
    By sweet enforcement and remembrance dear,
And pardon that thy secrets should be sung
    Even into thine own soft-conchèd ear:
Surely I dreamt to-day, or did I see
    The wingèd Psyche with awakened eyes?
I wandered in a forest thoughtlessly,
    And, on the sudden, fainting with surprise,
Saw two fair creatures, couchèd side by side
    In deepest grass, beneath the whispering roof   10
    Of leaves and tremblèd blossoms, where there ran
        A brooklet, scarce espied:
'Mid hushed, cool-rooted flowers, fragrant-eyed,
    Blue, silver-white, and budded Tyrian,

They lay calm-breathing on the bedded grass;
   Their arms embraced, and their pinions too:
   Their lips touched not, but had not bade adieu,
As if disjoinèd by soft-handed slumber,
And ready still past kisses to outnumber
     At tender eye-dawn of aurorean love:
        The wingèd boy I knew;
     But who wast thou, O happy, happy dove?
        His Psyche true!

O latest born and loveliest vision far
   Of all Olympus' faded hierarchy!
Fairer than Phoebe's sapphire-regioned star,
   Or Vesper, amorous glow-worm of the sky;
Fairer than these, though temple thou hast none,
     Nor altar heaped with flowers;
Nor virgin-choir to make delicious moan
     Upon the midnight hours;
No voice, no lute, no pipe, no incense sweet
     From chain-swung censer teeming;
No shrine, no grove, no oracle, no heat
     Of pale-mouthed prophet dreaming.

O brightest! though too late for antique vows,
   Too, too late for the fond believing lyre,
When holy were the haunted forest boughs,
   Holy the air, the water, and the fire;
Yet even in these days so far retired
   From happy pieties, thy lucent fans,
   Fluttering among the faint Olympians,
I see, and sing, by my own eyes inspired.
So let me be thy choir, and make a moan
     Upon the midnight hours;
Thy voice, thy lute, thy pipe, thy incense sweet
     From swingèd censer teeming –
Thy shrine, thy grove, thy oracle, thy heat
     Of pale-mouthed prophet dreaming.

Yes, I will be thy priest, and build a fane   50
   In some untrodden region of my mind,
Where branchèd thoughts, new grown with pleasant pain,
   Instead of pines shall murmur in the wind:
Far, far around shall those dark-clustered trees
   Fledge the wild-ridgèd mountains steep by steep;
And there by zephyrs, streams, and birds, and bees,
   The moss-lain Dryads shall be lulled to sleep;
And in the midst of this wide quietness
   A rosy sanctuary will I dress
With the wreathed trellis of a working brain,   60
   With buds, and bells, and stars without a name,
With all the gardener Fancy e'er could feign,
   Who breeding flowers, will never breed the same:
And there shall be for thee all soft delight
   That shadowy thought can win,
A bright torch, and a casement ope at night,
   To let the warm Love in!

———

On Fame (I)

Fame, like a wayward girl, will still be coy
   To those who woo her with too slavish knees,
But makes surrender to some thoughtless boy,
   And dotes the more upon a heart at ease;
She is gipsy, will not speak to those
   Who have not learnt to be content without her;
A jilt, whose ear was never whispered close,
   Who thinks they scandal her who talk about her –
A very gipsy is she, Nilus-born,
   Sister-in-law to jealous Potiphar.   10
Ye love-sick bards! repay her scorn for scorn;
   Ye artists lovelorn! madmen that ye are,
Make your best bow to her and bid adieu –
Then, if she likes it, she will follow you.

                              (Not published by Keats)

On Fame (II)

You cannot eat your cake and have it too
                 Proverb

How fevered is the man who cannot look
  Upon his mortal days with temperate blood,
Who vexes all the leaves of his life's book,
  And robs his fair name of its maidenhood;
It is as if the rose should pluck herself,
  Or the ripe plum finger its misty bloom,
As if a Naiad, like a meddling elf,
  Should darken her pure grot with muddy gloom:
But the rose leaves herself upon the briar,
  For winds to kiss and grateful bees to feed,
And the ripe plum still wears its dim attire,
    The undisturbèd lake has crystal space;
   Why then should man, teasing the world for grace,
Spoil his salvation for a fierce miscreed?
                 (Not published by Keats)

'Two or three posies'

Two or three posies
With two or three simples –
Two or three noses
With two or three pimples –
Two or three wise men
And two or three ninnies –
Two or three purses
And two or three guineas –
Two or three raps
At two or three doors –

Two or three naps
Of two or three hours –
Two or three cats
And two or three mice –
Two or three sprats
At a very great price –
Two or three sandies
And two or three tabbies –
Two or three dandies
And two Mrs— mum!   20
Two or three smiles
And two or three frowns –
Two or three miles
To two or three towns –
Two or three pegs
For two or three bonnets –
Two or three dove's eggs
To hatch into sonnets.
   (Not published by Keats)

―――

Ode on a Grecian Urn

I
Thou still unravished bride of quietness,
   Thou foster-child of silence and slow time,
Sylvan historian, who canst thus express
   A flowery tale more sweetly than our rhyme:
What leaf-fringed legend haunts about thy shape
   Of deities or mortals, or of both,
      In Tempe or the dales of Arcady?
   What men or gods are these? What maidens loth?
What mad pursuit? What struggle to escape?
      What pipes and timbrels? What wild ecstasy?   10

II

Heard melodies are sweet, but those unheard
    Are sweeter; therefore, ye soft pipes, play on;
Not to the sensual ear, but, more endeared,
    Pipe to the spirit ditties of no tone:
Fair youth, beneath the trees, thou canst not leave
    Thy song, nor ever can those trees be bare;
        Bold Lover, never, never canst thou kiss,
Though winning near the goal – yet, do not grieve:
    She cannot fade, though thou hast not thy bliss,
        For ever wilt thou love, and she be fair!

III

Ah, happy, happy boughs! that cannot shed
    Your leaves, nor ever bid the Spring adieu;
And, happy melodist, unwearièd,
    For ever piping songs for ever new;
More happy love! more happy, happy love!
    For ever warm and still to be enjoyed,
        For ever panting, and for ever young –
All breathing human passion far above,
    That leaves a heart high-sorrowful and cloyed,
        A burning forehead, and a parching tongue.

IV

Who are these coming to the sacrifice?
    To what green altar, O mysterious priest,
Lead'st thou that heifer lowing at the skies,
    And all her silken flanks with garlands dressed?
What little town by river or sea shore,
    Or mountain-built with peaceful citadel,
        Is emptied of this folk, this pious morn?
And, little town, thy streets for evermore
    Will silent be; and not a soul to tell
        Why thou art desolate, can e'er return.

V

O Attic shape! Fair attitude! with brede
  Of marble men and maidens overwrought,
With forest branches and the trodden weed;
    Thou, silent form, dost tease us out of thought
As doth eternity: Cold Pastoral!
    When old age shall this generation waste,
      Thou shalt remain, in midst of other woe
Than ours, a friend to man, to whom thou say'st,
    'Beauty is truth, truth beauty, – that is all
      Ye know on earth, and all ye need to know.'   50

Ode to a Nightingale

I

My heart aches, and a drowsy numbness pains
  My sense, as though of hemlock I had drunk,
Or emptied some dull opiate to the drains
  One minute past, and Lethe-wards had sunk:
'Tis not through envy of thy happy lot,
  But being too happy in thine happiness –
    That thou, light-wingèd Dryad of the trees,
      In some melodious plot
  Of beechen green, and shadows numberless,
    Singest of summer in full-throated ease.   10

II

O, for a draught of vintage! that hath been
  Cooled a long age in the deep-delvèd earth,
Tasting of Flora and the country green,
  Dance, and Provençal song, and sunburnt mirth!
O for a beaker full of the warm South,
  Full of the true, the blushful Hippocrene,
    With beaded bubbles winking at the brim,
      And purple-stainèd mouth,

That I might drink, and leave the world unseen,
20   And with thee fade away into the forest dim –

III
Fade far away, dissolve, and quite forget
    What thou among the leaves hast never known,
The weariness, the fever, and the fret
    Here, where men sit and hear each other groan;
Where palsy shakes a few, sad, last grey hairs,
    Where youth grows pale, and spectre-thin, and dies;
        Where but to think is to be full of sorrow
            And leaden-eyed despairs;
        Where Beauty cannot keep her lustrous eyes,
30   Or new Love pine at them beyond to-morrow.

IV
Away! away! for I will fly to thee,
    Not charioted by Bacchus and his pards,
But on the viewless wings of Poesy,
    Though the dull brain perplexes and retards.
Already with thee! tender is the night,
    And haply the Queen-Moon is on her throne,
        Clustered around by all her starry Fays;
            But here there is no light,
        Save what from heaven is with the breezes blown
40   Through verdurous glooms and winding mossy ways.

V
I cannot see what flowers are at my feet,
    Nor what soft incense hangs upon the boughs,
But, in embalmèd darkness, guess each sweet
    Wherewith the seasonable month endows
The grass, the thicket, and the fruit-tree wild –
    White hawthorn, and the pastoral eglantine;
        Fast fading violets covered up in leaves;
            And mid-May's eldest child,
        The coming musk-rose, full of dewy wine,
50   The murmurous haunt of flies on summer eves.

VI *In the dark*

Darkling I listen; and, for many a time
  I have been half in love with easeful Death,
Called him soft names in many a musèd rhyme,
    To take into the air my quiet breath;
Now more than ever seems it rich to die,
    To cease upon the midnight with no pain,
      While thou art pouring forth thy soul abroad
        In such an ecstasy!
    Still wouldst thou sing, and I have ears in vain –
      To thy high requiem become a sod.   60

VII

Thou wast not born for death, immortal Bird!
  No hungry generations tread thee down;
The voice I hear this passing night was heard
    In ancient days by emperor and clown:
Perhaps the self-same song that found a path
    Through the sad heart of Ruth, when, sick for home,
      She stood in tears amid the alien corn;
        The same that oft-times hath
    Charmed magic casements, opening on the foam
      Of perilous seas, in faery lands forlorn.   70

VIII

Forlorn! the very word is like a bell
  To toll me back from thee to my sole self!
Adieu! the fancy cannot cheat so well
    As she is famed to do, deceiving elf.
Adieu! adieu! thy plaintive anthem fades
    Past the near meadows, over the still stream,
      Up the hill-side; and now 'tis buried deep
        In the next valley-glades:
    Was it a vision, or a waking dream?
      Fled is that music – Do I wake or sleep?   80

Ode on Melancholy

I

No, no, go not to Lethe, neither twist
    Wolf's-bane, tight-rooted, for its poisonous wine:
Nor suffer thy pale forehead to be kissed
    By nightshade, ruby grape of Proserpine;
Make not your rosary of yew-berries,
    Nor let the beetle, nor the death-moth be
      Your mournful Psyche, nor the downy owl
A partner in your sorrow's mysteries;
    For shade to shade will come too drowsily,
10   And drown the wakeful anguish of the soul.

II

But when the melancholy fit shall fall
    Sudden from heaven like a weeping cloud,
That fosters the droop-headed flowers all,
    And hides the green hill in an April shroud;
Then glut thy sorrow on a morning rose,
    Or on the rainbow of the salt sand-wave,
      Or on the wealth of globèd peonies;
Or if thy mistress some rich anger shows,
    Emprison her soft hand, and let her rave,
20   And feed deep, deep upon her peerless eyes.

III

She dwells with Beauty — Beauty that must die;
    And Joy, whose hand is ever at his lips
Bidding adieu; and aching Pleasure nigh,
    Turning to poison while the bee-mouth sips:
Ay, in the very temple of Delight
    Veiled Melancholy has her sovran shrine,
      Though seen of none save him whose strenuous tongue
Can burst Joy's grape against his palate fine;

His soul shall taste the sadness of her might,
    And be among her cloudy trophies hung.   30

====

Ode on Indolence

They toil not, neither do they spin

I

One morn before me were three figures seen,
    With bowèd necks, and joinèd hands, side-faced;
And one behind the other stepped serene,
    In placid sandals, and in white robes graced;
They passed, like figures on a marble urn,
    When shifted round to see the other side;
        They came again; as when the urn once more
Is shifted round, the first seen shades return;
    And they were strange to me, as may betide
        With vases, to one deep in Phidian lore.   10

II

How is it, Shadows! that I knew ye not?
    How came ye muffled in so hush a masque?
Was it a silent deep-disguisèd plot
    To steal away, and leave without a task
My idle days? Ripe was the drowsy hour;
    The blissful cloud of summer-indolence
        Benumbed my eyes; my pulse grew less and less;
Pain had no sting, and pleasure's wreath no flower:
    O, why did ye not melt, and leave my sense
        Unhaunted quite of all but – nothingness?   20

III

A third time passed they by, and, passing, turned
    Each one the face a moment whiles to me;
Then faded, and to follow them I burned

And ached for wings because I knew the three;
The first was a fair Maid, and Love her name;
  The second was Ambition, pale of cheek,
    And ever watchful with fatiguèd eye;
The last, whom I love more, the more of blame
  Is heaped upon her, maiden most unmeek –
30   I knew to be my demon Poesy.

IV
They faded, and, forsooth! I wanted wings.
  O folly! What is love! and where is it?
And, for that poor Ambition – it springs
  From a man's little heart's short fever-fit.
For Poesy! – no, she has not a joy –
  At least for me – so sweet as drowsy noons,
    And evenings steeped in honeyed indolence.
O, for an age so sheltered from annoy,
  That I may never know how change the moons,
40   Or hear the voice of busy common-sense!

V
A third time came they by – alas! wherefore?
  My sleep had been embroidered with dim dreams:
My soul had been a lawn besprinkled o'er
  With flowers, and stirring shades, and baffled beams:
The morn was clouded, but no shower fell,
  Though in her lids hung the sweet tears of May;
    The open casement pressed a new-leaved vine,
  Let in the budding warmth and throstle's lay;
O Shadows! 'twas a time to bid farewell!
50   Upon your skirts had fallen no tears of mine.

VI
So, ye three Ghosts, adieu! Ye cannot raise
  My head cool-bedded in the flowery grass;
For I would not be dieted with praise,
  A pet-lamb in a sentimental farce!

Fade softly from my eyes, and be once more
  In masque-like figures on the dreamy urn.
        Farewell! I yet have visions for the night,
And for the day faint visions there is store.
        Vanish, ye Phantoms! from my idle sprite,
Into the clouds, and never more return!   60
              (Not published by Keats)

═══

Lamia

PART I

Upon a time, before the faery broods
Drove Nymph and Satyr from the prosperous woods,
Before King Oberon's bright diadem,
Sceptre, and mantle, clasped with dewy gem,
Frighted away the Dryads and the Fauns
From rushes green, and brakes, and cowslipped lawns,
The ever-smitten Hermes empty left
His golden throne, bent warm on amorous theft:
From high Olympus had he stolen light,
On this side of Jove's clouds, to escape the sight   10
Of his great summoner, and made retreat
Into a forest on the shores of Crete.
For somewhere in that sacred island dwelt
A nymph, to whom all hoofèd Satyrs knelt;
At whose white feet the languid Tritons poured
Pearls, while on land they withered and adored.
Fast by the springs where she to bathe was wont,
And in those meads where sometime she might haunt,
Were strewn rich gifts, unknown to any Muse,
Though Fancy's casket were unlocked to choose.   20
Ah, what a world of love was at her feet!
So Hermes thought, and a celestial heat
Burnt from his wingèd heels to either ear,
That from a whiteness, as the lily clear,

Blushed into roses 'mid his golden hair,
Fallen in jealous curls about his shoulders bare.

From vale to vale, from wood to wood, he flew,
Breathing upon the flowers his passion new,
And wound with many a river to its head
To find where this sweet nymph prepared her secret bed.
In vain; the sweet nymph might nowhere be found,
And so he rested, on the lonely ground,
Pensive, and full of painful jealousies
Of the Wood-Gods, and even the very trees.
There as he stood, he heard a mournful voice,
Such as, once heard, in gentle heart destroys
All pain but pity; thus the lone voice spake:
'When from this wreathèd tomb shall I awake!
When move in a sweet body fit for life,
And love, and pleasure, and the ruddy strife
Of hearts and lips! Ah, miserable me!'
The God, dove-footed, glided silently
Round bush and tree, soft-brushing, in his speed,
The taller grasses and full-flowering weed,
Until he found a palpitating snake,
Bright, and cirque-couchant in a dusky brake.

She was a gordian shape of dazzling hue,
Vermilion-spotted, golden, green, and blue;
Striped like a zebra, freckled like a pard,
Eyed like a peacock, and all crimson barred;
And full of silver moons, that, as she breathed,
Dissolved, or brighter shone, or interwreathed
Their lustres with the gloomier tapestries –
So rainbow-sided, touched with miseries,
She seemed, at once, some penanced lady elf,
Some demon's mistress, or the demon's self.
Upon her crest she wore a wannish fire
Sprinkled with stars, like Ariadne's tiar;

Her head was serpent, but ah, bitter-sweet!
She had a woman's mouth with all its pearls complete;   60
And for her eyes – what could such eyes do there
But weep, and weep, that they were born so fair,
As Proserpine still weeps for her Sicilian air.
Her throat was serpent, but the words she spake
Came, as through bubbling honey, for Love's sake,
And thus – while Hermes on his pinions lay,
Like a stooped falcon ere he takes his prey –

   'Fair Hermes, crowned with feathers, fluttering light,
I had a splendid dream of thee last night:
I saw thee sitting, on a throne of gold,   70
Among the Gods, upon Olympus old,
The only sad one; for thou didst not hear
The soft, lute-fingered Muses chanting clear,
Nor even Apollo when he sang alone,
Deaf to his throbbing throat's long, long melodious moan.
I dreamt I saw thee, robed in purple flakes,
Break amorous through the clouds, as morning breaks,
And, swiftly as a bright Phoebean dart,
Strike for the Cretan isle; and here thou art!
Too gentle Hermes, hast thou found the maid?'   80
Whereat the star of Lethe not delayed
His rosy eloquence, and thus inquired:
'Thou smooth-lipped serpent, surely high inspired!
Thou beauteous wreath, with melancholy eyes,
Possess whatever bliss thou canst devise,
Telling me only where my nymph is fled –
Where she doth breathe!' 'Bright planet, thou hast said,'
Returned the snake, 'but seal with oaths, fair God!'
'I swear,' said Hermes, 'by my serpent rod,
And by thine eyes, and by thy starry crown!'   90
Light flew his earnest words, among the blossoms blown.
Then thus again the brilliance feminine:
'Too frail of heart! for this lost nymph of thine,

Free as the air, invisibly, she strays
About these thornless wilds; her pleasant days
She tastes unseen; unseen her nimble feet
Leave traces in the grass and flowers sweet;
From weary tendrils, and bowed branches green,
She plucks the fruit unseen, she bathes unseen;
100   And by my power is her beauty veiled
To keep it unaffronted, unassailed
By the love-glances of unlovely eyes
Of Satyrs, Fauns, and bleared Silenus' sighs.
Pale grew her immortality, for woe
Of all these lovers, and she grievèd so
I took compassion on her, bade her steep
Her hair in weïrd syrops, that would keep
Her loveliness invisible, yet free
To wander as she loves, in liberty.
110   Thou shalt behold her, Hermes, thou alone,
If thou wilt, as thou swearest, grant my boon!'
Then, once again, the charmèd God began
An oath, and through the serpent's ears it ran
Warm, tremulous, devout, psalterian.
Ravished, she lifted her Circean head,
Blushed a live damask, and swift-lisping said,
'I was a woman, let me have once more
A woman's shape, and charming as before.
I love a youth of Corinth – O the bliss!
120   Give me my woman's form, and place me where he is.
Stoop, Hermes, let me breathe upon thy brow,
And thou shalt see thy sweet nymph even now.'
The God on half-shut feathers sank serene,
She breathed upon his eyes, and swift was seen
Of both the guarded nymph near-smiling on the green.
It was no dream; or say a dream it was,
Real are the dreams of Gods, and smoothly pass
Their pleasures in a long immortal dream.
One warm, flushed moment, hovering, it might seem

Dashed by the wood-nymph's beauty, so he burned; 130
Then, lighting on the printless verdure, turned
To the swooned serpent, and with languid arm,
Delicate, put to proof the lithe Caducean charm.
So done, upon the nymph his eyes he bent
Full of adoring tears and blandishment,
And towards her stepped: she, like a moon in wane,
Faded before him, cowered, nor could restrain
Her fearful sobs, self-folding like a flower
That faints into itself at evening hour:
But the God fostering her chillèd hand, 140
She felt the warmth, her eyelids opened bland,
And, like new flowers at morning song of bees,
Bloomed, and gave up her honey to the lees,
Into the green-recessèd woods they flew;
Nor grew they pale, as mortal lovers do.

    Left to herself, the serpent now began
To change; her elfin blood in madness ran,
Her mouth foamed, and the grass, therewith besprent,
Withered at dew so sweet and virulent;
Her eyes in torture fixed, and anguish drear, 150
Hot, glazed, and wide, with lid-lashes all sear,
Flashed phosphor and sharp sparks, without one cooling tear.
The colours all inflamed throughout her train,
She writhed about, convulsed with scarlet pain:
A deep volcanian yellow took the place
Of all her milder-moonèd body's grace;
And, as the lava ravishes the mead,
Spoilt all her silver mail, and golden brede;
Made gloom of all her frecklings, streaks and bars,
Eclipsed her crescents, and licked up her stars. 160
So that, in moments few, she was undressed
Of all her sapphires, greens, and amethyst,
And rubious-argent; of all these bereft,
Nothing but pain and ugliness were left.

Still shone her crown; that vanished, also she
Melted and disappeared as suddenly;
And in the air, her new voice luting soft,
Cried, 'Lycius! gentle Lycius!' – Borne aloft
With the bright mists about the mountains hoar
170   These words dissolved: Crete's forests heard no more.

Whither fled Lamia, now a lady bright,
A full-born beauty new and exquisite?
She fled into that valley they pass o'er
Who go to Corinth from Cenchreas' shore;
And rested at the foot of those wild hills,
The rugged founts of the Peræan rills,
And of that other ridge whose barren back
Stretches, with all its mist and cloudy rack,
South-westward to Cleone. There she stood
180   About a young bird's flutter from a wood,
Fair, on a sloping green of mossy tread,
By a clear pool, wherein she passionèd
To see herself escaped from so sore ills,
While her robes flaunted with the daffodils.

Ah, happy Lycius! – for she was a maid
More beautiful than ever twisted braid,
Or sighed, or blushed, or on spring-flowered lea
Spread a green kirtle to the minstrelsy:
A virgin purest lipped, yet in the lore
190   Of love deep learnèd to the red heart's core;
Not one hour old, yet of sciential brain
To unperplex bliss from its neighbour pain,
Define their pettish limits, and estrange
Their points of contact, and swift counterchange;
Intrigue with the specious chaos, and dispart
Its most ambiguous atoms with sure art;
As though in Cupid's college she had spent

Sweet days a lovely graduate, still unshent,
And kept his rosy terms in idle languishment.

Why this fair creature chose so faerily 200
By the wayside to linger, we shall see;
But first 'tis fit to tell how she could muse
And dream, when in the serpent prison-house,
Of all she list, strange or magnificent:
How, ever, where she willed, her spirit went;
Whether to faint Elysium, or where
Down through tress-lifting waves the Nereids fair
Wind into Thetis' bower by many a pearly stair;
Or where God Bacchus drains his cups divine,
Stretched out, at ease, beneath a glutinous pine; 210
Or where in Pluto's gardens palatine
Mulciber's columns gleam in far piazzian line.
And sometimes into cities she would send
Her dream, with feast and rioting to blend;
And once, while among mortals dreaming thus,
She saw the young Corinthian Lycius
Charioting foremost in the envious race,
Like a young Jove with calm uneager face,
And fell into a swooning love of him.
Now on the moth-time of that evening dim 220
He would return that way, as well she knew,
To Corinth from the shore; for freshly blew
The eastern soft wind, and his galley now
Grated the quaystones with her brazen prow
In port Cenchreas, from Egina isle
Fresh anchored; whither he had been awhile
To sacrifice to Jove, whose temple there
Waits with high marble doors for blood and incense rare.
Jove heard his vows, and bettered his desire;
For by some freakful chance he made retire 230
From his companions, and set forth to walk,
Perhaps grown wearied of their Corinth talk:

Over the solitary hills he fared,
Thoughtless at first, but ere eve's star appeared
His fantasy was lost, where reason fades,
In the calmed twilight of Platonic shades.
Lamia beheld him coming, near, more near –
Close to her passing, in indifference drear,
His silent sandals swept the mossy green;
240   So neighboured to him, and yet so unseen
She stood: he passed, shut up in mysteries,
His mind wrapped like his mantle, while her eyes
Followed his steps, and her neck regal white
Turned – syllabling thus, 'Ah, Lycius bright,
And will you leave me on the hills alone?
Lycius, look back! and be some pity shown.'
He did – not with cold wonder fearingly,
But Orpheus-like at an Eurydice –
For so delicious were the words she sung,
250   It seemed he had loved them a whole summer long.
And soon his eyes had drunk her beauty up,
Leaving no drop in the bewildering cup,
And still the cup was full – while he, afraid
Lest she should vanish ere his lip had paid
Due adoration, thus began to adore
(Her soft look growing coy, she saw his chain so sure):
'Leave thee alone! Look back! Ah, Goddess, see
Whether my eyes can ever turn from thee!
For pity do not this sad heart belie –
260   Even as thou vanished so I shall die.
Stay! though the greenest woods be thy domain,
To thy far wishes will thy streams obey.
Stay! though the greenest woods by thy domain,
Alone they can drink up the morning rain:
Though a descended Pleiad, will not one
Of thine harmonious sisters keep in tune
Thy spheres, and as thy silver proxy shine?
So sweetly to these ravished ears of mine

Came thy sweet greeting, that if thou shouldst fade
Thy memory will waste me to a shade –   270
For pity do not melt!' – 'If I should stay,'
Said Lamia, 'here, upon this floor of clay,
And pain my steps upon these flowers too rough,
What canst thou say or do of charm enough
To dull the nice remembrance of my home?
Thou canst not ask me with thee here to roam
Over these hills and vales, where no joy is –
Empty of immortality and bliss!
Thou art a scholar, Lycius, and must know
That finer spirits cannot breathe below   280
In human climes, and live. Alas! poor youth,
What taste of purer air hast thou to soothe
My essence? What serener palaces,
Where I may all my many senses please,
And by mysterious sleights a hundred thirsts appease?
It cannot be – Adieu!' So said, she rose
Tip-toe with white arms spread. He, sick to lose
The amorous promise of her lone complain,
Swooned, murmuring of love, and pale with pain.
The cruel lady, without any show   290
Of sorrow for her tender favourite's woe,
But rather, if her eyes could brighter be,
With brighter eyes and slow amenity,
Put her new lips to his, and gave afresh
The life she had so tangled in her mesh;
And as he from one trance was wakening
Into another, she began to sing,
Happy in beauty, life, and love, and every thing,
A song of love, too sweet for earthly lyres,
While, like held breath, the stars drew in their panting fires.   300
And then she whispered in such trembling tone,
As those who, safe together met alone
For the first time through many anguished days,
Use other speech than looks; bidding him raise

His drooping head, and clear his soul of doubt,
For that she was a woman, and without
Any more subtle fluid in her veins
Than throbbing blood, and that the self-same pains
Inhabited her frail-strung heart as his.
310 And next she wondered how his eyes could miss
Her face so long in Corinth, where, she said,
She dwelt but half retired, and there had led
Days happy as the gold coin could invent
Without the aid of love; yet in content
Till she saw him, as once she passed him by,
Where 'gainst a column he leant thoughtfully
At Venus' temple porch, 'mid baskets heaped
Of amorous herbs and flowers, newly reaped
Late on that eve, as 'twas the night before
320 The Adonian feast; whereof she saw no more,
But wept alone those days, for why should she adore?
Lycius from death awoke into amaze,
To see her still, and singing so sweet lays;
Then from amaze into delight he fell
To hear her whisper woman's lore so well;
And every word she spake enticed him on
To unperplexed delight and pleasure known.
Let the mad poets say whate'er they please
Of the sweets of Faeries, Peris, Goddesses,
330 There is not such a treat among them all,
Haunters of cavern, lake, and waterfall,
As a real woman, lineal indeed
From Pyrrha's pebbles or old Adam's seed.
Thus gentle Lamia judged, and judged aright,
That Lycius could not love in half a fright,
So threw the goddess off, and won his heart
More pleasantly by playing woman's part,
With no more awe than what her beauty gave,
That, while it smote, still guaranteed to save.
340 Lycius to all made eloquent reply,

Marrying to every word a twinborn sigh;
And last, pointing to Corinth, asked her sweet,
If 'twas too far that night for her soft feet.
The way was short, for Lamia's eagerness
Made, by a spell, the triple league decrease
To a few paces; not at all surmised
By blinded Lycius, so in her comprised.
They passed the city gates, he knew not how,
So noiseless, and he never thought to know.

    As men talk in a dream, so Corinth all,   350
Throughout her palaces imperial,
And all her populous streets and temples lewd,
Muttered, like tempest in the distance brewed,
To the wide-spreaded night above her towers.
Men, women, rich and poor, in the cool hours,
Shuffled their sandals o'er the pavement white,
Companioned or alone; while many a light
Flared, here and there, from wealthy festivals,
And threw their moving shadows on the walls,
Or found them clustered in the corniced shade   360
Of some arched temple door, or dusky colonnade.

    Muffling his face, of greeting friends in fear,
Her fingers he pressed hard, as one came near
With curled grey beard, sharp eyes, and smooth bald crown,
Slow-stepped, and robed in philosophic gown:
Lycius shrank closer, as they met and passed,
Into his mantle, adding wings to haste,
While hurried Lamia trembled: 'Ah,' said he,
'Why do you shudder, love, so ruefully?
Why does your tender palm dissolve in dew?' –   370
'I'm wearied,' said fair Lamia, 'tell me who
Is that old man? I cannot bring to mind
His features – Lycius! wherefore did you blind
Yourself from his quick eyes?' Lycius replied,

'''Tis Apollonius sage, my trusty guide
And good instructor; but tonight he seems
The ghost of folly haunting my sweet dreams.'

    While yet he spake they had arrived before
A pillared porch, with lofty portal door,
380   Where hung a silver lamp, whose phosphor glow
Reflected in the slabbèd steps below,
Mild as a star in water; for so new,
And so unsullied was the marble hue,
So through the crystal polish, liquid fine,
Ran the dark veins, that none but feet divine
Could e'er have touched there. Sounds Aeolian
Breathed from the hinges, as the ample span
Of the wide doors disclosed a place unknown
Some time to any, but those two alone,
390   And a few Persian mutes, who that same year
Were seen about the markets: none knew where
They could inhabit; the most curious
Were foiled, who watched to trace them to their house.
And but the flitter-wingèd verse must tell,
For truth's sake, what woe afterwards befell,
'Twould humour many a heart to leave them thus,
Shut from the busy world, of more incredulous.

PART II
Love in a hut, with water and a crust,
Is – Love, forgive us! – cinder, ashes, dust;
Love in a palace is perhaps at last
More grievous torment than a hermit's fast.
That is a doubtful tale from faery land,
Hard for the non-elect to understand.
Had Lycius lived to hand his story down,
He might have given the moral a fresh frown,
Or clenched it quite: but too short was their bliss
10   To breed distrust and hate, that make the soft voice hiss.
Besides, there, nightly, with terrific glare,

Love, jealous grown of so complete a pair,
Hovered and buzzed his wings, with fearful roar,
Above the lintel of their chamber door,
And down the passage cast a glow upon the floor.

    For all this came a ruin: side by side
They were enthronèd, in the eventide,
Upon a couch, near to a curtaining
Whose airy texture, from a golden string,
Floated into the room, and let appear   20
Unveiled the summer heaven, blue and clear,
Betwixt two marble shafts. There they reposed,
Where use had made it sweet, with eyelids closed,
Saving a tithe which love still open kept,
That they might see each other while they almost slept;
When from the slope side of a suburb hill,
Deafening the swallow's twitter, came a thrill
Of trumpets – Lycius started – the sounds fled,
But left a thought, a buzzing in his head.
For the first time, since first he harboured in   30
That purple-linèd palace of sweet sin,
His spirit passed beyond its golden bourne
Into the noisy world almost forsworn.
The lady, ever watchful, penetrant,
Saw this with pain, so arguing a want
Of something more, more than her empery
Of joys; and she began to moan and sigh
Because he mused beyond her, knowing well
That but a moment's thought is passion's passing-bell.
'Why do you sigh, fair creature?' whispered he: 40
'Why do you think?' returned she tenderly,
'You have deserted me – where am I now?
Not in your heart while care weighs on your brow:
No, no, you have dismissed me; and I go
From your breast houseless – ay, it must be so.'
He answered, bending to her open eyes,

Where he was mirrored small in paradise,
'My silver planet, both of eve and morn!
Why will you plead yourself so sad forlorn,
While I am striving how to fill my heart
With deeper crimson, and a double smart?
How to entangle, trammel up and snare
Your soul in mine, and labyrinth you there
Like the hid scent in an unbudded rose?
Ay, a sweet kiss – you see your mighty woes.
My thoughts! shall I unveil them? Listen then!
What mortal hath a prize, that other men
May be confounded and abashed withal,
But lets it sometimes pace abroad majestical,
And triumph, as in thee I should rejoice
Amid the hoarse alarm of Corinth's voice.
Let my foes choke, and my friends shout afar,
While through the throngèd streets your bridal car
Wheels round its dazzling spokes.' – The lady's cheek
Trembled; she nothing said, but, pale and meek,
Arose and knelt before him, wept a rain
Of sorrows at his words; at last with pain
Beseeching him, the while his hand she wrung,
To change his purpose. He thereat was stung,
Perverse, with stronger fancy to reclaim
Her wild and timid nature to his aim:
Besides, for all his love, in self-despite,
Against his better self, he took delight
Luxurious in her sorrows, soft and new.
His passion, cruel grown, took on a hue
Fierce and sanguineous as 'twas possible
In one whose brow had no dark veins to swell.
Fine was the mitigated fury, like
Apollo's presence when in act to strike
The serpent – Ha, the serpent! Certes, she
Was none. She burnt, she loved the tyranny,
And, all subdued, consented to the hour

When to the bridal he should lead his paramour.
Whispering in midnight silence, said the youth,
'Sure some sweet name thou hast, though, by my truth,
I have not asked it, ever thinking thee
Not mortal, but of heavenly progeny,
As still I do. Hast any mortal name,
Fit appellation for this dazzling frame?
Or friends or kinsfolk on the cited earth,   90
To share our marriage feast and nuptial mirth?'
'I have no friends,' said Lamia, 'no, not one;
My presence in wide Corinth hardly known:
My parents' bones are in their dusty urns
Sepulchred, where no kindled incense burns,
Seeing all their luckless race are dead, save me,
And I neglect the holy rite for thee.
Even as you list invite your many guests;
But if, as now it seems, your vision rests
With any pleasure on me, do not bid   100
Old Apollonius – from him keep me hid.'
Lycius, perplexed at words so blind and blank,
Made close inquiry; from whose touch she shrank,
Feigning a sleep; and he to the dull shade
Of deep sleep in a moment was betrayed.

    It was the custom then to bring away
The bride from home at blushing shut of day,
Veiled, in a chariot, heralded along
By strewn flowers, torches, and a marriage song,
With other pageants: but this fair unknown   110
Had not a friend. So being left alone,
(Lycius was gone to summon all his kin)
And knowing surely she could never win
His foolish heart from its mad pompousness,
She set herself, high-thoughted, how to dress
The misery in fit magnificence.
She did so, but 'tis doubtful how and whence

Came, and who were her subtle servitors.
About the halls, and to and from the doors,
120 There was a noise of wings, till in short space
The glowing banquet-room shone with wide-archèd grace.
A haunting music, sole perhaps and lone
Supportress of the faery-roof, made moan
Throughout, as fearful the whole charm might fade.
Fresh carvèd cedar, mimicking a glade
Of palm and plantain, met from either side,
High in the midst, in honour of the bride;
Two palms and then two plantains, and so on,
From either side their stems branched one to one
130 All down the aislèd place; and beneath all
There ran a stream of lamps straight on from wall to wall.
So canopied, lay an untasted feast
Teeming with odours. Lamia, regal dressed,
Silently paced about, and as she went,
In pale contented sort of discontent,
Missioned her viewless servants to enrich
The fretted splendour of each nook and niche.
Between the tree-stems, marbled plain at first,
Came jasper panels; then anon, there burst
140 Forth creeping imagery of slighter trees,
And with the larger wove in small intricacies.
Approving all, she faded at self-will,
And shut the chamber up, close, hushed and still,
Complete and ready for the revels rude,
When dreadful guests would come to spoil her solitude.

The day appeared, and all the gossip rout.
O senseless Lycius! Madman! wherefore flout
The silent-blessing fate, warm cloistered hours,
And show to common eyes these secret bowers?
150 The herd approached; each guest, with busy brain,
Arriving at the portal, gazed amain,
And entered marvelling – for they knew the street,

Remembered it from childhood all complete
Without a gap, yet ne'er before had seen
That royal porch, that high-built fair demesne.
So in they hurried all, mazed, curious and keen –
Save one, who looked thereon with eye severe,
And with calm-planted steps walked in austere.
'Twas Apollonius: something too he laughed,
As though some knotty problem, that had daffed   160
His patient thought, had now begun to thaw,
And solve and melt – 'twas just as he foresaw.

  He met within the murmurous vestibule
His young disciple. ''Tis no common rule,
Lycius,' said he, 'for uninvited guest
To force himself upon you, and infest
With an unbidden presence the bright throng
Of younger friends; yet must I do this wrong,
And you forgive me.' Lycius blushed, and led
The old man through the inner doors broad-spread;   170
With reconciling words and courteous mien
Turning into sweet milk the sophist's spleen.

  Of wealthy lustre was the banquet-room,
Filled with pervading brilliance and perfume:
Before each lucid panel fuming stood
A censer fed with myrrh and spicèd wood,
Each by a sacred tripod held aloft,
Whose slender feet wide-swerved upon the soft
Wool-woofèd carpets; fifty wreaths of smoke
From fifty censers their light voyage took   180
To the high roof, still mimicked as they rose
Along the mirrored walls by twin-clouds odorous.
Twelve spherèd tables, by silk seats ensphered,
High as the level of a man's breast reared
On libbard's paws, upheld the heavy gold
Of cups and goblets, and the store thrice told
Of Ceres' horn, and in huge vessels, wine

Come from the gloomy tun with merry shine.
Thus loaded with a feast the tables stood,
190   Each shrining in the midst the image of a God.

When in an antechamber every guest
Had felt the cold full sponge to pleasure pressed,
By ministering slaves, upon his hands and feet,
And fragrant oils with ceremony meet
Poured on his hair, they all moved to the feast
In white robes, and themselves in order placed
Around the silken couches, wondering
Whence all this mighty cost and blaze of wealth could spring.

Soft went the music the soft air along,
200   While fluent Greek a vowelled undersong
Kept up among the guests, discoursing low
At first, for scarcely was the wine at flow;
But when the happy vintage touched their brains,
Louder they talk, and louder come the strains
Of powerful instruments. The gorgeous dyes,
The space, the splendour of the draperies,
The roof of awful richness, nectarous cheer,
Beautiful slaves, and Lamia's self, appear,
Now, when the wine has done its rosy deed,
210   And every soul from human trammels freed,
No more so strange; for merry wine, sweet wine,
Will make Elysian shades not too fair, too divine.

Soon was God Bacchus at meridian height;
Flushed were their cheeks, and bright eyes double bright:
Garlands of every green, and every scent
From vales deflowered, or forest-trees branch-rent,
In baskets of bright osiered gold were brought
High as the handles heaped, to suit the thought
Of every guest – that each, as he did please,
220   Might fancy-fit his brows, silk-pillowed at his ease.

What wreath for Lamia? What for Lycius?
What for the sage, old Apollonius?
Upon her aching forehead be there hung
The leaves of willow and of adder's tongue;
And for the youth, quick, let us strip for him
The thyrsus, that his watching eyes may swim
Into forgetfulness; and, for the sage,
Let spear-grass and the spiteful thistle wage
War on his temples. Do not all charms fly
At the mere touch of cold philosophy?   230
There was an awful rainbow once in heaven:
We know her woof, her texture; she is given
In the dull catalogue of common things.
Philosophy will clip an Angel's wings,
Conquer all mysteries by rule and line,
Empty the haunted air, and gnomèd mine –
Unweave a rainbow, as it erewhile made
The tender-personed Lamia melt into a shade.

    By her glad Lycius sitting, in chief place,
Scarce saw in all the room another face,   240
Till, checking his love trance, a cup he took
Full brimmed, and opposite sent forth a look
'Cross the broad table, to beseech a glance
From his old teacher's wrinkled countenance,
And pledge him. The bald-head philosopher
Had fixed his eye, without a twinkle or stir
Full on the alarmèd beauty of the bride,
Brow-beating her fair form, and troubling her sweet pride.
Lycius then pressed her hand, with devout touch,
As pale it lay upon the rosy couch: 250
'Twas icy, and the cold ran through his veins;
Then sudden it grew hot, and all the pains
Of an unnatural heat shot to his heart.
'Lamia, what means this? Wherefore dost thou start?
Know'st thou that man?' Poor Lamia answered not.

He gazed into her eyes, and not a jot
Owned they the lovelorn piteous appeal;
More, more he gazed; his human senses reel;
Some hungry spell that loveliness absorbs;
260   There was no recognition in those orbs.
'Lamia!' he cried – and no soft-toned reply.
The many heard, and the loud revelry
Grew hush; the stately music no more breathes;
The myrtle sickened in a thousand wreaths.
By faint degrees, voice, lute, and pleasure ceased;
A deadly silence step by step increased,
Until it seemed a horrid presence there,
And not a man but felt the terror in his hair.
'Lamia!' he shrieked; and nothing but the shriek
270   With its sad echo did the silence break.
'Begone, foul dream!' he cried, gazing again
In the bride's face, where now no azure vein
Wandered on fair-spaced temples; no soft bloom
Misted the cheek; no passion to illume
The deep-recessèd vision. All was blight;
Lamia, no longer fair, there sat a deadly white.
'Shut, shut those juggling eyes, thou ruthless man!
Turn them aside, wretch! or the righteous ban
Of all the Gods, whose dreadful images
280   Here represent their shadowy presences,
May pierce them on the sudden with the thorn
Of painful blindness; leaving thee forlorn,
In trembling dotage to the feeblest fright
Of conscience, for their long offended might,
For all thine impious proud-heart sophistries,
Unlawful magic, and enticing lies.
Corinthians! look upon that grey-beard wretch!
Mark how, possessed, his lashless eyelids stretch
Around his demon eyes! Corinthians, see!
290   My sweet bride withers at their potency.'
'Fool!' said the sophist, in an undertone

Gruff with contempt; which a death-nighing moan
From Lycius answered, as heart-struck and lost,
He sank supine beside the aching ghost.

'Fool! Fool!' repeated he, while his eyes still
Relented not, nor moved: 'From every ill
Of life have I preserved thee to this day,
And shall I see thee made a serpent's prey?'
Then Lamia breathed death-breath; the sophist's eye,
Like a sharp spear, went through her utterly,   300
Keen, cruel, perceant, stinging: she, as well
As her weak hand could any meaning tell,
Motioned him to be silent; vainly so,
He looked and looked again a level – *No!*
'A Serpent!' echoed he; no sooner said,
Than with a frightful scream she vanishèd:
And Lycius' arms were empty of delight,
As were his limbs of life, from that same night.
On the high couch he lay! – his friends came round –
Supported him – no pulse, or breath they found,   310
And, in its marriage robe, the heavy body wound.

═══

'Bright star! would I were steadfast as thou art'

Bright star! would I were steadfast as thou art –
    Not in lone splendour hung aloft the night
And watching, with eternal lids apart,
    Like nature's patient, sleepless Eremite,
The moving waters at their priestlike task
    Of pure ablution round earth's human shores,
Or gazing on the new soft-fallen mask
    Of snow upon the mountains and the moors –
No – yet still steadfast, still unchangeable,
    Pillowed upon my fair love's ripening breast,   10
To feel for ever its soft swell and fall,
    Awake for ever in a sweet unrest,

Still, still to hear her tender-taken breath,
And so live ever – or else swoon to death.

(Not published by Keats)

'Pensive they sit, and roll their languid eyes'

Pensive they sit, and roll their languid eyes,
Nibble their toasts and cool their tea with sighs;
Or else forget the purpose of the night,
Forget their tea, forget their appetite.
See, with crossed arms they sit – Ah! hapless crew,
The fire is going out and no one rings
For coals, and therefore no coals Betty brings.
A fly is in the milk-pot – must he die
Circled by a Humane Society?
No, no; there, Mr Werter takes his spoon,
Inverts it, dips the handle, and lo! soon
The little struggler, saved from perils dark,
Across the teaboard draws a long wet mark.
Romeo! Arise! take snuffers by the handle,
There's a large cauliflower in each candle.
A winding-sheet – ah, me! I must away
To No. 7, just beyond the Circus gay.
'Alas, my friend, your coat sits very well;
Where may your tailor live?' 'I may not tell.
O pardon me – I'm absent now and then.
Where *might* my tailor live? I say again
I canot tell. Let me no more be teased –
He lives in Wapping, *might* live where he pleased.'

(Not published by Keats)

To Autumn

I

Season of mists and mellow fruitfulness,
    Close bosom-friend of the maturing sun,
Conspiring with him how to load and bless
    With fruit the vines that round the thatch-eves run;
To bend with apples the mossed cottage-trees,
    And fill all fruit with ripeness to the core;
        To swell the gourd, and plump the hazel shells
    With a sweet kernel; to set budding more,
And still more, later flowers for the bees,
Until they think warm days will never cease,   10
        For Summer has o'er-brimmed their clammy cells.

II

Who hath not seen thee oft amid thy store?
    Sometimes whoever seeks abroad may find
Thee sitting careless on a granary floor,
    Thy hair soft-lifted by the winnowing wind;
Or on a half-reaped furrow sound asleep,
    Drowsed with the fume of poppies, while thy hook
        Spares the next swath and all its twinèd flowers;
And sometimes like a gleaner thou dost keep
    Steady thy laden head across a brook;   20
    Or by a cider-press, with patient look,
        Thou watchest the last oozings hours by hours.

III

Where are the songs of Spring? Ay, where are they?
    Think not of them, thou hast thy music too –
While barrèd clouds bloom the soft-dying day,
    And touch the stubble-plains with rosy hue:
Then in a wailful choir the small gnats mourn
    Among the river sallows, borne aloft
        Or sinking as the light wind lives or dies;

30   And full-grown lambs loud bleat from hilly bourn;
         Hedge-crickets sing; and now with treble soft
         The red-breast whistles from a garden-croft;
            And gathering swallows twitter in the skies.

The Fall of Hyperion. A Dream

CANTO I
Fanatics have their dreams, wherewith they weave
A paradise for a sect; the savage too
From forth the loftiest fashion of his sleep
Guesses at Heaven; pity these have not
Traced upon vellum or wild Indian leaf
The shadows of melodious utterance.
But bare of laurel they live, dream, and die;
For Poesy alone can tell her dreams,
With the fine spell of words alone can save
10   Imagination from the sable charm
And dumb enchantment. Who alive can say,
'Thou art no Poet – mayst not tell thy dreams'?
Since every man whose soul is not a clod
Hath visions, and would speak, if he had loved,
And been well nurtured in his mother tongue.
Whether the dream now purposed to rehearse
Be Poet's or Fanatic's will be known
When this warm scribe my hand is in the grave.

20   Methought I stood where trees of every clime,
Palm, myrtle, oak, and sycamore, and beech,
With plantain, and spice-blossoms, made a screen –
In neighbourhood of fountains, by the noise
Soft-showering in mine ears, and, by the touch
Of scent, not far from roses. Turning round,
I saw an arbour with a drooping roof
Of trellis vines, and bells, and larger blooms,

Like floral censers, swinging light in air;
Before its wreathèd doorway, on a mound
Of moss, was spread a feast of summer fruits,
Which, nearer seen, seemed refuse of a meal   30
By angel tasted, or our Mother Eve;
For empty shells were scattered on the grass,
And grape-stalks but half bare, and remnants more,
Sweet-smelling, whose pure kinds I could not know.
Still was more plenty than the fabled horn
Thrice emptied could pour forth at banqueting
For Proserpine returned to her own fields,
Where the white heifers low. And appetite
More yearning than on earth I ever felt
Growing within, I ate deliciously;   40
And, after not long, thirsted, for thereby
Stood a cool vessel of transparent juice,
Sipped by the wandered bee, the which I took,
And, pledging all the mortals of the world,
And all the dead whose names are in our lips,
Drank. That full draught is parent of my theme.
No Asian poppy, nor elixir fine
Of the soon-fading jealous Caliphat;
No poison gendered in close monkish cell,
To thin the scarlet conclave of old men,   50
Could so have rapt unwilling life away.
Among the fragrant husks and berries crushed,
Upon the grass I struggled hard against
The domineering potion; but in vain –
The cloudy swoon came on, and down I sunk,
Like a Silenus on an antique vase.
How long I slumbered 'tis a chance to guess.
When sense of life returned, I started up
As if with wings; but the fair trees were gone,
The mossy mound and arbour were no more.   60
I looked around upon the carvèd sides
Of an old sanctuary with roof august,

Builded so high, it seemed that filmèd clouds
Might spread beneath, as o'er the stars of heaven.
So old the place was, I remembered none
The like upon the earth: what I had seen
Of grey cathedrals, buttressed walls, rent towers,
The superannuations of sunk realms,
Or Nature's rocks toiled hard in waves and winds,
70   Seemed but the faulture of decrepit things
To that eternal domèd monument.
Upon the marble at my feet there lay
Store of strange vessels and large draperies,
Which needs had been of dyed asbestos wove,
Or in that place the moth could not corrupt,
So white the linen; so, in some, distinct
Ran imageries from a sombre loom.
All in a mingled heap confused there lay
Robes, golden tongs, censer and chafing-dish,
80   Girdles, and chains, and holy jewelleries –

    Turning from these with awe, once more I raised
My eyes to fathom the space every way –
The embossèd roof, the silent massy range
Of columns north and south, ending in mist
Of nothing, then to eastward, where black gates
Were shut against the sunrise evermore.
Then to the west I looked, and saw far off
An Image, huge of feature as a cloud,
At level of whose feet an altar slept,
90   To be approached on either side by steps,
And marble balustrade, and patient travail
To count with toil the innumerable degrees.
Towards the altar sober-paced I went,
Repressing haste, as too unholy there;
And, coming nearer, saw beside the shrine
One ministering; and there arose a flame.
When in mid-May the sickening East wind
Shifts sudden to the south, the small warm rain

Melts out the frozen incense from all flowers,
And fills the air with so much pleasant health   100
That even the dying man forgets his shroud –
Even so that lofty sacrificial fire,
Sending forth Maian incense, spread around
Forgetfulness of everything but bliss,
And clouded all the altar with soft smoke,
From whose white fragrant curtains thus I heard
Language pronounced: 'If thou canst not ascend
These steps, die on that marble where thou art.
Thy flesh, near cousin to the common dust,
Will parch for lack of nutriment – thy bones   110
Will wither in few years, and vanish so
That not the quickest eye could find a grain
Of what thou now art on that pavement cold.
The sands of thy short life are spent this hour,
And no hand in the universe can turn
Thy hourglass, if these gummèd leaves be burnt
Ere thou canst mount up these immortal steps.'
I heard, I looked: two senses both at once,
So fine, so subtle, felt the tyranny
Of that fierce threat, and the hard task proposed.   120
Prodigious seemed the toil; the leaves were yet
Burning – when suddenly a palsied chill
Struck from the pavèd level up my limbs,
And was ascending quick to put cold grasp
Upon those streams that pulse beside the throat.
I shrieked; and the sharp anguish of my shriek
Stung my own ears – I strove hard to escape
The numbness, strove to gain the lowest step.
Slow, heavy, deadly was my pace: the cold
Grew stifling, suffocating, at the heart;   130
And when I clasped my hands I felt them not.
One minute before death, my iced foot touched
The lowest stair; and as it touched, life seemed
To pour in at the toes: I mounted up,

As once fair Angels on a ladder flew
From the green turf to Heaven. 'Holy Power,'
Cried I, approaching near the hornèd shrine,
'What am I that should so be saved from death?
What am I that another death come not
140   To choke my utterance sacrilegious, here?'
Then said the veilèd shadow: 'Thou hast felt
What 'tis to die and live again before
Thy fated hour. That thou hadst power to do so
Is thy own safety; thou hast dated on
Thy doom.' 'High Prophetess,' said I, 'purge off,
Benign, if so it please thee, my mind's film.'
'None can usurp this height,' returned that shade,
'But those to whom the miseries of the world
Are misery, and will not let them rest.
150   All else who find a haven in the world,
Where they may thoughtless sleep away their days,
If by a chance into this fane they come,
Rot on the pavement where thou rotted'st half.'
'Are there not thousands in the world,' said I,
Encouraged by the sooth voice of the shade,
'Who love their fellows even to the death;
Who feel the giant agony of the world;
And more, like slaves to poor humanity,
Labour for mortal good? I sure should see
160   Other men here: but I am here alone.'
'They whom thou spak'st of are no visionaries,'
Rejoined that voice – 'They are no dreamers weak,
They seek no wonder but the human face;
No music but a happy-noted voice –
They come not here, they have no thought to come –
And thou art here, for thou art less than they –
What benefit canst thou do, or all thy tribe,
To the great world? Thou art a dreaming thing,
A fever of thyself. Think of the Earth;
170   What bliss even in hope is there for thee?

What haven? Every creature hath its home;
Every sole man hath days of joy and pain,
Whether his labours be sublime or low –
The pain alone; the joy alone; distinct:
Only the dreamer venoms all his days,
Bearing more woe than all his sins deserve.
Therefore, that happiness be somewhat shared,
Such things as thou art are admitted oft
Into like gardens thou didst pass erewhile,
And suffered in these temples; for that cause   180
Thou standest safe beneath this statue's knees.'
'That I am favoured for unworthiness,
By such propitious parley medicined
In sickness not ignoble, I rejoice –
Ay, and could weep for love of such award.'
So answered I, continuing, 'If it please,
Majestic shadow, tell me: sure not all
Those melodies sung into the world's ear
Are useless: sure a poet is a sage,
A humanist, physician to all men.   190
That I am none I feel, as vultures feel
They are no birds when eagles are abroad.
What am I then? Thou spakest of my tribe:
What tribe?' – The tall shade veiled in drooping white
Then spake, so much more earnest, that the breath
Moved the thin linen folds that drooping hung
About a golden censer from the hand
Pendant. – 'Art thou not of the dreamer tribe?
The poet and the dreamer are distinct,
Diverse, sheer opposite, antipodes.   200
The one pours out a balm upon the world,
The other vexes it.' Then shouted I,
Spite of myself, and with a Pythia's spleen,
'Apollo! faded, far-flown Apollo!
Where is thy misty pestilence to creep
Into the dwellings, through the door crannies,

Of all mock lyrists, large self-worshippers
And careless hectorers in proud bad verse.
Though I breathe death with them it will be life
210   To see them sprawl before me into graves.
Majestic shadow, tell me where I am,
Whose altar this; for whom this incense curls;
What image this, whose face I cannot see,
For the broad marble knees; and who thou art,
Of accent feminine so courteous?'

Then the tall shade, in drooping linens veiled,
Spake out, so much more earnest, that her breath
Stirred the thin folds of gauze that drooping hung
About a golden censer from her hand
220   Pendant; and by her voice I knew she shed
Long-treasured tears. 'This temple, sad and lone,
Is all spared from the thunder of a war
Foughten long since by giant hierarchy
Against rebellion; this old image here,
Whose carvèd features wrinkled as he fell,
Is Saturn's; I Moneta, left supreme
Sole priestess of his desolation.'
I had no words to answer, for my tongue,
Useless, could find about its roofèd home
230   No syllable of a fit majesty
To make rejoinder to Moneta's mourn.
There was a silence, while the altar's blaze
Was fainting for sweet food: I looked thereon,
And on the pavèd floor, where nigh were piled
Faggots of cinnamon, and many heaps
Of other crispèd spice-wood – then again
I looked upon the altar, and its horns
Whitened with ashes, and its languorous flame,
And then upon the offerings again;
240   And so by turns – till sad Moneta cried:
'The sacrifice is done, but not the less
Will I be kind to thee for thy goodwill.

My power, which to me is still a curse,
Shall be to thee a wonder; for the scenes
Still swooning vivid through my globèd brain,
With an electral changing misery,
Thou shalt with those dull mortal eyes behold,
Free from all pain, if wonder pain thee not.'
As near as an immortal's spherèd words
Could to a mother's soften, were these last: 250
But yet I had a terror of her robes,
And chiefly of the veils, that from her brow
Hung pale, and curtained her in mysteries
That made my heart too small to hold its blood.
This saw that Goddess, and with sacred hand
Parted the veils. Then saw I a wan face,
Not pined by human sorrows, but bright-blanched
By an immortal sickness which kills not;
It works a constant change, which happy death
Can put no end to; deathwards progressing   260
To no death was that visage; it had passed
The lily and the snow; and beyond these
I must not think now, though I saw that face –
But for her eyes I should have fled away.
They held me back, with a benignant light,
Soft-mitigated by divinest lids
Half-closed, and visionless entire they seemed
Of all external things – they saw me not,
But in blank splendour beamed like the mild moon,
Who comforts those she sees not, who knows not   270
What eyes are upward cast. As I had found
A grain of gold upon a mountain's side,
And twinged with avarice strained out my eyes
To search its sullen entrails rich with ore,
So at the view of sad Moneta's brow
I ached to see what things the hollow brain
Behind enwombèd; what high tragedy
In the dark secret chambers of her skull

Was acting, that could give so dread a stress
To her cold lips, and fill with such a light
Her planetary eyes; and touch her voice
With such a sorrow – 'Shade of Memory!'
Cried I, with act adorant at her feet,
'By all the gloom hung round thy fallen house,
By this last temple, by the golden age,
By great Apollo, thy dear foster child,
And by thyself, forlorn divinity,
The pale Omega of a withered race,
Let me behold, according as thou said'st,
What in thy brain so ferments to and fro.'
No sooner had this conjuration passed
My devout lips, than side by side we stood
(Like a stunt bramble by a solemn pine)
Deep in the shady sadness of a vale,
Far sunken from the healthy breath of morn,
Far from the fiery noon and eve's one star.
Onward I looked beneath the gloomy boughs,
And saw, what first I thought an image huge,
Like to the image pedestalled so high
In Saturn's temple. Then Moneta's voice
Came brief upon mine ear: 'So Saturn sat
When he had lost his realms.' Whereon there grew
A power within me of enormous ken
To see as a God sees, and take the depth
Of things as nimbly as the outward eye
Can size and shape pervade. The lofty theme
At those few words hung vast before my mind,
With half-unravelled web. I set myself
Upon an eagle's watch, that I might see,
And seeing ne'er forget. No stir of life
Was in this shrouded vale, not so much air
As in zoning of a summer's day
Robs not one light seed from the feathered grass,
But where the dead leaf fell there did it rest.

A stream went voiceless by, still deadened more
By reason of the fallen divinity
Spreading more shade; the Naiad 'mid her reeds
Pressed her cold finger closer to her lips.
Along the margin-sand large footmarks went
No farther than to where old Saturn's feet   320
Had rested, and there slept – how long a sleep!
Degraded, cold, upon the sodden ground
His old right hand lay nerveless, listless, dead,
Unsceptred; and his realmless eyes were closed,
While his bowed head seemed listening to the Earth,
His ancient mother, for some comfort yet.

   It seemed no force could wake him from his place;
But there came one who, with a kindred hand
Touched his wide shoulders, after bending low
With reverence, though to one who knew it not.   330
Then came the grieved voice of Mnemosyne,
And grieved I hearkened. 'That divinity
Whom thou saw'st step from yon forlornest wood,
And with slow pace approach our fallen King,
Is Thea, softest-natured of our brood.'
I marked the goddess in fair statuary
Surpassing wan Moneta by the head,
And in her sorrow nearer woman's tears.
There was a listening fear in her regard,
As if calamity had but begun;   340
As if the vanward clouds of evil days
Had spent their malice, and the sullen rear
Was with its storèd thunder labouring up.
One hand she pressed upon that aching spot
Where beats the human heart, as if just there,
Though an immortal, she felt cruel pain;
The other upon Saturn's bended neck
She laid, and to the level of his hollow ear
Leaning with parted lips, some words she spake

350   In solemn tenor and deep organ tune,
    Some mourning words, which in our feeble tongue
    Would come in this-like accenting – how frail
    To that large utterance of the early Gods! –
    'Saturn! look up – and for what, poor lost King?
    I have no comfort for thee, no – not one;
    I cannot cry, *Wherefore thus sleepest thou?*
    For Heaven is parted from thee, and the Earth
    Knows thee not, so afflicted, for a God;
    And Ocean too, with all its solemn noise,
360   Has from thy sceptre passed, and all the air
    Is emptied of thine hoary Majesty.
    Thy thunder, captious at the new command,
    Rumbles reluctant o'er our fallen house;
    And thy sharp lightning, in unpractised hands,
    Scorches and burns our once serene domain.
    With such remorseless speed still come new woes
    That unbelief has not a space to breathe.
    Saturn! sleep on. Me thoughtless, why should I
    Thus violate thy slumbrous solitude?
370   Why should I ope thy melancholy eyes?
    Saturn, sleep on, while at thy feet I weep.'

      As when, upon a trancèd summer-night,
    Forests, branch-charmèd by the earnest stars,
    Dream, and so dream all night without a noise,
    Save from one gradual solitary gust,
    Swelling upon the silence; dying off;
    As if the ebbing air had but one wave –
    So came these words, and went; the while in tears
    She pressed her fair large forehead to the earth,
380   Just where her fallen hair might spread in curls,
    A soft and silken mat for Saturn's feet.
    Long, long those two were postured motionless,
    Like sculpture builded-up upon the grave
    Of their own power. A long awful time

I looked upon them: still they were the same;
The frozen God still bending to the earth,
And the sad Goddess weeping at his feet;
Moneta silent. Without stay or prop,
But my own weak mortality, I bore
The load of this eternal quietude,   390
The unchanging gloom, and the three fixèd shapes
Ponderous upon my senses a whole moon.
For by my burning brain I measured sure
Her silver seasons shedded on the night,
And every day by day methought I grew
More gaunt and ghostly. Oftentimes I prayed
Intense, that death would take me from the vale
And all its burthens. Gasping with despair
Of change, hour after hour I cursed myself –
Until old Saturn raised his faded eyes,   400
And looked around and saw his kingdom gone,
And all the gloom and sorrow of the place,
And that fair kneeling Goddess at his feet.
As the moist scent of flowers, and grass, and leaves,
Fills forest dells with a pervading air
Known to the woodland nostril, so the words
Of Saturn filled the mossy glooms around,
Even to the hollows of time-eaten oaks,
And to the windings in the foxes' hole,
With sad low tones, while thus he spake, and sent   410
Strange musings to the solitary Pan.

  'Moan, brethren, moan; for we are swallowed up
And buried from all godlike exercise
Of influence benign on planets pale,
And peaceful sway above man's harvesting,
And all those acts which deity supreme
Doth ease its heart of love in. Moan and wail.
Moan, brethren, moan; for lo! the rebel spheres
Spin round, the stars their ancient courses keep,

420   Clouds still with shadowy moisture haunt the earth,
      Still suck their fill of light from sun and moon,
      Still buds the tree, and still the sea-shores murmur.
      There is no death in all the universe,
      No smell of death – there shall be death – moan, moan,
      Moan, Cybele, moan; for thy pernicious babes
      Have changed a God into a shaking palsy.
      Moan, brethren, moan, for I have no strength left,
      Weak as the reed – weak – feeble as my voice –
      O, O, the pain, the pain of feebleness.
430   Moan, moan, for still I thaw – or give me help:
      Throw down those imps, and give me victory.
      Let me hear other groans, and trumpets blown
      Of triumph calm, and hymns of festival,
      From the gold peaks of heaven's high-pilèd clouds –
      Voices of soft proclaim, and silver stir
      Of strings in hollow shells; and let there be
      Beautiful things made new for the surprise
      Of the sky-children –' So he feebly ceased,
      With such a poor and sickly sounding pause,
440   Methought I heard some old man of the earth
      Bewailing earthly loss; nor could my eyes
      And ears act with that pleasant unison of sense
      Which marries sweet sound with the grace of form
      And dolorous accent from a tragic harp
      With large-limbed visions. More I scrutinized:
      Still fixed he sat beneath the sable trees,
      Whose arms spread straggling in wild serpent forms,
      With leaves all hushed; his awful presence there
      (Now all was silent) gave a deadly lie
450   To what I erewhile heard – only his lips
      Trembled amid the white curls of his beard.
      They told the truth, though, round, the snowy locks
      Hung nobly, as upon the face of heaven
      A midday fleece of clouds. Thea arose,
      And stretched her white arm through the hollow dark,

Pointing some whither; whereat he too rose
Like a vast giant, seen by men at sea
To grow pale from the waves at dull midnight.
They melted from my sight into the woods;
Ere I could turn, Moneta cried: 'These twain   460
Are speeding to the families of grief,
Where roofed in by black rocks they waste, in pain
And darkness, for no hope.' – And she spake on,
As ye may read who can unwearied pass
Onward from the antechamber of this dream,
Where even at the open doors awhile
I must delay, and glean my memory
Of her high phrase – perhaps no further dare.

CANTO II
'Mortal, that thou mayst understand aright,
I humanize my sayings to thine ear,
Making comparisons of earthly things;
Or thou mightst better listen to the wind,
Whose language is to thee a barren noise,
Though it blows legend-laden through the trees –
In melancholy realms big tears are shed,
More sorrow like to this, and such-like woe,
Too huge for mortal tongue, or pen of scribe.
The Titans fierce, self-hid or prison-bound,   10
Groan for the old allegiance once more,
Listening in their doom for Saturn's voice.
But one of our whole eagle-brood still keeps
His sovereignty, and rule, and majesty;
Blazing Hyperion on his orbèd fire
Still sits, still snuffs the incense teeming up
From man to the sun's God – yet unsecure.
For as upon the earth dire prodigies
Fright and perplex, so also shudders he:
Nor at dog's howl or gloom-bird's even screech,   20
Or the familiar visitings of one

Upon the first toll of his passing-bell:
But horrors, portioned to a giant nerve,
Make great Hyperion ache. His palace bright,
Bastioned with pyramids of glowing gold,
And touched with shade of bronzèd obelisks,
Glares a blood-red through all the thousand courts,
Arches, and domes, and fiery galleries;
And all its curtains of Aurorian clouds
30 Flush angerly: when he would taste the wreaths
Of incense breathed aloft from sacred hills,
Instead of sweets, his ample palate takes
Savour of poisonous brass and metals sick.
Wherefore, when harboured in the sleepy West,
After the full completion of fair day,
For rest divine upon exalted couch
And slumber in the arms of melody,
He paces through the pleasant hours of ease
With strides colossal, on from hall to hall;
40 While far within each aisle and deep recess
His wingèd minions in close clusters stand
Amazed, and full of fear; like anxious men,
Who on a wide plain gather in sad troops,
When earthquakes jar their battlements and towers.
Even now, while Saturn, roused from icy trance,
Goes, step for step, with Thea from yon woods,
Hyperion, leaving twilight in the rear,
Is sloping to the threshold of the West –
Thither we tend.' – Now in clear light I stood,
50 Relieved from the dusk vale. Mnemosyne
Was sitting on a square-edged polished stone,
That in its lucid depth reflected pure
Her priestess-garments. My quick eyes ran on
From stately nave to nave, from vault to vault,
Through bowers of fragrant and enwreathèd light
And diamond-pavèd lustrous long arcades.
Anon rushed by the bright Hyperion;

His flaming robes streamed out beyond his heels,
And gave a roar, as if of earthly fire,
That scared away the meek ethereal Hours,   60
And made their dove-wings tremble. On he flared . . .
                    (Not published by Keats)

═══

'What can I do to drive away'

What can I do to drive away
Remembrance from my eyes? for they have seen,
Ay, an hour ago, my brilliant Queen!
Touch has a memory. O say, love, say,
What can I do to kill it and be free
In my old liberty?
When every fair one that I saw was fair,
Enough to catch me in but half a snare,
Not keep me there;
When, howe'er poor or parti-coloured things,   10
My muse had wings,
And ever ready was to take her course
Whither I bent her force,
Unintellectual, yet divine to me –
Divine, I say! What sea-bird o'er the sea
Is a philosopher the while he goes
Winging along where the great water throes?

    How shall I do
    To get anew
Those moulted feathers, and so mount once more   20
    Above, above
    The reach of fluttering Love,
And make him cower lowly while I soar?
Shall I gulp wine? No, that is vulgarism,
A heresy and schism,
    Foisted into the canon law of love;

No – wine is only sweet to happy men;
  More dismal cares
    Seize on me unawares –
30 Where shall I learn to get my peace again?
To banish thoughts of that most hateful land,
Dungeoner of my friends, that wicked strand
Where they were wrecked and live a wreckèd life;
That monstrous region, whose dull rivers pour,
Ever from their sordid urns into the shore,
Unowned of any weedy-hairèd gods;
Whose winds, all zephyrless, hold scourging rods,
Iced in the great lakes, to afflict mankind;
Whose rank-grown forests, frosted, black, and blind,
40 Would fright a Dryad; whose harsh-herbaged meads
Make lean and lank the starved ox while he feeds;
There flowers have no scent, birds no sweet song,
And great unerring Nature once seems wrong.

O, for some sunny spell
To dissipate the shadows of this hell!
Say they are gone – with the new dawning light
Steps forth my lady bright!
O, let me once more rest
My soul upon that dazzling breast!
50 Let once again these aching arms be placed,
The tender gaolers of thy waist!
And let me feel that warm breath here and there
To spread a rapture in my very hair –
O, the sweetness of the pain!
Give me those lips again!
Enough! Enough! It is enough for me
To dream of thee!

(Not published by Keats)

'This living hand, now warm and capable'

This living hand, now warm and capable
Of earnest grasping, would, if it were cold
And in the icy silence of the tomb,
So haunt thy days and chill thy dreaming nights
That thou would wish thine own heart dry of blood
So in my veins red life might stream again,
And thou be conscience-calmed – see here it is –
I hold it towards you.

(Not published by Keats)

'In after-time, a sage of mickle lore'

In after-time, a sage of mickle lore
Y-cleped Typographus, the Giant took,
And did refit his limbs as heretofore,
And made him read in many a learned book,
And into many a lively legend look;
Thereby in goodly themes so training him,
That all his brutishness he quite forsook,
When, meeting Artegall and Talus grim,
The one he struck stone-blind, the other's eyes wox dim.

(Not published by Keats)

====

Notes

Abbreviations

1817	*Poems* (1817)
1820	*Lamia, Isabella, The Eve of St Agnes, and Other Poems* (1820)
1848	*Life, Letters, and Literary Remains, of John Keats*, ed. R. M. Milnes, 2 vols, 1848.
1876	*The Poetical Works of John Keats*, Aldine edition, ed. R. M. Milnes, 1876.
Forman	*The Poetical Works and Other Writings of John Keats*, ed. H. B. Forman, 4 vols, 1883.

Lines Written on 29 May The Anniversary of the Restoration of Charles II

Written 29 May 1815. Published A. Lowell, *John Keats* (1925). Written during the Hundred Days following Napoleon's escape from Elba. Louis XVIII sought asylum in London, where he was met by huge crowds. On 29 May bells were rung all over England to commemorate Charles II's restoration. As a liberal Keats disapproved of both events: legitimacy alone was not sufficient. For Hazlitt, Waterloo was 'the sacred triumph of Kings over mankind.' *Algernon Sidney* (1622–83), *Lord William Russell* (1639–83) and *Sir Henry Vane* (1613–62) (l. 5) were all executed for treason by Charles II. They were regarded as heroes by the Whigs.

On First Looking into Chapman's Homer

Written October 1816. Published *Examiner*, 1 December 1816, *1817*.

To my Brothers

Written 18 November 1816 to mark Tom Keats's seventeenth birthday. Published *1817*.

Addressed to [Haydon]

Written 19 or 20 November 1816. Published *1817*. The three '*spirits*' celebrated are Wordsworth (ll. 2–4), Leigh Hunt (ll. 5–6) and the painter, B. R. Haydon (ll. 7–8).

'I stood tip-toe upon a little hill'

Completed December 1816. Published *1817*. *Motto* from Leigh Hunt's *The Story of Rimini* (1816), III, 430. Keats's ideas on the origin and nature of poetry are probably indebted to his reading of Wordsworth's *Excursion* (1814), IV, 687–765, 840–81, which suggest that Classical deities originated from man's pantheistic response to nature. Compare Keats's early treatment of the story of Psyche (ll. 141–50) with that in 'Ode to Psyche'.

Sleep and Poetry

Started October, completed December 1816. Published *1817*. Woodhouse identified the '*lone spirits*' (l. 218) as Henry Kirke White (1785–1806) and Chatterton, the '*swan's ebon bill*' (l. 226) as a reference to Wordsworth and the '*fine sounds*' (l. 228) as references to Byron and Coleridge's *Christabel*. The '*clubs . . . Disturbing the grand sea*' (ll. 234–5) have been taken as an attack on the Lake School (Leigh Hunt) or on Byron. Woodhouse thought that the '*fallen angel*' (l. 242) alluded to Byron. The '*poet's house*' (l. 354) was Leigh Hunt's Hampstead cottage, where Keats was staying. Keats goes on to describe Hunt's library.

Written in Disgust of Vulgar Superstition

Written 22 December 1816. Published *1876*. An important poem for its light on Keats's attitudes to conventional religion.

To Kosciusko

Written December 1816. Published *Examiner*, 16 February 1817, and *1817*. Tadeusz Kosciusko (1746–1817), Polish patriot, fought against Russia and for the United States in the War of Independence. He died a hero of English liberals.

'After dark vapours have oppressed our plains'

Written 31 January 1817. Published *Examiner*, 23 February 1817, and *1848*.

To Leigh Hunt, Esq.

Written extempore February, and published as the dedicatory sonnet to *1817*.

On the Sea

Written 16 or 17 April 1817 at Carisbrooke, Isle of Wight. Published *Champion*, 17 August 1817, and *1848*.

'The Gothic looks solemn'

Written September 1817 in a (lost) letter to J. H. Reynolds. Published *Forman*. Keats was visiting Benjamin Bailey at Oxford, and working on *Endymion*.

Endymion: A Poetic Romance

Begun *c.* 18 April 1817 on Isle of Wight; completed November 1817 at Burford Bridge, Surrey. Published in May 1818.

Endymion is a Romantic quest-poem portraying the poet's search for true imaginative powers. The hero's confusions arise from the decision of Diana, the moon-goddess, to visit the poet-prince first in the form of an unknown goddess (Book I, Book II), and later in the guise of an Indian Maid (Book IV). In love with all three, Endymion's divided feelings are finally resolved by the discovery that they are one. The romance ends with the deification of Endymion and his marriage to Diana.

Endymion argues for the interconnectedness of human love and the truth of ideal beauty. In Book I, the hero is set apart from his Latmian subjects by the '*cankering venom*' (I, 396) caused by his dream of a heavenly goddess. The hero is initiated into the mysteries of the heavens (Book I), the earth (Book II) and the sea (Book III), before being returned to earth. He is also shown progressively learning to sympathize with the joys and sufferings of other lovers – Venus and Adonis (II, 387–587), Alpheus and Arethusa (II, 932–1017) and Glaucus (III, 187–1015). Endymion is named variously as 'the Latmian' and 'the Carian', Diana as 'Cynthia' and 'Phoebe'.

Motto from Shakespeare, Sonnet xvii.12. Keats's original Preface (and dedication), which attacked the reading public, met with strong objections from his friend J. H. Reynolds, and from Taylor and Hessey, his publishers, and was replaced by the present text.

BOOK I

The stanzaic hymn to Pan (ll. 232–306) is indebted to Chapman's Homeric hymns. Wordsworth thought it merely a 'Very pretty piece of Paganism'. '*Peona*' (l. 408), Endymion's sister and confidante, is a character invented by Keats. On 30 January 1818 Keats sent his publishers an additional passage (ll. 777–81) to serve as introduction to ll. 782–4. Benjamin Bailey commented privately on the 'inclination' of ll. 833–42 towards 'that abominable principle of *Shelley*'s – that *sensual love* is the principle of *things*'.

BOOK II

II, 387–587 The wandering Endymion is vouchsafed this vision of the sleeping Adonis and his union with Venus by '*a heavenly guide benignant*' (l. 377). It foreshadows Endymion's later union with Cynthia.

II, 827–end The narrator explains how myths are created (ll. 827–48), and Endymion awakes to find he has been deserted by an unknown goddess/woman. Book II ends with the story of Arethusa and Endymion's descent into the sea.

BOOK III

III, 1–21 Keats is reported to have said, 'It will easily be seen what I think of the present Ministers by the beginning of the 3rd Book [of *Endymion*].' The passage reflects Leigh Hunt's attacks on the tyrants and the clergy in the *Examiner*. The references are obscure, but '*idiot blink*' (l. 6) may refer to the King or to the Tory ministry who keep the price of corn high in a period of distress and poor harvests.

III, 42 'thy Sister' Diana, the moon. Apollo was, for Keats, god of the sun and of poetry.

III, 314–638 In his journey under the sea Endymion meets an aged man with a mysterious book who has been awaiting the coming of a young man to release him. The old man tells his story, and identifies himself as Glaucus. This excerpt ends with the death of Scylla following Glaucus's entrancement by Circe. The remainder of Book III is taken up with Endymion and Glaucus releasing 'All lovers, whom fell storms have doomed to die' (l. 702).

BOOK IV

IV, 1–29 Keats's induction places the British Muse in a historical relationship to Biblical inspiration (l. 10), Greek poetry (ll. 11–14), and the Italy of Virgil and Dante (ll. 14–17). Keats seems to make an implicit contrast between modern day '*barren souls*' and the achievement of the Elizabethans (ll. 17–20).

IV, 143–290 Endymion chances on the Indian Maid, with whom, to his consternation, he instantly falls in love. She '*For pity sang this roundelay*', in which she tells the story of Bacchus's progress (to which she apparently attached herself in India) through Egypt, Abyssinia and Asia.

IV, 900–end Endymion, bewildered by his experiences, determines to retreat from life as a hermit dedicated to Diana. He bids farewell to his sister Peona and the Indian Maid. The latter finally reveals herself as his Phoebe (i.e., Cynthia/Diana).

IV, 954ff. '*This dusk religion*' This obscure passage may be an attack on conventional moral (and Christian) attitudes to human love.

Nebuchadnezzar's Dream

Date uncertain, but probably December 1817. Published *Literary Anecdotes of the Nineteenth Century* (1896). This obscure poem seems to satirize the repressive measures taken by the Tory government to silence its critics. '*Daniel*' probably stands for William Hone (1780–1842), unsuccessfully tried for blasphemous and seditious writings, 18–20 December 1817. Keats, like other liberals, followed the trial with interest. Based on Daniel II–IV, Nebuchadnezzar probably stands for George III, the '*valiant crew*' (l. 10) for his ministry.

To Mrs Reynolds's Cat

Written 16 January 1818. Published *The Comic Annual* (1830).

On Sitting Down to Read King Lear Once Again

Written 22 January 1818. Published *Plymouth and Devonport Weekly*, 8 November 1838.

'When I have fears that I may cease to be'

Written between 22 and 31 January 1818. Published *1848*.

To — ('Time's sea hath been five years at its slow ebb')

Written 4 February 1818. Published *Hood's Magazine*, September 1844, *1848*.

'O thou whose face hath felt the Winter's wind'

Written 19 February 1818. Published *1848*.

To J. H. Reynolds, Esq.

Written as a letter to Reynolds on 24 March 1818 from Devon. Published *1848*.

Isabella; or, The Pot of Basil

Probably begun March 1818, completed by 27 April. Subsequently revised for publication in *1820*. Based on the fifth novella of the fourth day in Boccaccio's *Decameron*. Keats heightens the grotesque elements.

On Visiting the Tomb of Burns

Written 1 July 1818 (the day Keats visited Burns's tomb at Dumfries). Published *1848*. The punctuation and wording of this sonnet are highly problematic. Editors usually emend '*Fickly*' (l. 11) to 'Sickly'. Keats said 'This Sonnet I have written in a strange mood, half asleep ... the Clouds, the sky, the Houses [of Scotland], all seem anti-Grecian and anti-Charlemagnish ...' Scotland, Keats thought, was antipathetic to true poetry: he ends by apologizing to Burns who had nevertheless written true poetry there.

A Song about Myself

Written 3 July 1818 at Kirkcudbright during Keats's and Charles Brown's walking tour of Scotland, in a letter to his sister, Fanny, then just fifteen. Published *Forman*.

From *Fragment of the 'Castle Builder'*

Date 1818: Miriam Allott argues for late October 1818. Published *1848*. Possibly a fragment of a satire on Regency taste.

'And what is love? It is a doll dressed up'

Written 1818, perhaps October. Published *1848*.

Hyperion. A Fragment

Mainly written between late September 1818 and the death of Tom Keats, 1 December 1818. Finally abandoned in April 1819. Published *1820*, whose Advertisement says that the unfinished poem was printed at the publisher's 'particular request, and contrary to the wish of the poet'. Keats said, '... in Endymion I think you may have many bits of the deep and sentimental cast – the nature of *Hyperion* will lead me to treat it in a more naked and grecian manner – and the march of passion and endeavour will be undeviating ...'

Keats's re-imagining of the epic struggle in which Saturn and the Titans are overthrown by their children, the Olympian gods, begins in

mid-action. The Titans have been defeated. Only Hyperion, the
Titan god of the sun is as yet undefeated by his Olympian successor,
Apollo. Books I and II describe the Titans' suffering: the unfinished
Book III depicts Apollo's apotheosis into godhead. Hyperion's down-
fall is seen as the tragic consequence of an inevitable historical
evolution towards higher forms of beauty. For Keats Apollo was the
god of poetry as well as the god of the sun and of healing. Although
Hyperion is not overtly political, its mythic world puts forward an
alternative 'Greek' vision of heroic struggle and human progress,
created out of Keats's dissatisfactions with contemporary politics,
religion and government.

The Eve of St Agnes

Written between 18 January and 2 February 1819; revised September
1819. Published *1820*. Keats's alterations in September made the
poem more sexually explicit, and deeply upset his publishers, Taylor
and Hessey. Taylor refused to publish the volume at all unless the
more innocent version was restored. In critical terms the earlier
version is preferable. Keats, concerned to be seen as manly and not
mawkish, coarsened the poem's balance. The narrative turns on the
superstition that if a virgin observed the proper rites on the eve of St
Agnes she would dream of her future husband. The idea of the poem
was possibly suggested by Mrs Isabella Jones.

The Eve of St Mark

Written 13–17 February 1819. Published *1848*. Unfinished. Possibly
begun on a suggestion of Mrs Isabella Jones.

'Why did I laugh tonight? . . .'

Written March 1819, before the 19th. Published *1848*.

Character of Charles Brown

Written 16 April 1819. Published *1848*. The extempore *jeu d'esprit*
was a reply to a skit Brown was writing on Keats and Fanny Brawne.
Charles Brown (1787–1842), a firm friend of Keats, was anything but
melancholy, being bald, heavily built, in his thirties and flirtatious. He
had a child by his housekeeper, Abigail O'Donaghue.

A Dream, after reading Dante's Episode of Paolo and Francesca

Written *c.* April 1819, when Keats copied it out for George and
Georgiana Keats. Published in Leigh Hunt's *Indicator*, 28 June 1820
(signed 'Caviare'), but not in *1820*. Keats had been reading Cary's
translation of Dante's *Inferno* (the '*Delphic reed*' of l. 3). Just as Hermes
rescued Io by lulling her hundred-eyed guardian Argus to sleep with
music, so his reading makes the narrator forget worldly anxieties, and
flee to Dante's second circle. Paolo and Francesca are sinners
condemned for satisfying their sexual needs, but for whom Dante
feels compassion because of their innocence and youth. The dreamer
and Paolo are assimilated into one. '*Whirlwind*' (l. 10) is the manu-
script wording: the *Indicator* version has 'world-wind', which would
indicate that the world itself is wholly inimical to romantic love.

La Belle Dame sans Merci. A Ballad

Written 21 April 1819. Published *Indicator*, 10 May 1820 (signed
'Caviare'), *1848*. Not published in *1820*. The *Indicator* version intro-
duces an ironic note absent in the letter version sent to George and
Georgiana Keats and the MSS versions. Like all editors, the text here
rejects the *Indicator* version.

To Sleep

Probably written late April 1819. Published *Plymouth and Devonport Weekly Journal*, 11 October 1838, *1848*. An experimental sonnet, with the next, leading to the stanzaic structure of 'Ode to Psyche'.

'If by dull rhymes our English must be chained'

Probably written before 30 April 1819. Published *1848*.

Ode to Psyche

Written 21 and 30 April 1819. Published *1820*. Keats commented, it '. . . is the first and only [poem] with which I have taken even moderate pains . . . You must recollect that Psyche was not embodied as a Goddess before the time of Apuleius the Platonist who lived after the Augustan age, and consequently the Goddess was never worshipped or sacrificed to with any of the ancient fervour – and perhaps never thought of in the old religion – I am more orthodox tha[n] to let a he[a]then Goddess be so neglected –' Traditionally, Psyche represented the soul. Keats's unnamed Cupid should be identified with Eros.

On Fame (I) ('Fame, like a wayward girl, will still be coy')

Written 30 April 1819. Published *Ladies' Companion* (New York), August 1837, etc., *1848*.

On Fame (II) ('How fevered is the man who cannot look')

Written 30 April 1819. Published *1848*. An extempore sonnet, written while Charles Brown was transcribing the preceding.

'Two or three posies'

Written *c.* 1 May 1819 in a letter to his sister, Fanny. Published *Forman*. 'Mrs —' is Mrs Abbey, wife of Richard Abbey who acted as the Keats children's guardian from 1810. Relations between Abbey and Keats were strained.

Ode on a Grecian Urn

Written in 1819. Date conjectural, but probably early May. Published *Annals of the Fine Arts*, xv (January 1820), *1820*.

The relation of the final couplet to the rest of the ode has been much debated. Basically the question is whether the speaker endorses the ode's 'motto' or whether, in varying degrees, the 'motto' is that spoken by the Urn only. *1820* reads, ' "Beauty is truth, truth beauty," – that is all/Ye know on earth, and all ye need to know.' The *Annals* and MSS texts, with other punctuation variants, omit the inverted commas round the opening phrase. The present text attributes both lines to the Urn.

Ode to a Nightingale

Dated 'May 1819' in MSS, but exact date conjectural. Published *1820*. Normally believed to precede 'Ode on a Grecian Urn', but the internal references suggest a date in mid-May.

Ode on Melancholy

Date conjectural, but probably May 1819. Published *1820*.

Ode on Indolence

Probably written late May or early June 1819. Published *1848*.

Lamia

Written *c.* 28 June and 11 July 1819, 12 August and *c.* 5 September 1819, revised March 1820. Published *1820*. Keats printed his prime source at the end of the poem in *1820*. He quotes Burton's *Anatomy of Melancholy* III.2.i.1:

> Philostratus, in his fourth book *de Vita Apollonii*, hath a memorable instance in this kind, which I may not omit, of one Menippus Lycius, a young man of twenty-five years of age, that going between Cenchreas and Corinth, met such a phantasm in the habit of a fair gentlewoman, which taking him by the hand, carried him home to her house, in the suburbs of Corinth, and told him she was a Phoenician by birth, and if he would tarry with her he should hear her sing and play, and drink such wine as never any drank, and no man should molest him; but she, being fair and lovely, would live and die with him, that was fair and lovely to behold. The young man, a philosopher, otherwise staid and discreet, able to moderate his passions, though not this of love, tarried with her a while to his great content, and at last married her, to whose wedding amongst other guests, came Apollonius; who, by some probable conjectures, found her out to be a serpent, a lamia; and that all her furniture was, like Tantalus' gold, described by Homer, no substance but mere illusions. When she saw herself descried, she wept, and desired Apollonius to be silent, but he would not be moved, and thereupon she, plate, house, and all that was within it, vanished in an instant: many thousands took notice of this fact, for it was done in the midst of Greece.

'Bright star! would I were steadfast as thou art'

Date conjectural and controversial. Published *Plymouth and Devonport Weekly Journal*, 27 September 1838, *1848*. Long regarded as Keats's last poem, it has been dated 1 October 1818, 2 July 1819, October–November 1819. A date in July 1819 now seems to me the most probable.

'Pensive they sit, and roll their languid eyes'

Written 17 September in Keats's journal-letter to George and Georgiana Keats. Published *World* (New York), 25 June 1877, *Forman*.

To Autumn

Written *c.* 19 September 1819. Published *1820*.

The Fall of Hyperion. A Dream

Begun mid-July 1819, 'given up' *c.* 21 September 1819. Published *Biographical and Historical Collections of the Philobiblon Society, 1856–7* (1856).

Keats's second attempt at the Hyperion story looks to Dante rather than Milton. The fragment is a dream vision in which the narrator is initiated into knowledge by Moneta, an admonitory version of Mnemosyne (goddess of memory and foster-mother of Apollo). At Canto I, 294 Keats began to work in material from his earlier poem. The fragment concludes with the appearance of Hyperion in Canto II. Its precise allegorical implications are obscure. It has been read recently as a rejection of the poetry and politics of Coleridge and Wordsworth. However, the dream seems not only to examine the nature of a true poet, but to give a Keatsian version of the origins of myth and religion, as well as a critique of his own poetic career. The evolutionary optimism of *Hyperion* is not sustained in *The Fall of Hyperion*. The syntax and thought of the invocation (I, 1–18) are less than transparent. The *'Fanatics'* (l. 1) seem not to be compared with *'savages'* (I. 2) but to be their opposite. The savage, an animist *'guess[ing] at Heaven'* from the evidence of the natural world, cannot, without the medium of writing (and print), perpetuate his dreams. The *'fanatic'* imprisons his sect in a false paradise. Only *'Poesy'* can give permanent life to the truth perceived by unlettered savages. This poem could itself be either a fanatic's dream or truth. The reader must decide whether the narrator is a poet or dreamer (I. 198–200).

The '*arbor*' entered by the narrator (I. 19–38) seems to represent the '*realm of Flora*', embodied in Keats's career by *Endymion*, and '*the Chamber of Maiden-Thought*'. There is probably no precise meaning available for the '*full draught*' (I. 42–5). The encounter between the dreamer and Moneta in a temple (I. 62–293) is probably in some part a reply to Coleridge's second *Lay Sermon* (1817), with a humanist goddess in the place of Coleridge's Christian supernaturalism, and while the narrator's outburst against contemporary false poets (I. 204–210) is deliberately general, aspects of Wordsworth, Coleridge and Byron are probably in Keats's sights.

'*What can I do to drive away*'

Date conjectural. Late 1819 or even early 1820. Published *1848*. The poem is an expression of Keats's confused feelings towards Fanny Brawne (see Introduction). The '*friends*' dungeoned in '*that most hateful land*' refers to the family of Keats's brother George, who were experiencing difficulties after emigrating to America. Keats depicts the New World as barren of mythology.

'*This living hand, now warm and capable*'

Probably written November to December 1819. Published H. B. Forman, *Poetical Works of John Keats*, 6th ed. (1898). Formerly thought to be addressed to Fanny Brawne, now generally regarded as a fragment for later use in a poem or play.

'*In after-time, a sage of mickle lore*'

Probably written *c*. July 1820. Published *Plymouth and Devonport Weekly Journal*, 4 July 1839, and *1848*. Charles Brown said this was 'the last stanza of any kind that [Keats] wrote before his lamented death'. The stanza inverts Spenser's anti-democratic allegory in *The Faerie Queene*, V.ii. 29–54. There, Spenser's 'mighty Gyant', who demands equality for all, is opposed by Artegall (Justice, and the English crown's representative in Ireland) and Talus (the executive arm of government). Keats's '*Giant*' of the future restores the lost wisdom of Typographus (that is, restores a free press), who kills the two oppressors.

Index of First Lines